Thomas Wolfe's
Civil War

DISCARDED

Thomas Wolfe's Civil War

Edited and with an Introduction by
David Madden

THE UNIVERSITY OF ALABAMA PRESS   TUSCALOOSA

Copyright © 2004
The University of Alabama Press
Tuscaloosa, Alabama 35487-0380
All rights reserved
Manufactured in the United States of America

Designer: Michele Myatt Quinn
Typeface: ACaslon

∞

The paper on which this book is printed meets the minimum requirements of
American National Standard for Information Science–Permanence of Paper for
Printed Library Materials, ANSI Z39.48–1984.

Library of Congress Cataloging-in-Publication Data

Wolfe, Thomas, 1900–1938.
Thomas Wolfe's Civil War / edited and with an introduction by David Madden.
p. cm.
"Fire Ant books."
"Selected works of Thomas Wolfe": p.
ISBN 0-8173-5094-2 (pbk. : alk. paper)
1. United States—History—Civil War, 1861–1865—Literary collections.
I. Madden, David, 1933– II. Title.
PS3545.O337A6 2004
813'.52—dc22

2003021996

The author gratefully acknowledges permission to reprint material from the
following source: *The Good Child's River* by Thomas Wolfe, edited by Suzanne
Stutman. Copyright © 1991 by Paul Gitlin, Administrator, C.T.A. of the Estate
of Thomas Wolfe. Published by the University of North Carolina Press. Used by
permission of the publisher. All other material from the works of Thomas Wolfe
is used by permission of the Estate of Thomas Wolfe.

Contents

Acknowledgments

I AM VERY GRATEFUL TO Henry R. Williams for researching rights to reprint Wolfe's works and to Eugene H. Winick, Administrator of the Thomas Wolfe Estate, for granting permission to reprint the works included in this collection, with the exception of *The Good Child's River*, edited and with an introduction by Suzanne Stutman, permission for which was granted by the University of North Carolina Press.

I am grateful to the Thomas Wolfe Society for inviting me to deliver a talk on Thomas Wolfe's Civil War at its Gettysburg Meeting in 1996, to Terry Roberts, editor of *Thomas Wolfe Review*, for publishing my talk, and to the awards committee of the society for choosing my essay for the Zelda Gitlin Prize for the best scholarly essay published on Thomas Wolfe for the year 1997.

John L. Idol, friend for almost fifty years, has always encouraged my Thomas Wolfe endeavors, and I am grateful for his helpful reading of this manuscript. I welcome any chance to remember Richard Kennedy, whose response to the lecture was encouraging.

This book is yet another expression of the venturesomeness of the University of Alabama Press.

I appreciate the help of my assistant, Emilie Staat. It is always good to be able to thank my students. Ashley Berthelot and Brian Fontenot gave the manuscript sensitive and perceptive readings that made a difference. Ethan Guagliardo, my research assistant, delved into the library for me. My wife, Robbie, a former editor, who knows what works and what doesn't, infallibly, gave this, the latest in a seemingly endless number of manuscripts, the okay—high praise indeed.

My thanks to Tom Watson for providing me with photographs of the late Richard LeFevre's paintings, from which the designer chose the cover art, and to Carol LeFevre for granting permission for use of the work.

Mrs. Diane LeNoir at LSU College of Arts and Sciences' text processing operation saved me from an arduous typing task.

Introduction

DAVID MADDEN

THOMAS WOLFE'S ACHIEVEMENT MAY be most fully appreciated if we read him in a relatively fresh light—as a major contributor to Civil War literature. This slight volume is, of course, evidence of the fact that in his vast body of work one finds only a play, a few short stories, several passages scattered throughout his novels, and an unfinished last novel in which he literally renders the experience of the war. Understandably then, critics and general readers seldom comment on the role of the war in his work. Mindful of the almost universal evaluation of his novels as artistically flawed, I suggest that some of his Civil War pieces might be counted among his greatest achievements and that "Chickamauga" and "The Four Lost Men" are among the finest short stories in all Civil War literature. Whatever their individual merits, his war writings will illuminate a first reading or a rereading of everything else he wrote. When certain aspects of his life are reexamined, especially his relationship with his father and his mother in light of their memory of the war, Wolfe may be seen as having tried to define his life and his vision of America in terms of the Civil War.[1]

Northerners generally think of the Civil War as consisting of a series of battles. Southerners, on the other bloody hand, remember the South's defeat in war and suffering in Reconstruction. Except for those who have written Civil War novels, the war has little effect upon the consciousness of the northern writer—Frank Norris, Theodore Dreiser, Edith Wharton, Sherwood Anderson, Ernest Hemingway, and F. Scott Fitzgerald, for instance. The war has been the central experience in the history of the South—the long-developing cause, the bloody agony of battle, and the lingering Lost Cause aftereffects. The aim then of most novels about the war by southerners has been to defend, explain, or criticize, sometimes to extol or preserve, the southern way of life. By contrast, for the northerner, the North as a coherent region with a history and an identity, and his or her place in it *as a northerner,* has very little reality. The northern writer's perspective is that the Civil War was interesting as a human drama that ended with an important moral victory.

The most meaningful definition in my own use of the term "Civil War" in my fiction, nonfiction, and criticism, and in this collection is that it embraces the antebellum, the war, and the Reconstruction eras, and the legacy aftereffects of those eras on into the twenty-first century. Given that definition, nothing a northern writer writes, not even a Civil War novel, derives from that broadest Civil War experience. *Everything* a southern writer writes, on the other hand, derives to some extent and in various ways from the Civil War experience.

A passage in Wolfe's third novel, *The Web and the Rock,* more directly evokes this pervasive presence of the Civil War. George Webber (Wolfe's autobiographical hero) and some friends visit Richmond, where

[t]hey felt in touch with wonder and with life, they felt in touch with magic and with history. They saw the state house and they heard the guns. They knew that Grant was pounding at the gates of Richmond. They knew that Lee was digging in some twenty miles away at Pe-

tersburg. They knew that Lincoln had come down from Washington and was waiting for the news at City Point. They knew that Jubal Early was swinging in his saddle at the suburbs of Washington. They felt, they knew, they had their living hands and hearts upon the living presence of these things, and upon a thousand other things as well. They knew that they were at the very gateways of the fabulous and unknown North.[2]

In a sense that runs deep and that matters very much, in all southern literature, there is always something unspoken—and something about the war and its lingering, ghostly effects is what is unspoken. Readers feel those effects most obviously when moving around in the fictive atmosphere that William Faulkner created, but if we listen more attentively as we inhabit Wolfe's world, we may feel it even more intensely. All southern literature *comes out* of the Civil War and Reconstruction and all southern novels are *about* the Civil War and Reconstruction because the lingering effect of the war and Reconstruction has permeated southern history and the consciousness of southerners, and we can see the process of that effect delineated in the plays and fiction of Thomas Wolfe, if not as deliberately and clearly as we may demand, more completely than in the works of any other southern novelist. By contrast, there is no such thing as a northern novel, nor a true Civil War novel by a northerner because there is no such thing as the North or a northerner, except in the minds of southerners; the South and southerners are, however, both real and surreal to northerners.

One way to get Wolfe's achievement in perspective is to look briefly at comparable works by major southern novelists of that era. "Like Faulkner, he felt compelled to depict his view of the South: Black versus White, the Civil War, the pull of the land."[3] In his novel *Absalom, Absalom!* (originally "Dark House"), Faulkner covers the same time frame as Wolfe's Civil War play *Mannerhouse* (originally "The House"). Faulkner's own all-embracing Yoknapatawpha saga was, comparatively, not a planned work but a work that evolved. Evelyn Scott's antebellum, Civil War, Reconstruction trilogy, consisting of *Migrations: An Arabesque in Histories* (1927), *The Wave* (1929), and *A Calendar of Sin* (1931, two volumes) took only four years to write; her trilogy, however, was carefully planned and almost as long—twenty-three hundred pages—as Wolfe's four related novels—three thousand pages—but it was part of a life's work that included an earlier, psychological trilogy, more novels, plays, poems, and nonfiction, and that was even more varied than Wolfe's or Faulkner's.

Once it was over, northern writers became relatively disconnected from the war. Three other great novelists of Wolfe's time, Fitzgerald, Hemingway, and Dos Passos—midwesterners— did not write novels about the Civil War. Hemingway was in a war and wrote about it, but it was the Spanish, not the American, Civil War (which Carlos Baker does not mention in his biography). Fitzgerald began by writing plays and several stories, some satirical, about the Civil War, and he married a southern belle, as if trying to get into the southern tradition, but he lacked the vision. *The Great Gatsby* is the great symbolic novel of the American dream-nightmare, but more applicable to the northern concept. Even though his father fought in the Civil War at age fourteen, Dos Passos did not write about it; his trilogy *U.S.A.* (1930–36) focused on Chicago—1896 through 1935. Most of Wolfe's southern contemporaries left the region; some stayed away, some returned. But Wolfe searched farther—over to England, France, Norway, and on into Germany. By contrast to his northern contemporaries who went into romantic exile in Paris, Wolfe holed up in Brooklyn. They had glamorous lovers; Wolfe's mistress for twelve years, Aline Berstein, was almost twice his age when they met, although her life in the theater and her exotic Jewish heritage were alluring.

Although some have argued for candidates, two mythic achievements in the novel form have eluded the creative powers of the greatest northern and southern writers: the great American novel and the great Civil War novel. I am aware that many regard this notion of greatness as spurious, but allow me to treat it seriously as one perspective on Wolfe's achievement.

The notion of a great national novel is distinctly American. As far as I know, neither the British, nor the Russians, nor the Japanese are on the lookout for one. But in this nation, there is a deeply serious longing, among readers if not critics, for the great American novel and an optimism that someday it will appear on the best-seller list. Americans know the mystique of the great American novel better than any other literary notion.

I am convinced that the great American novel must also be the great Civil War novel because that war provides the single most provocative and complex perspective on the entire American experience. As one of the best examples of a southern writer whose entire body of work is indirectly about the Civil War, Wolfe is also a prime example of the southern writer who had the potential to write the great American novel as a Civil War novel.

What, then, can and must the great American novel be? Here are some possible criteria. It must have a proven popularity and have achieved, over at least a generation, the status of a classic. It must dramatize a concept about America; offer a conception of the American character; capture a sense of American speech; convey a sense of the American land and a sense of American history; offer a prophetic vision of America's future; and deal with a major American theme. Wolfe's fiction achieves all those criteria.

If distinctions between northern and southern literature are relevant, how are we to determine what characteristics and qualities *the* great nonpartisan American Civil War novel should have? Here are some possible criteria. The great American Civil War novel must dramatize an important or noble theme; authentically depict family life on the plantation; encompass the antebellum era, major battles, and Reconstruction; demonstrate exhaustive factual research; present the common soldier's view; be written out of a coherent philosophy of the Civil War; and be controlled by a complex artistic conception. The author's vision must emerge out of the complexities of the war experience but transcend them.

To the terminology of the criteria for the ideal American Civil War novel as a great American novel a word Coleridge applied to Shakespeare, a word also applied to Faulkner, might be profitably added: "myriadmindedness," the ability to feel, imagine, and think in many realms of experience. Perhaps Wolfe, in setting out, as he said himself, in a new direction at the end of his life, would have felt, imagined, and pondered not only all facets of the war and its many implications already depicted in his and in other novels but also startling new facets and implications; perhaps he could have become that novelist who could control, aesthetically, that vast range of possibilities with a technique and a style that only myriadmindedness can produce. If "might have been" speculation is ultimately futile, I am convinced it will at least enable us to experience a greater richness in what he did write.

The great American Civil War novel will succeed in stimulating and engaging the emotions, the imagination, and the intellect. Its point of view, style, and other techniques will make the reader a collaborator with the author in creating a conception of the Civil War that will enable the reader, long after the fiction ends, to illuminate ways through which the war may become and *stay* part of the living essence simultaneously of the main character's and the reader's everyday consciousness. It will be the novel Americans need to stimulate a revolution in our way of feeling, imagining, and meditating on an event that has determined the development of this nation and that continues to affect our behavior in ways we do well to see and understand. Again, these criteria are expressed, more implicitly than explicitly, throughout Wolfe's work.

The fabled great American novel will have to be suffused with the Civil War, as broadly defined above, and only a southern writer is temperamentally capable of writing it. Of all the southern writers, Thomas Wolfe, I am convinced, could have written and probably would have written, that great American Civil War novel.

Wolfe was the only major novelist of his time to set out deliberately to evolve a positive, coherent, and transcendent vision of America from novel to novel. In prose, Fitzgerald compressed a vision into a single novel, *The Great Gatsby*, especially in the opening and closing passages, as Hart Crane, in poetry, compressed his vision into a single long poem, *The Bridge*, especially in the proem. But no grand vision of America informed the novels of Hemingway, Evelyn Scott, or even Dos Passos in his radical, sociopolitical chronicles. Wolfe's passionate interest in the individual person, of every possible type, partook simultaneously of his vision of America and of the world. In his all inclusiveness, his myriadmindedness, Wolfe achieved a greater completeness in his fiction overall than any other novelist of his time, except perhaps Faulkner.

In the imagination, humankind transcends captivity in "self," in the limited sense of that word. We do not often reimagine the facts of our own past, as Wolfe does. But he goes further: in making the humanistic leap to imagine the lives of *others*, he most truly creates himself. Wolfe's autobiographical character in the first two novels, Eugene (renamed George in the last two novels), succeeds as a human being by becoming, at the end of the process, the man who remembered, imagined, and meditated on his past and his ancestors' pasts—the man who tried not to miss the essence of the war and its legacy. Such a man is capable then of passing that experience, in

artistic form, on to others. Wolfe delineates the growth of
Eugene's subjective life always in a reiterated context of all
human life, for Wolfe's vision of America draws upon all time,
from the Greeks to a prophetic vision of the future. What
makes Wolfe unique among southern novelists is his vision of
the South within a larger vision of America and of mankind.

A Brief Look at the Life and the Work

Born in October 1900, Wolfe would have learned about the
Civil War and Reconstruction through the oral tradition of
mountain storytelling among his relatives and their friends and
perhaps have been perplexed by the irony of the fact that more
dead and wounded came from the non–slave holding region of
the western North Carolina mountains where his hometown,
Asheville, is located than any other part of the South. Both his
mother, who ran a boarding house where he lived most of his
traumatic childhood, and his father, a stonecutter who kept a
monument shop on the public square, were talkers and dramatic, even theatrical, tellers of stories. And he absorbed both
sides of the saga of the war, his father having been an adolescent witness to the war around Gettysburg, Pennsylvania, and
his mother having been a child witness in the mountains of
North Carolina during that era. He would have witnessed evidence that the South had malingered, because of the lingering
effects of Reconstruction, in a long October of decay and non-
productivity.

Young Wolfe read or otherwise acquired knowledge of—
one may assume, given his excellent education—the vast array
of novels, short stories, poems, histories, biographies and auto-
biographies, music, art, and photographs depicting the war.
And his teacher, the nurturing Margaret Roberts, who guided
him through the literary firmament, would have provided him
with the context of the historical and cultural past of the wider

world for his always expanding knowledge of the war and its legacies of class, race relations, economic deprivation, distrust of government, and violence. Deeply, he felt the lonely isolation and spiritual claustrophobia of living in a small town, imprisoned within mountain walls, but his nature was to take great mental and physical strides out of there, which was typical of southern writers, but not of southerners generally in his time.

At the University of North Carolina, he read everything time could possibly allow, especially in the ancient classics and English literature, absorbing the satirical, lyrical, and tragic vision and rhetoric at its most sublime. But he was also attracted to living audiences and acted in several of the plays he wrote in the now famous Carolina Playmakers; the theater continued to attract him when he moved on as a graduate student to Harvard, where, under the tutelage of George Pierce Baker, he completed three long plays about mountain folk.

When he became a teacher himself, at New York University (off and on from 1924 to 1930), he was twenty-four, and his numerous plays had drawn upon the history of his people, from pioneer days to the 1900s. Keep in mind that he had not yet written fiction nor directly focused his writings upon the subject for which he became famous: himself. History, quite simply, was his interest, although regional at that time. All the people who figured importantly in his life inspired or shared in some way his interest in the Civil War themes: his mother, his father, his teacher Mrs. Roberts, his editors Maxwell Perkins and Edward Aswell, and even his Jewish mistress, Aline Bernstein, whose grandfather fought for the Union and whose story is told in *The Good Child's River*. In August 1925, on the voyage home from his first of several trips to Europe, young Wolfe met Aline Bernstein, almost twice his age. Part of her appeal may have been her glamorous life in the theater as a set and costume designer. During Wolfe's lifetime, she published two works of fiction about that way of life and about their relationship; later, she published a third novel and a memoir; all were favorably reviewed.

In his first novels—although he took his navel to be the center of the universe—he set the stage for his own adolescent histrionics by defining his father's adolescence in the Civil War, portraying him later as a kind of exile from his native North, a rank stranger among rank strangers. In all his writings, Wolfe would express this sense of isolation as universal. Within a few years, in *The Web of Earth*, he made a similar moment in his mother's childhood the foundation for his mother's future as a native mountain person, who, by contrast, always seemed oblivious to any notion of alienation, who seemed perfectly at home within herself, among her people, and even among the many strangers who came and went as boarders in her rambling house, the Old Kentucky Home.

In London, young Wolfe was still writing a long play, *Mannerhouse*, when he turned to fiction, and to remembering, with a terrible nostalgia. All his wanderings in Europe were a reaching out of the maternal heritage he had lived each day of his life in his mother's boarding house until he went to the university and thus on into that complex, universal life of the mind and of art. An overreaching search for roots in the deep, dark past of history lured him to Paris for the culture, of which he wished to become a part through his writings, and to Berlin and Bavaria for grounding in his paternal heritage. I suggest that we make much of the fact that six years after he turned from writing *Mannerhouse*, a play about the Civil War, and began writing fiction, starting with the novel generally considered his best, *Look Homeward, Angel*, this thirty-one-year-old writer, already deep into his second long novel, *Of Time and the River*, envisioned an extraordinarily long book that consisted of two more huge novels and a final, unfinished fifth novel.

As of 1931 he had conceived and planned in some detail a

series of novels, to which he gave the overall formal title *The October Fair*, but which he referred to as "the book," consisting, as he wrote in his notebook, of "Look Homeward, Angel (1884–1920); Of Time and the River (1920–1925); The October Fair (1925–1928); The Hills Beyond Pentland (1838–1926); The Death of the Enemy (1928–1933); Pacific End (1791–1884)."[4] One may think of Balzac, Hugo, Dumas, Proust, and Jules Romains, but this obsessive audacity was unique in American literature. Wolfe did not just eat, read, talk, and walk in a big way, as some other writers do—often instead of writing—he also envisioned and wrote out of a plan ("the book") much grander in scale than any of his contemporaries, southern or northern, although Dos Passos, Evelyn Scott, and Faulkner come close.

Wolfe's reputation among readers, critics, and writers has always been mixed, but that he deserves a permanent place in the American literary firmament is generally undisputed. His books sold quite well originally, and all the major works and most of the works published in the past fifty-five years are now in print. His autobiographical character Eugene was the Holden Caulfield of his day. It is also generally agreed that, given his stated intentions and the evidence of his latest work, he stood a good chance, had he lived, of producing far greater work.

Wolfe controlled his talent most effectively in his five short novels: *A Portrait of Bascom Hawke*, *No Door*, "*I Have a Thing to Tell You*," *The Party at Jack's*, and *The Web of Earth*. And yet Wolfe's myriadmindedness compelled him to see even those most artistically coherent and somewhat experimental works in various and shifting contexts, so that he frequently reshuffled parts of those and other works and reassembled them in different patterns, a practice somewhat like Faulkner's. Wolfe declared that *The Web of Earth* fit into his grandiose narrative plan, the one big book that was to be his life's work, a work cut short by early death. The seeding of his magnum opus (that is, all the novels taken as one) with passages that deal both overtly and by implication with the Civil War demonstrates his conscious and unconscious preoccupation with the war and its aftereffects.

Out of "the book," following Wolfe's untimely death in 1938, Edward Aswell edited *The Web and the Rock, You Can't Go Home Again,* and *The Hills Beyond.* A good case has been made to the effect that Aswell did "meticulous editing" with *The Hills Beyond.* In his book on Wolfe and his editors, Leslie Field makes an effective case against the legend that Aswell was a kind of coauthor, concluding that "Wolfe wrote, Aswell edited."[5] Dieter Meindl, one of the most recent and persuasive champions of *The Hills Beyond,* describes its evolution. "As he worked toward catching up with the fleeting present in a series of bulky books fictionalizing his own life, Wolfe also devoted himself to elaborating a mythic version of the ancestral and sectional past. The exceedingly complex textual history of *The Hills Beyond* evokes a writer's frustration—it looms as Wolfe's constantly thwarted or abandoned desire to write a genealogical novel in regional terms."[6]

Although comparatively little of his work deals directly with the warfare years, consider the fullest, richest implications of the fact that Wolfe's earliest major work was not a novel, but a play, and not an autobiographical play, but a play about the Civil War that fits my broad definition: it is set during antebellum times, the war, and Reconstruction. Even as he was writing his first huge autobiographical opus, *Look Homeward, Angel,* he continued to work on that play until about 1930. And when we consider that as early as 1931, he was planning *The Hills Beyond,* which also fits my definition for the scope of the term "Civil War fiction," we may begin to think of him as a writer for whom the Civil War was a lifelong major concern, both explicitly and implicitly. Consider further that throughout the massive body of his published and his unpublished works, long passages deal with the war, its causes and legacy, and thousands of allusions and implications pervade. Add then two of the major Civil War stories, "Chickamauga" and "Four Lost Men." This collection draws upon the entire range.

We may call one factor operating on Thomas Wolfe the lure of the historical, for want of a better name, meaning the history of the region in which he grew up. All his published and unpublished work is so suffused with explicit and implicit family, regional, Civil War, national, and world history that we might justifiably think of everything he wrote, taken together, as being set in an overall historical matrix. Think further of his immersion in history as occurring over a relatively short period of time from *Mannerhouse* in 1921 to *The Hills Beyond* in 1938. *Of Time and the River* and *From Death to Morning* (containing "Chickamauga") were published in a single year, 1935. The massive manuscript out of which his editor Edward Aswell carved the last three books appeared over a mere three years: *The Web and the Rock* (1939), *You Can't Go Home Again* (1940), and *The Hills Beyond* (1941), all three of which deal in part or extensively with the Civil War and Reconstruction and their hovering legacy. It is astonishing that Wolfe didn't set out early in his life to write a huge work on the Civil War, until we recall that he derived a great deal of what he wrote from direct experience and got caught in that self-woven web.

The web of associations Wolfe wove among the various elements of his all-embracing fiction was so real he got more and more entangled in its sticky strands, but simultaneously he was weaving strands on a spiritual level. Those strands were spun out of the Civil War until their origin became unrecognizable to most readers. Our belated recognition of that origin now gives the web greater clarity of intent, design, and effect. This collection is designed to bring attention to the literal role of the war in his work, from the beginning to the end of his writing life. And the purpose of this introduction is to make a start in our discussion of the implications of the claim that, as is true of all southern writers, male and female, during and since the war, all Wolfe's work is "about" the Civil War.

In the first four selections in this collection, Wolfe expresses the effect the war had upon him through the effect it had on his father and on his mother. By opening *O Lost*—the restored edition of the autobiographical *Look Homeward, Angel*—with his father watching Union soldiers march off to battle at Gettysburg near his hometown, Wolfe emphasizes the importance of the war not only in his father's consciousness but in his own. Although only a few pages are directly devoted to the effect of the war on Wolfe's mother, who as a child watched Confederate soldiers march out of the North Carolina mountains to war, a sense of the war and its legacy permeates the brilliant novella *The Web of Earth*. The excerpts from his play *Mannerhouse* show the first effects in his writing of his listening and reading experiences about the war. Passages from *The Good Child's River* (published fifty-three years after his death) show Wolfe's ability to set himself aside and write about the war through an imagined character. That the war that haunted his father also haunted Wolfe is suggested in "His Father's Earth." "Four Lost Men" is the fullest and most direct expression of Wolfe's personal feelings about his father and all the other lost men of the Civil War era. Wolfe deals directly with the war in "Chickamauga" and with Reconstruction in "The Plumed Knight," for which he gathered materials by listening to stories throughout his life, but especially those told by his mother and her people.

O Lost and *The Web of Earth*

Thomas Wolfe's father, William Oliver Wolfe, was only twelve years old when the battle of Gettysburg was fought near his village. William's sister's husband was killed in that battle, and his older brother was killed at Chancellorsville. In 1865 William, now fourteen, went to work with another brother "in the Union mule camps at Harrisburg."[7]

I often imagine Thomas Wolfe as a child, watching his father chisel stone in his monument shop, listening to that great voice conjure up his childhood memories of the Civil War, which is carved in stone on the first page of *O Lost*. Haunting images of his youth are so charged with memory, emotion, and meaning, the father transmits them through the oral story-telling tradition to the son, who is so haunted by his father's youth that when he becomes a writer, he transmits the charge to his readers.

Wolfe imagined two modes for expressing aspects of his father's and his mother's lives, using the first person point of view for both—a visionary meditation, "Four Lost Men," and a dramatic monolog, *The Web of Earth*, both of which Wolfe included in *From Death to Morning* (1935), which Hugh Holman, an early and major Wolfe scholar, feels "has never received the critical attention that it deserves."[8] The "mad rebel singing of Armageddon" beckons us to Wolfe's mother's side of the family, to Bacchus Pentland, who is depicted more fully in the story "Chickamauga," published three years later. The Wolfe who listened to his mother conjure an image similar to his father's was no longer a boy, but a famous author. Wolfe's mother reveled in her compulsive storytelling. On a visit to his Brooklyn apartment in January 1932, the sounds of harbor boats making her feel alien there, Wolfe's mother traced the vast web of Pentland earth. Two years or so earlier, Wolfe had made some notes on the story his mother often told of hearing two voices speaking to her in a dream, "in the year that the locusts came." Now he urged her to conjure up the two ghostly voices of the past through her own. She talked for hours.[9]

Near the start of *The Web of Earth*, the short novel Wolfe

published in the same year his mother visited Brooklyn, comes this image: "Don't I remember him? Old Bill Pentland standin' there with all the rest of us to watch the troops go by." And near the end: "Don't I remember it all, yes! every minute is like it was today, the men marchin', and the women cryin', the way the dust rose."[10] Like Wolfe's father, his mother as a child watched Rebel soldiers—but as they marched out of the mountains of North Carolina and into the father's field of vision near Gettysburg. We may readily imagine how those polar images of his mother and father as children watching marching men affected Wolfe, first as a child and later as a mature artist.

Wolfe expresses the character of Eliza (his mother) through a rapid spinning of her memories, tales, observations, and opinions, a retrieval of seventy years, into an intricate web. He was aware of similarities between Eliza's compulsive ninety-four-page dramatic monolog (her son is the implied listener) and Molly Bloom's forty-five-page verge-of-sleep stream of consciousness in James Joyce's *Ulysses,* but he bragged that he knew his mother better than Joyce knew Molly (based on his wife).[11] Wolfe wrote to his mother, "In the telling the story weaves back and forth like a web and for that reason I have called it *The Web of Earth* . . . written as an honorable tribute to her courage, strength, and character . . . the web of life . . . web of fortune, misfortune, joy and grief."[12] "It is different from anything I have ever done," he added, "that story about the old woman [the fictional version of his mother] has got everything in it, murder and cruelty, and hate and love, and greed and enormous unconscious courage, yet the whole thing is told with the stark innocence of a child."[13] Eliza Gant's web of memories reflects the effect of time on her private life and on the public life around her, a time haunted by the Civil War. And yet, her tone overall, like Molly Bloom's, is one of affirmation.

The potential for a prose epic work about the war was activated as early as *The Web of Earth,* the longest of Wolfe's five short novels. Maxwell Perkins said, "Not one word of this should be changed." Richard Kennedy declared that Wolfe was in full command of his powers. "The story of the Westalls . . . had no artistic flaws . . . a tightness of plot that Wolfe had not achieved before." "Nothing Wolfe wrote," said Holman, who edited the collection of short novels, "has been more highly praised than this short novel. Elizabeth Nowell [Wolfe's agent] said, 'Technically, it was the most perfect thing that Wolfe ever wrote.' Wolfe reported that Perkins thought it 'the best single piece of writing, the truest, the most carefully planned, and in the end the most unassailable that I've ever done.'"[14] Of Appalachian mountain oral stories in the southern literary tradition, the language is, for me, among the most expressive. Four of the five novellas and seventeen of the thirty-four stories he prepared for publication himself, as opposed to the stories published posthumously, are told in the first person, showing his facility with spoken language as in contrast to the ornately literary style in the omniscient point of view for which he is best known.[15] In all his work, Wolfe displayed a "mastery of the spoken language," but *The Web of Earth* shows it most clearly.[16]

Wolfe himself and his pro and con critics often cite the theme of the search for the father—a commonplace theme in American literature—as central to his fiction. The precipitating image of the father in that search is Wolfe's actual father's fathering image, transmitted to his young son, of himself as a child watching Confederate soldiers march toward nearby Gettysburg. That search extended, even before his father's death, to other men, real and mythic, and the mythic dimension expanded to include a search for sacred land, his father's land, in the "dark Helen of the North," and his paternal ancestors' land, in the "dark Helen" of Bavaria, Germany. The land as ideal fathering image extended to cities, mostly in the

North, focusing on New York, and on to London, Paris, and Berlin. Small towns, Asheville in the South and Brooklyn in the North, and the big city, New York, became focal points for his search for the fathering influence of America itself. The web he wove over the fewer than twenty years of his creative life was America, the physical transcending to the metaphysical. London, Paris, and Germany extended his vision to include the loneliness and hope of all mankind. In the vision-fashioning process, from *Mannerhouse* to *The Hills Beyond*, he kept his eyes fixed on the father-fostered image of the Civil War at Gettysburg, historic high tide of the Confederacy.

By contrast, the search for the mother, among both male and female writers, is not nearly as commonplace in literature as the search for the father. Some critics have suggested that Wolfe-Eugene was in search of a mother and that he found one in his mistress of twelve years, Aline Bernstein. The Jungian concept of the earth mother is certainly central to Wolfe's fiction, and that comes out most dramatically in *The Web of Earth*. The mother speaks and the past comes alive, her own and her ancestors'. It is the history of his mother's people in the mountains of the South that inspired the novel that Wolfe, near the time of his death, vowed to make an important work, in what he declared would be a new phase, one of greater artistic control, in his creative life. While the search for the mother is not as explicit as the search for the father, clearly his actual mother was more persistently a vivid presence in his life than was his father, as evidenced for one thing in the large collection of his letters to her.

The twin images of his father in the North and his mother in the South watching soldiers go to war are all the more important in the inspiration and formation of Wolfe's more indirect expression of facets of the war. If we agree with Graham Greene, then "the creative writer perceives his world once and for all in childhood and adolescence, and his whole career is an effort to illustrate his private world in terms of the great public world we all share."[17]

MANNERHOUSE

Remembering the generally unfavorable critical view of it and considering its length, I had not intended to include *Mannerhouse* in this collection. But when I reread it, I found not only that it is indispensably relevant to the broader Civil War context I have been delineating but also that I am perfectly willing to chance the claim that it is a far more accomplished work than anyone has allowed, that it is the most artistically conceptualized of all Wolfe's works.[18] My argument for the intensity of Wolfe's lifelong preoccupation with the Civil War rests first of all and firmly upon *Mannerhouse.*

The play is no longer in print. Because efforts are under way to publish all Wolfe's plays in a single volume, this play is not available for reprint in its entirety in a collection; therefore, I have included here only the prologue and act 4 (structurally a kind of epilogue), in which not only the main elements of the play but also the elements in all Wolfe's Civil War fiction are prefigured and resolved.

It should be stressed again that until he began writing *Look Homeward, Angel* in London in 1926, Thomas Wolfe thought of himself as a playwright, and that it was the antebellum–Civil War–Reconstruction era in the mountains of North Carolina that he chose to dramatize in the first of his three full-length plays. Although he had inklings earlier, Wolfe was actively at work from 1921 through 1925 on *Mannerhouse* (called variously "The Heirs," "The Wasters," and "The House").[19] In his 1924 application for a teaching job, he wrote, "It is only fair to tell you that my interests are centered in the drama, and that someday I hope to write successfully for the theatre and to do nothing but that." In 1929 and 1930, after publication of his first novel, he returned to this play, rewriting it and trying again to get it produced. The successful playwright Clifford Odets could describe Wolfe in 1935 as "very stagestruck" and as saying "that he had always wanted to be a playwright, not a novelist."[20] The theater was still very much alive in Wolfe's creative consciousness in 1935, as he revealed in an autobiographical sketch.[21]

The young playwright's stage directions (detailed down to the faint sound of water dripping somewhere in the huge house throughout the play) prefigure the prose of a novelist, and the facility of the playwright is seen in the power of the novels' dialogue scenes, many as long as one-act plays. As a member of Professor Frederick H. Koch's new playwriting group, the Carolina Playmakers, at Chapel Hill, young Wolfe wrote four plays in a single year. Unlike his first four novels, his plays deal not with himself but with characters in cultural, social, and historical settings in the mountains of western North Carolina. In *The Return of Buck Gavin*, his first play, written in 1919 when he was eighteen, a hunted outlaw daringly returns home to place wildflowers on the grave of his partner and is captured. In *The Third Night*, Capt. Richard Harkins, "a degenerate Southern gentleman," kills his fiancée's father, who haunts him until he goes mad. Playing the lead in those two dramas, Wolfe showed talent as an actor. In *The Convict's Theory*, a bootlegger kills a man and blames his brother; released from prison, the convict seeks revenge until he learns that his brother has married his former fiancée. Research for Wolfe's first published work, the youthful essay "The Crisis in Industry," provided background for his contribution to a forty-eight-page play that was a joint class effort called *The Strikers*.

Wolfe began another long play, *The Mountains*, at the Carolina Playmakers and continued work on it in the even more famous playwriting workshop at Harvard, conducted by George Pierce Baker, who had been Koch's teacher.[22] Over the next four years, Wolfe worked on several plays, three of them full length. At one point, he had written parts of six plays. He concentrated first on *Welcome to Our City* (originally called "Niggertown"). It was produced at Harvard in 1923.[23] A satire set in Altamont, the fictional Asheville, it "dealt with the scheme of white promoters in a Southern city to evict Negro tenants from a slum area in order to develop a white residential section there."[24]

Wolfe wrote his other plays very quickly, but initially he spent more than two years on *Mannerhouse*. In the relatively constricted genre of drama, when he was only eighteen, long before he even thought of writing a novel, we may see a parallel to the epic scope of "the book." The prologue is set in the pioneer antebellum era as the Ramsey house is being built; acts 1, 2, and 3, embrace the three eras of the Civil War— antebellum, war, Reconstruction—and act 4, as brief as the prologue, is set in the house at the turn of the century, when it literally collapses, decayed by time and neglect. Young Wolfe, like the hero Eugene (George) seems passionately obsessed, romantically and satirically, with the misconceived "manner" of life lived in the manor houses of the South.

One of the reasons critics and readers seldom focus on Wolfe's interest in the Civil War is that, as Paschal Reeves points out in his writings about contemporary life, Wolfe deals only indirectly with slavery or, except for the famous "Child by Tyger" chapter in *The Web and the Rock,* the plight of African Americans in the South after the war. But in the prologue of *Mannerhouse,* "he shows the subjugation of 'savage black men' fresh from Africa. The relationships . . . are the traditional ones of master and slave." Among his manuscripts is a set of notes on the South and slavery, written most probably soon after the play and before *Look Homeward, Angel,* which deals briefly with slavery "in a satiric vein."[25] But Wolfe's profound immersion in the issues is quite clear in his letters. In 1923 he wrote to Merlin Taylor, who had been a classmate in the play-writing workshop at Harvard, "I think my play 'The House' [*Mannerhouse*] will 'pack a punch' for it is founded on a sincere belief [by some of the characters] in the essential inequality of things and people, in a sincere belief in men and masters, rather than in men and men, in a sincere belief in the necessity of some form of human slavery—yes, I mean this—and it deals, moreover, with the one period in our history that believed these things and fought for them and was destroyed because of its belief in them."[26]

In 1924 Wolfe, himself a teacher now, wrote to his teacher-muse, Elizabeth Roberts, "I write like a fiend on one of the finest plays you ever saw."[27] When his bag, containing the play, was stolen in Paris, in 1925, he almost went "crazy." He described the incident and, more importantly, the sense of loss in letters to several people. To his mother: "Nothing has hit me as hard as this since papa's death."[28] To Homer Watt: "nothing has hit me like this since the death of my brother Ben six years ago." Astonishingly, he rewrote the entire play. "Good or bad, what I have done in these past five weeks is the best I have ever done. I am rather glad the thing was stolen: it has helped me." To Miss Lewisohn of the Neighborhood Playhouse in New York: "this play belongs to no world that ever existed by land or sea. . . . This is what the play means to me:—one, three or four years ago, when I was twenty-one or twenty-two, and wanted to prove things in plays, I wanted to write a play that should describe a cycle in our native history. . . . [N]o one, I think, will confuse it with realism. It became the mould for an expression of my secret life, of my own dark faith, chiefly through the young man Eugene. If you would know what that faith is, distilled, my play tries to express my passionate belief in all myth, in the necessity of defending and living not for truth—but for divine falsehood."[29] In the play, Eugene says, "The youth of the world, under my leadership, will band together for freedom, truth, beauty, art, and love, and will wage merciless war on hypocrisy, custom, and tradition; or they have been tricked."[30]

Writing *Mannerhouse*, Wolfe, who was well read in modern world literature, drew upon the dramaturgical innovations of his time. Theater historian Oliver Sayler greeted Wolfe's other full-length play *Welcome to Our City* as the first experimental play produced by Baker's playwriting workshop, "a play as radical in form and treatment as the contemporary stage has yet acquired." During the winter of 1926, the Theatre Guild, the Provincetown Theatre, and the Neighborhood Playhouse rejected *Mannerhouse*. But "Lawrence Langner, a member of the Theater Guild board of directors and a man of taste whose patronage has been important in the history of the American stage," encouraged Wolfe. Courtenay Lemon assured him that the guild was interested in his work and considered him "the best man the Workshop had yet turned out." Even so, after seven months of trying to sell both *Mannerhouse* and *Welcome to Our City*, "Wolfe was forced to admit," writes his agent Nowell, "that he would never be a successful dramatist."[31]

Given the negative evaluations of the play in recent decades, it should be stressed that when *Mannerhouse*, edited and with an introduction by Wolfe's last editor, Edward Aswell, was published in 1948, the reviews were generally laudatory, as the following revelatory quotations from Paschal Reeve's compilation *Thomas Wolfe: The Critical Reception* show. Few disagreed with Guy Savino, who laments that this play about "decayed Southern aristocracy . . . has never been adequately dealt with." Anna C. Hunter hears "sheer poetry"; the theme mounts "in anguish like a great psalm. Here is Wolfe in his youth, yet there is much that is redolent of his later years." For Dayton Kohler the play is a "dramatic treatment of a Southern myth. The house of the Ramsays stands for a culture, a social order, built according to the old plan and the old values. Its disintegration begins with the Civil War; its degradation is shown by a new proprietorship of the materialistic but ambitious poor white." Elinor Hughes sees at work in the play "power, eloquence and vivid imagination. . . . The decline and fall of a civilization built on a series of heroic conceptions of man's place in the world and doomed because its foundation was the institution of slavery. . . . 'Mannerhouse,' in short, tends to dwarf most modern plays as its author did his contemporaries."[32]

Harold Clurman agreed, but his vast experience as stage manager, actor, and play reader for the Theater Guild (which had rejected *Mannerhouse*), as director of the celebrated Group Theater of the thirties, and later as director of plays by Tennessee Williams, Shaw, Anouilh, Inge, and O'Neill enabled him to better envision its playability on stage and offer an insightful and balanced assessment. "There is nothing in the play that I cannot find fault with; yet I discover myself strongly attracted to it. . . . [M]ake no mistake about it: this adolescent, confused, awkward, sometimes even absurd essay in dramatic writing is many times more alive and more provocative than two or three current Broadway successes I could name. . . . *Mannerhouse* reveals a fascinating psychological duality: the young poet (Wolfe) ready to break with his basic attachment to the soil that nourished him and the faith that once sustained him, feels the need to pay tortured tribute to them before embarking on his new course."[33] Literary critics' evaluations have not been as well informed as Clurman's on purely dramaturgical grounds.

Referring to the historical element in *Look Homeward, Angel*, but relevant, I contend, to all Wolfe's writings, Shawn Holliday says, "No event affects Eugene as much as the American Civil War. . . . Wolfe shows that the conflict's historical residue still exists in the twentieth century. Just as the U.S. geographical split itself," and just as his mother and father's relationship was one of warfare, "Eugene's identity is split . . . by his dual Northern and Southern heritages, mirroring how the country's geographical problems caused ambivalent identity construction in several generations of Americans." Wolfe "develops themes of 'the decayed Southern aristocracy' that he first employed in his 1925 play *Mannerhouse*."[34] The fact that mountain people make a distinction between themselves and southerners in general may have given Wolfe the objectivity he needed to embrace but transcend both perspectives in forging his vision of America.

Although he had noted Eugene as a possible name for the hero of a narrative that became *Look Homeward, Angel,* it was in this play that Wolfe first used the name Eugene. Wolfe projected himself into an imagined historical character named Eugene before he plunged deep and long into his actual self; and when he returned to a focus on the Civil War in *The Hills Beyond,* he imagined himself again, now called by a similar name, Edward, as a historical figure who is still a boy when Wolfe was born in 1900. Young Wolfe's failure to secure a production of the play may have discouraged him from returning directly to the Civil War eras until he was more mature, as a young southerner become cosmopolitan and as a celebrated novelist who had finally gained artistic control, as seen in his conception for *The Hills Beyond.*[35] Five years before his death, having written most of "the book," Wolfe planned a single novel that would encompass an even broader range of eras, from the early Native American civilization to the Depression thirties, much of which is there in the unfinished *The Hills Beyond.*

Of Time and the River and "The Four Lost Men"

No distinct genre exists to accommodate "The Four Lost Men." To call it a story is to mislead readers into disappointment. One may read it most effectively as a lyric meditation in Wolfe's own first person voice (no fictional character is named, although Eugene may be implied), a cross between new journalism and metafiction. No writer before Wolfe ever wrote as he does here and none since. In contrast to the simple narrative of "Chickamauga," "The Four Lost Men" is a visionary, conceptualized fiction. Amid the endless sameness of much writing about the war, fiction and nonfiction, it provides the kind of unique perspective on the Civil War that we crave. Wolfe meditates upon the excruciatingly poignant impossibility of experiencing events of great magnitude on a level commensurate with their scope, complexity, and implications. The urge to recover the unrecoverable, experience the ineffable, express what is almost too metaphysical for words struggles magnificently. By expressing a concept of the war and its lingering effects through implication, "The Four Lost Men" is, I believe, the single greatest short story about the Civil War.

From around 1932 to 1937 Wolfe made five or six different visits to Gettysburg battlefield and to his father's home place nearby; those visits, the letters about them, and the fiction that derived from them demonstrate his preoccupation with his search for his father, always inseparable from his father's memory of the war and Reconstruction. With his editor and substitute father, Maxwell Perkins, Wolfe walked Gettysburg battlefield on more than one occasion; Perkins planned a visit that would include Ernest Hemingway and F. Scott Fitzgerald, but Wolfe was unable to join them. Wolfe wrote to his early mother substitute, his teacher Mrs. Roberts, about a visit to the Gettysburg area with his brother Fred and Perkins. "We got as far as York Springs, the little village a few miles from Gettysburg near which my father was born. I went out to the little country graveyard where his father and mother and a good many of his people are buried, and talked to a lot of people who remembered them all, and visited some relatives of mine who live in York Springs." Perkins, who pursued a life-long interest in the Civil War, was the editor of several major Civil War novels by both northern and southern writers. So one might be permitted to speculate that Wolfe and Perkins had long conversations about the war and that it was a major basis of their legendary editor-author friendship. Even so, A. Scott Berg tells us that "Gant's history before he arrived in Altamont was reduced to three pages and his remembrance of the Civil War to twenty-three words: 'How this boy stood by the roadside near his mother's farm, and saw the dusty Rebels march past on their way to Gettysburg.' For years it weighed on Max's conscience that he had persuaded Tom to cut out that first scene of the two little boys on the roadside with the battle impending." While we can well imagine Wolfe listening to stories on both sides of the family, Robert Raynolds is only one of Wolfe's friends who has eloquently testified to the passion with which he retold stories about his people, about "regions where he had also searched for his father (even as among the marbles of Vermont), and presently, with a joyous glow on his face, he was talking about the farm lands out towards Gettysburg, the fat farms, the fat orchards, the fat-to-bursting barns, and the wholesome and huge-eating farmer folk he had met out there. It was one of those radiant moments when Wolfe, the talker, happy in his listeners, poured forth the good speech of direct and joyous experience."[36]

The first of Wolfe's two great short stories about the Civil War," The Four Lost Men," appeared in the February 1934 issue of *Scribner's Magazine* and was included in the short fiction collection *From Death to Morning*, published in 1935. One-fifth longer, the version reprinted in this collection is included in *The Complete Short Stories of Thomas Wolfe* (106–19). Wolfe wrote "The Four Lost Men" sometime around 1933, the year I was born. "Four Lost Men" and "Chickamauga" were the first stories I ever read about the Civil War.[37] At thirteen I knew little history. Fifty years later my Civil War novel *Sharp-shooter* was published. In its 150 pages, I compress some of the visionary elements of Wolfe's "Four Lost Men" and the oral storytelling elements of "Chickamauga." My sense, reading those stories, of so much missing and lost influenced my perception of the war. Willis Carr, the narrator, who, a child-warrior, was in every major battle with General Longstreet, sums up the novel's theme in this question and all it implies: "Why, if I am the Sharpshooter who shot General William Price Sanders . . . did I feel then, as I do still, that I missed the War?"[38] With facts and imagination, he strives for fifty years to achieve a concept, a vision of the war that will displace the agony of the revelation that he missed the war. Rereading those stories, I am gratified to see that to a significant degree, what was missing may be found, resurrected, conceptualized, and preserved in Wolfe's two short works of art and finally in their readers.

In resurrecting his father's four dead Civil War heroes, Wolfe resurrects his father and instills in us a vision of all the lost men of all wars. Wolfe opens "The Four Lost Men" with this invocation: "Suddenly, at the green heart of June, I heard my father's voice again" (*Complete Short Stories*, 106; page numbers for this story are given in parentheses). Wolfe had breathed life into that voice five years earlier in *O Lost/ Look Homeward, Angel.* He was the world-famous author of *Look Homeward, Angel* when he heard his "father's great voice sounding from the porch again" and wrote "The Four Lost Men" (106). "My father was old, he was sick with a cancer. . . . Yet under the magic life and hope the War had brought to us, his life seemed to have revived again out of its grief and pain, its death of joy, its sorrow of irrevocable memory" (108). And then Wolfe reenvisions the haunting image that opened *O Lost/Look Homeward, Angel.* Included in this collection is a passage from *Of Time and the River* in which Eugene visits his dying father and listens to his stories of the war one last time.

Implicit in Wolfe's most often repeated cry, "Lost!" is the relatively banal word "missing." The men were lost to Wolfe's father, too, because in a sense all who fought in the war—Garfield, Harrison, Arthur, and Hayes themselves—or who witnessed some episodes of it—as Wolfe's father and mother did—missed the war because they became lost either in nostalgic details or pseudomythic states of mind. And so as a youth Wolfe too missed the war, and those millions who have walked the battlefields miss the war. There is "something in our hearts we cannot utter" (117). These men appealed to Wolfe because they were real—as Gettysburg was—to his father, then lost to him, then missing for sixteen-year-old Wolfe and for the famous Wolfe until he remembers and then re-creates. To anchor his emotions, Wolfe looked into the *Encyclopedia Britannica* for facts about the four presidents; for words that would soar above facts, he looked into his imagination.

Wolfe starts with his own emotions, shared with other young men, about the advent of World War I, recalls his father's haunting awareness of the Civil War, his father's sadness that the four heroes are now lost and forgotten. Then Wolfe asks questions about the humanity they must have shared with him and his friends, universal emotions, sensory experiences, sexual longings. Soon he is speaking for himself, his contemporaries, his father, Garfield, all who experienced the Civil War, all humanity. Seeing them not from his father's actual experience but from his own imagination, Wolfe saw them as his father never did, and thus reclaims them for his father, creates them for himself and his readers. He lets the four lost veterans speak for themselves as a chorus about the war, imputing to them his own feelings, and those feelings, as expressed, are unique.

Southern love of language, dialect, colloquialisms that he listened to, and the style of all the masters that he voraciously read—usually the big books, such as *Moby Dick, War and Peace,* Balzac's *Human Comedy* series, and the big poems, such as *Paradise Lost*—affected Wolfe's vision and his style. His complex, ornate, overtly expressive style is imbued with all those qualities. That style, best seen in "The Four Lost Men," is composed of a vast array of rhetorical devices: ornate imagery, abstract words, compound modifiers, numerous qualifiers, double and triple adjectives and adverbs, repetition for emphasis and sound, generalizations, rhythm, rhapsodic flourishes, lyrical riffs, personification, rhetorical questions, balanced phrasing, parallel structure, inverted syntax, overt thematic statements, archaic words, literary phrases, superlatives, clichés, formalisms, vivid contrasts, meditative modes, expressionistic effects, and more. His style leaves his readers laved in rhetoric and awash in sounds, giving them experiences they can find in no other writer.

Wolfe's artistic achievement lies in his brilliant orchestration of all the raw material elements and the poetics of this unique meditation, controlled within a rhetorical structure. In this story, Wolfe's use of repetition, which he learned from the oral storytelling tradition, is even more trancelike, incantatory, than usual. He successfully pushes the technique of repetition to the limit of its possibilities. The repetition of key phrases is necessary as part of the process for conjuring new phrases, words, images. He repeatedly uses the rhetorical device of asking questions about what the four men saw, felt, heard, or knew, such as, "Were they not burning with the wild and wordless hope?" shifting often from those introductory words to the oddly poignant "Had they not felt, as we have felt, as they waited in the night, the huge lonely earth of night time and America?" (114). The effect of the negative word "not" para-

effect upon him of one his visits to York, Pennsylvania, his father's earth, his father's people, and to the Gettysburg battlefield.

I don't know if I told you I also went to York Springs for two or three days at the beginning of October. Stayed with Aunt Mary (Gil's wife) and her son Edgar (they all call him Jim). . . . I went with him on his rounds and saw the country—also the little house where papa's mother & Augusta lived, place where they are all buried, etc. Met several people who knew & remembered papa.—A very strange thing happened while I was there: Jim and I were going to visit our cousin, Charles Wolfe, who was Geo. Wolfe's son, but of course a much older man than either of us—66. He was said to be a wealthy and prosperous man & lived in Dillsburg, a town about 8 miles from York Springs. Well, he died very suddenly a day or two after I got there—one of his sons came early one morning with the news—Jim and I went over and saw the body and he looked so much like papa it was startling. The same long lean look, the same thin long nose, grey moustache, grey hair—I'd have known him for one of papa's people if no one had ever told me who he was.[41]

One may imagine Wolfe, having described his trip to his father's earth in language as vivid as his fiction, getting a kind of sustenance from hearing from his mother that she too, only a month or so later, had visited her former husband's earth. He wrote to her in March 1933.

I am glad you had the trip to York Springs and saw Aunt Mary and Jim and his wife and also had the chance of going over the field of Gettysburg with Fred. I have been across the battle field myself but it was in a hired car driven by some country boy up there who had been taught a little speech to say and annoyed me so much by getting it all wrong. I have read so much about that battle that I now understand pretty well what happened and I would much rather go with Fred or someone I know than in a hired car. . . . I'm sorry that you could not have seen it on some such season as that when it looked as it must have looked on those hot days in July when the battle was fought. I was very glad and interested to know that so many of your own kinsman were in that battle and in other battles of the war and, of course, several of Papa's people, as you know, including his older brother George and George Lentz's father were on the Union side in the war. So we seem to have been represented on every side there was.[42]

It is not only as his northern father's son but as a southerner that Wolfe ventures out in search of the other half of his being, that he visits Germany, especially Munich and the mountain regions of Bavaria described in *The Web and the Rock* and in *You Can't Go Home Again.* The home he can't go to again is not only the literal home in Asheville and the literal home he never had in Germany and in all the other places he tried to make home—Chapel Hill, Cambridge, New York City, Brooklyn, London, Paris—but the mythic home of the North; and the mythic image of the South's home in the glorious-inglorious past, and the longed-for mythic home that combines his father's North and his mother's South in the mythic image of America, where the American dream turned nightmare, a nightmare to be overcome through hope in the future. Wolfe's uniqueness among other writers, both northern and southern, and his special value for us lies in this actual, creative, and spiritual journey into "lost time" and into a projected brighter future. The test of the value of a prophetic vision is not only in its final realization but in the quality and relevance of its image in the consciousness of those who embrace it.

The complexity of the compositional and publication history of versions of "His Father's Earth" illustrates the indirect nature of the Civil War's effect on Wolfe and, by implication, on southern writers. And implication, as I have stressed, is ultimately more powerful than direct expression. Just as Wolfe's writing career began in playwriting with his projection of his own Byronic romantic-satirical sensibility into an imagined character in the Civil War era, in *The Good Child's River* he projected himself into his portrayal of the father of his mistress, Aline Bernstein. Wolfe wandered, in his three years' composition of "The Good Child's River" component of "the book," away from his promise to her to focus on the story of Esther's (Aline's) childhood and family history to tell her father Joe's story as he imagined it, especially the long Civil War passages devoted to Joe's father's gory Civil War experiences (reprinted in this collection from *The Good Child's River*) and the visit that Joe makes to his father's people in the North.[43] Wolfe removed the story of the visit, shortened it, and sold it as the short story "His Father's Earth," in which he attributed that visit to his autobiographical character George Webber as "the boy." Considered to be one of Wolfe's finest stories, it was published in Modern Monthly, April 1935, and is included in *The Complete Short Stories of Thomas Wolfe*. A shorter version is included in *The Web and the Rock* (86–90; it ends as a climax, within three pages of the end of part 1). In the short story and *The Web and the Rock* versions, Eugene-George only imagines the visit. Wolfe's multiple use of the northern home place material suggests that perhaps the inspiration was a vision in which he himself made that visit, either as a boy or as a man, at some time before he made the actual visit. While Wolfe commonly made multiple use of short and long passages from "the book," the way he used this one is relatively unusual. His three important uses of the same material suggest that his need to connect with the family in the Civil War era was deep, strong, and lasting.

"Chickamauga"

More deeply than Elizabeth Nowell, the biographer before him, or David Donald, the one after him, Andrew Turnbull, as revealed in his style and choice of detail, was aware of the implications of Wolfe's visits to Gettysburg and to the home places of his family, on both sides. "That spring and summer he went on several jaunts through Pennsylvania Dutch country with Fred, now a Westinghouse salesman based in Harrisburg. The fat farmland with its huge barns and powerful horses and air of abundance stirred memories of his father who still had relatives living in York Springs, near storied Gettysburg. In July, Tom and Fred, accompanied by Max Perkins, tramped over the battlefield where seventy years earlier almost to the day their great uncles, George Pentland and Bacchus Westall, had fought under Lee."[44]

In a letter to his mother, April 31, 1934, Wolfe revealed his ever-deepening preoccupation with his families' experiences in the Civil War and the implications of those experiences for all human history.

It may be too vast an undertaking, but I keep thinking about it and if I tell how one family like your own, for instance, going back a hundred and fifty years or more to pioneer and Colonial days and with all their settling in various places, pushing Westward, marrying into other families everywhere, etc., finally weaving a kind of great web, it really would have the whole history of the country in it. For example, your own father and Uncle Bacchus and other of your relatives who were in the Civil War on the Southern side and Papa's brother, George, and his sister's husband, Lentz, and others in that group in Pennsylvania who fought on the Northern side, and the rest of you who stayed at home or what you did, what your lives were like during that time—the whole story of the Civil War could be told in the lives of those people. . . . [I]f you explore your own back-yard carefully enough and compare it with all the other things you find out, you may some day find out what the whole earth is like.[45]

Listening to family stories provided Wolfe with material for both the short story "Chickamauga" and *The Hills Beyond*.

That Wolfe repeatedly walked the battlefield where his southern ancestors fought and near the home place of his northern father's people, and that he often read books about that battle suggest that Gettysburg might have become the center of the Confederate soldier novel he envisioned. "It is a very beautiful spot," he wrote to his mother, "and it seemed to be especially created by God or the devil for a battlefield."[46] Sensitive to the ways the Civil War affected Wolfe's life and his writing, Turnbull, alone of the three major biographers, included an image of a kind that would stir the emotions and imagination of almost any writer, but certainly Wolfe.

In September [1934] he spent two weeks at the Chicago World's Fair, and in October visited "Welbourne," a pre–Civil War mansion in Middleburg, Virginia, that belonged to some friends of the Perkinses. On one of the windowpanes were Jeb Stuart's initials, which the Gallant Pelham had scratched with his diamond ring while waiting for his horse to be brought to the door, and five miles away was the Manassas battlefield.[47] Deep-seated emotions welling up in him, Wolfe wrote to his hostess after his return to Brooklyn, "There is an enormous age and sadness in Virginia—a grand kind of death—I always felt it, even when all I did was ride across the state at night in a train—it's the way the earth looks, the fields and the woods and in the great hush and fall of evening light."[48]

That charged image of Stuart's initials on the windowpane suggests Wolfe's reaching out beyond family-centered approaches to the war.

Turnbull wanted his readers to know not only Wolfe's most recent reading of Civil War history, but that the literary context for such reading was rich. "On the back of an envelope postmarked February 21, 1936, he listed" works by Carlyle, Dickens, Shakespeare, Twain, Whitman, Pepys, Thackeray, Tolstoy, and Browning, "and—reflecting his perennial interest in the Civil War—General Gordon's *Reminiscences,* Abner Doubleday's *Chancellorsville and Gettysburg,* and J. F. C. Fuller's *Grant and Lee.*"[49]

In April 1937 Wolfe, still intending someday to write that novel about a common soldier during the Civil War, made yet another compelling visit to Gettysburg and his father's family's cemetery at York Springs. Taking a bus, he moved down the Shenandoah Valley, well aware of the exploits of the legendary Stonewall Jackson and, apparently, of the instant fame of the recently published *Gone with the Wind,* which he had bought. Visiting his mother's family at Burnsville, he listened eagerly to his great uncle John Westall, then ninety-five years old, tell about his adventures in the 29th North Carolina Infantry during the Civil War, doling out many details of the fighting at Chickamauga in 1863. "Over the next months," writes David Donald, Wolfe's most recent biographer, "Wolfe blended Westall's recollections and other family lore with a completely fictional love story into 'Chickamauga,' which was told entirely in the voice of the old veteran. Its language did not represent John Westall's careful, usually correct English but reflected Wolfe's deliberate attempt to recapture the speech of mountain folk while avoiding too much dialect and too many colloquialisms"—which had marred his first few one-act plays. "The clear structure of the story and restrained use of language again demonstrated how much Wolfe had learned."[50]

In July 1937 Wolfe wrote to the southern novelist Hamilton Basso, expressing the excitement of plunging, at last, into battle.

When I got back to New York, I wrote a story called "Chickamauga" and if I do say so, it is one of the best stories I ever wrote. I got the idea for it from an old, old man, my great-uncle, John Westall, who lives over in Yancey County and who is ninety-five years old. When I saw him this spring, he began to tell me about the Civil War and about the battle of Chickamauga, which was, he said, the bloodiest, most savage battle he was ever in. He told about it all so wonderfully and in such pungent and poetic language, such as so many of the old country people around here use, that I couldn't wait to get back to New York to begin on it. My idea was simply to tell the story of a great battle in the language of a common soldier—the kind of country mountain boy who did so much of the fighting in the war . . . and it simply crackled with action from the first line and besides that, it was so real, so true—it was all told in the old man's language and when you read it, it was just as if he was there talking to you.[51]

But most of the major magazines, including *Scribner's*, turned it down as being neither fiction nor history.[52] When the story didn't sell, Wolfe had become mature enough as an artist to assure Elizabeth Nowell, his agent, that he was aware of the problems. "I am. . . . willing if necessary to revise the story and perhaps to bring it back more to its original purpose—that is the story of an old man telling about the war and the battle."[53] The *Saturday Evening Post* rejected it as not having enough of the "story element." "All this piece had was the whole Civil War. . . . If it had had any more of the 'story element,' it would have exploded into electricity."[54]

"Chickamauga" electrified the pages of the 1938 winter issue of the *Yale Review* a few months before all Wolfe's creative electrical storms ceased. It was included among the stories in *The Hills Beyond*, published posthumously in 1941. Edward Aswell, the novel's shaping editor, reports that with the rejections, "The answer everywhere was the same: The Civil War wasn't timely—we were done with wars!"[55] He called it "one of the best stories Tom ever wrote." Most reviewers agreed, including J. Donald Adams, who called "Chickamauga" "an exceedingly well done tale."[56]

Wolfe gives the impression that the story the old man is

telling is about his friend Jim and his obsession with Martha. But in effect, I have always argued that every first person story is about the teller, about the expressed or implied effect on him or her of the story he or she tells. Paradoxically, the nature of first person is that it is omniscient: the teller already knows all he will tell us. But because this tale is about the "whole war" in a sense—the old man tells of other major battles also—this first person storyteller seems all the more omniscient. The oral storyteller achieves a communal "we" on a folk level, a felicitous, even necessary complement to the visionary "we" of the more literary "Four Lost Men."

"Chickamauga" is a simple narrative but it is also in its own way unique in Civil War literature. Its achievement derives from its aesthetic unity and its effect. The structure—four battles—and the theme—four changes the war wrought in the characters' lives—are perfectly meshed. This story has more obvious organization than any of Wolfe's other stories and more than most other first person Civil War short stories.

Instead of telling the story to the prodigal returning as a world famous author, as his maternal great-uncle told Wolfe, the nameless old man tells the story to a nameless boy. He begins with the story of Fort Donelson, then here is an example of Wolfe's repetition and transition techniques: "Well then, Fort Donelson was the funniest fight that I was ever in because hit was all fun fer me without no fightin'. . . . And Stone Mountain was the most peculiar fight that I was in because— well, I'll tell you a strange story and you can figger fer yourself."[57] The storyteller invites the listener to participate. Then he tells about Shiloh and again recapitulates before going on to the biggest battle. "I've told you of three battles now, and one was funny, one was strange, and one was—well, one showed us what war and fightin' could be. But I'll tell you of a fourth one now" (92; page numbers for this story are given in parentheses). That battle comes exactly in the middle of the thirty-page story, which ends with this line: "the bloodiest battle anyone has ever fought—was at Chickamauga in that cedar thicket—at Chickamauga Creek in that great war" (107).

A parallel structural progression renders reversals and changes wrought by the war in the storyteller and his best friend, Jim. As he is going to war, Jim meets Martha. The two friends discover that war is different from what they had expected. "Hit's funny how war and a little black-haired gal will change a man—but that's the story that I'm goin' to tell you now" (83). The storyteller himself experiences the major change: "Before the war I was the serious one, and Jim had been the one to play" (94). He became so hardened to the spectacle of dead bodies that when Jim was shot, "I took one look at him and then stepped over him like he was a log" (105). The crowning ironic reversal is that he marries Martha himself. "That's where I made my big mistake" (85). "We never knowed" (95) is a phrase the old man repeats often. As the saying goes, "It's the damned not knowing."

The effect on the reader of the battle tales and of the ironic reversals on the personal level derives from Wolfe's mastery of the southern Appalachian oral storytelling tradition that had kept the Civil War alive up to that day in the spring of 1937 when he listened to his great-uncle Westall tell about it. The repetition of such phrases as "they say," "I say," "as I was tellin' you," "Well, like I say then," and "I heard 'em tell about it later" create the storytelling-listening ambience. The Bacchus and George Pentland stories seem to be digressions, but they serve a useful function by conveying a sense of the storyteller's background and culture. The simplicity of the oral diction, the unusually effective rhythm created by his use of the oral storytelling device of repetition, the use of the communal pronoun "we" mingled with "I" have such a profound effect on the

reader that we can imagine its effect on the boy who listens. "The eagerness of the listener," we can imagine, taking a
phrase from *Jane Eyre*, "quickens the tongue of the teller."

It is not merely that he wrote the two Civil War stories
"Four Lost Men" and "Chickamauga," but the way he wrote
them, with masterful artistic skill, that helps persuade me that
Thomas Wolfe had the potential for writing the great Civil
War novel.

"The Plumed Knight" and *The Hills Beyond*

At the heart of my original conception of *Thomas Wolfe's Civil
War* was the inclusion of the entire unfinished novel *The Hills
Beyond*, but LSU Press reprinted it before this collection was
well under way. So I have chosen for inclusion here only the
chapter in which most of the themes are deployed. Like Wolfe's
first really ambitious work, the play *Mannerhouse*, "The Plumed
Knight," chapter 5, at the center of the book, is both satirical
and lyrical and finally sadly profound in its implications; it reveals most coherently and at a most sustained length many of
the themes, prototypes, and elements prefigured in *Mannerhouse*. After the war, Theodore, the so-called scholar of the
Joyner clan, having failed his bar examination, founds the
Joyner Heights Military Academy. A professional veteran, he
fosters myths about the "manner" of the southern aristocracy
and its role in the war.[58] Because Wolfe was a Byronic romantic, he was also a satirist, and Shakespearean that he was, he
was also a writer of comic scenes of great vitality. Wolfe was
already planning this novel, first called "The Hills beyond
Pentland," in 1931; it was the project upon which his creative
energy was focused when he died seven years later.

In the long, obsessive revision process, Wolfe called *Of Time
and the River's* second part "The Hills beyond Pentland," which
he later turned into a separate novel.[59] Kennedy tells us:

Although the "Publisher's Note" in *Of Time and the River* [1935] had stated that "The Hills Beyond Pentland" was already written, it was by no means ready for publication. Wolfe had in typescript the sequence about the boy and the street on which he lived: a description of "The Return of the Prophet Bacchus" for a reunion of Civil War veterans; Eliza Gant's tales of Bacchus and other Pentland kin; an account of Uncle Bascom's visit from Boston, which included Bascom's bitter denunciation of his father, Major Thomas Pentland; and sketches of Eliza's boarders and their talk, from which "The Four Lost Men" had already been taken for publication. Followers of Wolfe's work who have wondered what the announced volume, "The Hills Beyond Pentland," contained can now see that, with varying degrees of alteration, this material finally made its way into print in the first nine chapters of *The Web and the Rock*.[60]

In May 1935 Wolfe's letter to Perkins expresses in the strongest terms how important this novel, within the design of the big "book," had become for him. "I think 'The October Fair' is going to be a grand book and we will try to meet the criticism of the critics and to show them that I am improving and learning my business all the time. The book I am living for, however, is the Pentland book . . . and I feel if there is any chance of my doing anything good before I am forty it will be this book. I feel such a swelling and exultant sense of certitude and such a feeling of gathering power and fulfillment that I tremble when I think about it and I hope to God that nothing happens to me or to my life . . . before I get to it."[61]

As late as 1937 he wrote about "the book" to Sherwood Anderson, the midwestern writer who had influenced Gertrude Stein, Hemingway, and Faulkner, and who had settled in Marion, Virginia, as a small town newspaper editor: "I'm wrestling with a huge leviathan of work—three monstrous books, all worked upon and sweat upon and prayed about and dreamt and cursed upon for years."[62] Holman describes Wolfe's purpose for "the book": "He wished to weave a myth of his native land, an embodiment of its nature and its spirit. At a time when the American critic was just beginning to be concerned with the newer concepts of myth, Wolfe wrote, in the manuscript later published as the title piece of *The Hills Beyond:* 'The Myth is founded on *extorted* fact: wrenched from the context of ten thousand days. . . . For it is not a question of having faith, or lack of it. It is a simple fact of seeing.' "[63]

Wolfe's powers in the use of the third person, omniscient point of view are fully operative in the ten chapters of *The Hills Beyond,* which one reviewer said "might have been the greatest realistic Southern picture of Reconstruction Days."[64] As I have suggested, a novel about Reconstruction *is* a Civil War novel. Serving on a panel at Loyola University in New Orleans with novelist-historian Shelby Foote several years ago, I asked him why he thought no historian had written a great narrative about Reconstruction such as he had written about the war years and why novelists had not done so. "It's not romantic," he said, and added, "This nation committed two sins for which it can never atone: slavery and Reconstruction." Had he lived, Wolfe would have discovered, I think, as Shelby Foote did when he wrote his three-volume narrative of the war, that the "Civil War was the crossroads of our being," that to tell that war story is to tell, by implication, the whole story of America and to express its spirit, dark mingled with light.

In 1941 the reviewers, one and all, were moved to reassess all Wolfe's fiction and to imagine what he could have achieved had he lived beyond his literary adolescence.[65] "'The Lion at Morning' and 'The Hills Beyond,' parts of an incomplete novel . . . are proof that Thomas Wolfe had not shot his bolt." One reviewer seemed to feel the need to strike a balance. "Wolfe's last work of all, the novelette 'The Hills Beyond,' creaks with a conscious effort at orderly factual progression which—except in the last beautiful chapter—makes it like the writings of a stranger."[66] The widely respected reviewer for the *New York Times Book Review* J. Donald Adams made the most persuasive case for *The Hills Beyond* as a harbinger of the new Wolfe, capable of writing an artistically accomplished Civil War novel.

The unfinished novel, Mr. Aswell informs us, was the work with which Wolfe was chiefly occupied during the year before his death. . . . [S]ections of "You Can't Go Home Again" were more objective than anything previous, and with "The Hills Beyond" the goal he had set himself was definitely in sight. . . . In this book—how great a pity that he did not live to finish it!—he aimed to tell the story of his forebears. . . . Wolfe could make his people live. We require that of any novelist worth his salt. But Tom Wolfe had more than that to give. There was that marvelous sensory equipment of his, that vibrant sensitivity, evident from the first. He had the power of evocation as only the best writers have. . . . But Wolfe was growing—growing fast, when death overtook him. The integration that he needed was under way. He was finding himself in relation to life, in relation to his world. . . . The indications of this growth in "The Hills Beyond" are plentiful. One of them is the increasing number of passages in which he does not simply feel, but thinks. . . . [I]f Thomas Wolfe had lived he would have gotten more of what has made us the people we are into his fiction than any novelist we have had.[67]

Bella Kussy, writing in 1942, expressed some doubt about Wolfe's ability to recharge his capacity for expressive power. In *The Hills Beyond* "Wolfe's style" had "become objective to the point of flat, lifeless dullness. . . . [W]e find that what has been lost is not merely 'subjectivity,' but movement and color, individuality and magnificence." Literary critic and broad canvas historian Herbert J. Muller, who, in 1947, wrote the first book-length study of Wolfe, gave a balanced assessment of *The Hills Beyond*. He noted a diminishment of the raw power that had enthralled Wolfe's readers. Had he lived, I am convinced he was capable of generating a different kind of power through artistic compression. "Here we see the new, sober, impersonal Wolfe, who is conscientiously practicing restraint, who has profited by criticism." Some pages later, Muller writes: "This is unquestionably Wolfe's most 'objective' fiction, impersonal even by high critical standards. With one or two exceptions, his characters are inventions; he is not himself the hero, nor does he identify himself with any one character; and though he comments freely on the narrative, he comments as the omniscient, dispassionate author. Likewise his style is modest and quiet. . . . In short, Wolfe is no longer possessed, but in full possession of his materials and his powers."[68]

Those who do not have a high opinion of *The Hills Beyond* sometimes cite as a reason the circumstantial incompleteness of it. In 1998 Dieter Meindl mounted an argument for coherence. "The 150-page text . . . is usually called a fragment of a novel. . . . [But] *The Hills Beyond* by itself, as a narrative cycle consisting of interrelated, but self-sustained parts . . . reveals greater unity and cohesion than on the basis of reading it as a truncated novel with the part joining it to the Webber novels left unfinished." It should be viewed "as autonomous—as partaking of the short story cycle and the chronicle—and as providing a sense of closure"—as in Joyce's *Dubliners,* Anderson's *Winesburg, Ohio.* Meindl exhorts us to view it "as an artistic achievement, a text that has received too little and too derogatory attention."[69] Aside from its artistic merits or its genre classification, *The Hills Beyond* lends a richness to Wolfe's novels by providing the ancestral roots of George Webber (Eugene Gant).

"I Am Thomas Wolfe, American"

Richard Kennedy urges us not to "lose sight of the fact that" Thomas Wolfe "passed from the literary scene only nine years after he entered upon it with *Look Homeward, Angel.*"[70]

The often-repeated claim that Wolfe was the least mature as an artist—and perhaps as a person—of the major writers of his time needs to be reexamined. Denigrators like to say that Wolfe wrote for youth. Although his body was prematurely aged when he died, a youthful vigor and hope animated everything he wrote. When the great novelists of Wolfe's time published their best work, they were all about the same age: Fitzgerald was twenty-nine (*The Great Gatsby*); Hemingway, twenty-seven (*The Sun Also Rises*); Wolfe, twenty-nine (*Look Homeward, Angel*); Faulkner, thirty-two (*The Sound and the Fury*). Two were older: Evelyn Scott was thirty-six (*The Wave*, part 2 of her trilogy and one of the great Civil War novels), and Dos Passos was forty-one (*U.S.A.*). When Wolfe died at thirty-seven, the best work of Fitzgerald, Hemingway, Faulkner, Dos Passos, and Scott was clearly behind them. Wolfe died youngest, with the greater promise of future work (except for Faulkner, especially *Absalom, Absalom!*, another major Civil War novel).

Looking at Wolfe's work again, including those published by university presses and by the Thomas Wolfe Society over the past quarter of a century, and reexamining his life, I see him as less provincial than the reputedly more sophisticated and cosmopolitan Hemingway and Fitzgerald, whose lives were full of drinking, sports, parties, and foreign travel—a form of child's play. Wolfe could do parties, too, though not African safaris, but Germany meant more to him than the Paris of Hemingway and Fitzgerald. Wolfe dreamed of the "dark Helen" of Germany, but he found the ugly darkness of Nazism (just as the South nurtured the darkness of slavery). All his writing considered, he was the most intellectual, although Scott, Faulkner, and Robert Penn Warren fare well by comparison.

In the late thirties and throughout the forties, when the widespread love of Wolfe's novels was most intense, the many photographs of Wolfe, his marble brow, glaring dark eyes, and black hair, his gigantic stature, were among the icons of American literature, along with Whitman, Twain, Frost, Hemingway, Fitzgerald, and Faulkner. While some critics and novelists, from Bernard de Voto to Wright Morris, have derided Wolfe's work, in 1947, almost a decade after Wolfe's death, Faulkner, when asked whom he admired, put Wolfe first. Hemingway, Wolfe, Dos Passos, and Steinbeck had all failed, but "Wolfe made the grandest failure because he had a vast courage," wrote A. Wigfall Green, paraphrasing Faulkner from notes. "He wrote as though he didn't have long to live. . . . Faulkner showed great humility at the mention of Wolfe's name."[71] We should return again and again to look where Faulkner looked for the real Thomas Wolfe—the overreacher who took all mankind as his province and aspired to utter what words could not express. It was in the latter aspiration that he failed most magnificently; I say "magnificently" because, as writers and readers, we must never refuse to believe that words are capable of achieving Wolfe's ideal.

An expression of his immaturity, some declare, was that Wolfe embraced all experience with an attitude of awe and wonder. When considering the question of maturity, we might recall the scope and variety of the writers to whom he was favorably compared and the bases for those comparisons: with Homer, the poet who captured the past, present, and future of a people; with the translators of the King James Bible and the Elizabethan playwrights, whose language was rich; with Dostoyevsky, for the epic scope of such works as *The Brothers Karamazov;* with Dickens, for depiction of characters; with Rabelais, for his huge and magnificent appetite for the raw materials of life; with Balzac, for compulsive work habits similar to Wolfe's and for his huge social canvas, Paris, small towns, and the countryside; with Melville, for his allegory on a large scale and his language; with Whitman, for his comprehensive cataloging and listing of the raw materials of American life and his vision of America; with Proust, for his rendering of time and memory; with Joyce, for his use of the devices of fiction, especially stream of consciousness, symbolism, style, structure; with Hart Crane, for his vision of America (by happenstance, Crane and Wolfe lived at different times in the same room, from the window of which the builder of the Brooklyn Bridge directed construction). And I add Thomas Mann, for parallels between Wolfe's youth, in *Buddenbrooks,* and his intellectual development, in *The Magic Mountain.* And Jules Romains, who conceived his massive *Men of Good Will* when he first began to write, and in 1932 published the first two volumes of the projected thirty-seven, covering the world from 1900 to 1933.

We do well to reexamine writers in various new perspectives as a way of enriching our perceptions of their work and our collective literature. Wolfe's first and final subject was the Civil War, in the broad sense I have described. I conceived this collection as a way of making a case for Thomas Wolfe as a Civil War novelist, both in accomplishment and potential, because he has seldom been seen in that light, and it is my conviction that seeing him in that light illuminates his life and magnifies his magnificent overall achievement. Presented in this way, he may—it is my hope—attract first readers, among the young and among those interested in the Civil War, who might not otherwise be attracted to his work, or even have heard of him.

That Wolfe strove, especially in the later years of his short life, to write objectively, to put subjectivity behind him, as when he left Perkins to stand alone, is well known. But I have shown that he had objectivity at the very beginning in his plays; drama is in its nature an objective genre. In some works, his technique is cinematic, also objective. He was conscious at the end of having begun, at least, to achieve objectivity but, some critics say, at the loss of lyrical passion. That loss, I am convinced, was only temporary, transitional. Had he not died at such an early age, he might have had thirty more years of productivity in which to triple what he had already achieved, and, I believe, move into his literary maturity.

The prevailing conception of Thomas Wolfe's massive body of fiction is that it is overwhelmingly autobiographical. That conception did not prevail over my recent closer examination. Wolfe, it is certainly true, expended much of his creative energy in remembering, revealing, reconciling, and regenerating the essence of his own life; but he extended his energies to each and every member of his immediate family—and later to his ancestors on both sides—to his townspeople; and beyond, among his friends and acquaintances and the people he observed in Chapel Hill, Harvard, New York, London, Paris, and Germany. His copious allusions to mythic Greece, the Elizabethan and other historical eras were an expression of his desire to embrace life in all its manifestations. This myriad-minded all-inclusiveness makes his achievement as a southern writer, all of whose works derive from the Civil War, much more meaningfully complex than any other southern writer. Wolfe's Civil War, unlike Faulkner's, and unlike that of any Civil War novel, is embedded in a vision of America as a whole. Wolfe was a southerner, but a southerner as American (in his pocket notebook, he wrote, "I am Thomas Wolfe, American")—an American, his "book" proclaims, as a citizen of the world. In this expansive context, Wolfe's work is less autobiographical than autouniversal.

Wolfe's plans for his future work were always on a grand scale. When he was only thirty years old, he mapped out "the book" in five parts (each about a thousand pages, as four of them turned out to be) for which he projected ten years of his life; most writers don't hit their stride until about thirty-five. His last and unfinished novel, *The Hills Beyond,* based upon the lives of his maternal ancestors, departs completely from his own life and marks the unfinished story of his creative life. But works written throughout his life, from drama, the first genre that attracted him, to the two novels published in his lifetime and the two novels published after his death, to the many short stories and nonfiction works, reveal a consciousness simultaneously and inextricably as obsessed with all mankind among many nations throughout the mythic and recorded history of the world as he was with his own short life. Such humanistic overreaching sprang from his temperament. Although relatively few of the millions and millions of words Wolfe wrote, millions of which remain unpublished, directly tell the story of the Civil War, they embrace antebellum America and the war and Reconstruction. But indirection through implication and allusion is at the heart of the definition I offer of southern fiction—that all of it derives from the Civil War. That heart beats strongest in the works of Thomas Wolfe, which, even as they fall short of the great American novel as the great Civil War novel, show that a myriadminded vision of America and of humanity is possible and hovers even now.

Notes

1. Out of the concept of this collection grew a lecture, delivered in Gettysburg at the Thomas Wolfe Society's annual conference in May 1996, and published as "Lost Men: From Gettysburg to Chickamauga," *Thomas Wolfe Review* 21, no. 2 (fall 1997): 7–17, which won the Thomas Wolfe Society's Zelda Gitlin Literary Prize. For this introduction, I have included adaptations of that essay and several passages from the introduction to my book, edited with Peggy Bach, *Classics of Civil War Fiction* (Tuscaloosa: University of Alabama Press, 2001), along with ideas and a few passages from "For the New Millennium: New Perspectives on the Civil War," *National Forum: Phi Kappa Phi Journal* 77, no. 3 (summer 1997), and forthcoming essays on William Faulkner's *Absalom, Absalom!* and Robert

Penn Warren's *All the King's Men.* Ideas expressed in those works have evolved over two decades and are still evolving, especially the concept of myriadmindedness.

2. Thomas Wolfe, *The Web and the Rock* (New York: Harper and Brothers, 1939), 183.

3. Leslie Field, preface to Thomas Wolfe, *The Autobiography of an American Novelist,* ed. Field (Cambridge: Harvard University Press, 1983), vii.

4. Thomas Wolfe, *The Notebooks of Thomas Wolfe,* ed. Richard S. Kennedy and Paschal Reeves (Chapel Hill: University of North Carolina Press, 1970), 2:673.

5. Leslie Field, *Thomas Wolfe and His Editors* (Norman: University of Oklahoma Press, 1987), 150, 165.

6. Dieter Meindl, "Thomas Wolfe's *The Hills Beyond:* A Reappraisal in Generic Terms," *Thomas Wolfe Review* 22, no. 2 (fall 1998): 28–38.

7. Elizabeth Nowell, *Thomas Wolfe* (Garden City, N.Y.: Doubleday, 1960), 22.

8. Thomas Wolfe, *The Short Novels of Thomas Wolfe,* ed., with introd. and notes, C. Hugh Holman (New York: Scribner, 1961), xvii.

9. Richard S. Kennedy, *The Window of Memory: The Literary Career of Thomas Wolfe* (Chapel Hill: University of North Carolina Press, 1962), 240.

10. Thomas Wolfe, *From Death to Morning* (New York: Charles Scribner's Sons, 1963), 221, 301.

11. Wolfe, *Short Novels,* 75–76.

12. C. Hugh Holman and Sue Fields Ross, eds., *The Letters of Thomas Wolfe to His Mother* (Chapel Hill: University of North Carolina Press, 1968), 180–81.

13. C. Hugh Holman, *Loneliness at the Core* (Baton Rouge: Louisiana State University Press, 1975), 60.

14. Perkins quoted in Nowell, *Thomas Wolfe,* 210; Kennedy, *The Window of Memory,* 241; Wolfe, *Short Novels,* 75.

15. See *The Complete Short Stories of Thomas Wolfe* (New York: Scribner, 1987).

16. Holman, *Loneliness at the Core*, 24.

17. Graham Greene, "The Young Dickens," *The Lost Childhood and Other Essays* (New York: Viking Press, 1952), 54.

18. Excerpts reprinted in this volume are not from Aswell's version but from the version published by LSU Press in 1985, edited by Louis D. Rubin Jr. and John L. Idol Jr., whose introductory material is an excellent source of information and insights.

19. For Wolfe's use of the house as symbol and for a contrast with his own childhood house and his people, see "The House of the Far and the Lost," *Complete Short Stories*, 147–66.

20. Pat M. Ryan, introduction to Thomas Wolfe, *The Mountains* (Chapel Hill: University of North Carolina Press, 1970), 3–4.

21. Thomas Wolfe, "Something of My Life," in *The Enigma of Thomas Wolfe*, ed. Richard Walser (Cambridge: Harvard University Press, 1953), 4.

22. David Herbert Donald, *Look Homeward: A Life of Thomas Wolfe* (Boston: Little, Brown, 1987), 58–60, 66.

23. Thomas Wolfe, *Welcome to Our City* (Baton Rouge: Louisiana State University Press, 1983), xi.

24. Thomas Clark Pollack and Oscar Cargill, *Thomas Wolfe at Washington Square* (New York: New York University Press, 1954), 6. See also 68 n 19.

25. Paschal Reeves, *Thomas Wolfe's Albatross: Race and Nationality in America* (Athens: University of Georgia Press, 1968), 16–17.

26. Elizabeth Nowell, *The Letters of Thomas Wolfe* (New York: Scribner's, 1956), 45.

27. Ibid., 67.

28. Holman and Ross, *Letters of Thomas Wolfe to His Mother*, 83.

29. Nowell, *Letters of Thomas Wolfe*, 73–74, 103–4.

30. Thomas Wolfe, *Mannerhouse*, ed. Louis D. Rubin Jr. and John L. Idol Jr. (Baton Rouge: Louisiana State University, 1985), 101.

31. Kennedy, *The Window of Memory*, 84–85; Nowell, *Thomas Wolfe*, 102.

32. Paschal Reeves, *Thomas Wolfe: The Critical Reception* (New York: David Lewis, 1974), 201–2, 206–7.

33. Ibid., 203.

34. Shawn Holliday, *Thomas Wolfe and the Politics of Modernism* (New York: Peter Lang, 2001), 15–16, 20.

35. *Mannerhouse* was finally produced in 1949 by the Yale Dramatic Association.

36. Nowell, *Letters of Thomas Wolfe*, 517; A. Scott Berg, *Max Perkins, Editor of Genius* (New York: Dutton, 1978), 134–35; Robert Raynolds, *Thomas Wolfe: Memoir of a Friendship* (Austin: University of Texas Press, 1965), 125.

37. In the last few chapters of my novel *Bijou* (New York: Crown 1974), 449–500, young Lucius Hutchfield roams around Asheville and the cemetery to commune with the spirit of his hero Thomas Wolfe; the novel ends when he gets into Wolfe's house and wanders from room to room.

38. David Madden, *Sharpshooter: A Novel of the Civil War* (Knoxville: University of Tennessee Press, 1996), 87.

39. Ferner Nuhn, "Thomas Wolfe, Six-Foot-Six," *New York Herald Tribune Books,* Nov. 17, 1935, 79.

40. Wolfe, "His Father's Earth," in *Complete Short Stories,* 206.

41. Holman and Ross, *Letters of Thomas Wolfe to His Mother,* 192.

42. Ibid.,199–200.

43. Thomas Wolfe, *The Good Child's River* (Chapel Hill: University of North Carolina Press, 1991), 118–23. The rest of the chapter contains a version of "Circus at Dawn" (*Complete Short Stories,* 201–5), which may be read as a kind of companion piece to "His Father's Earth." The circus is a major trope in southern literature.

44. Andrew Turnbull, *Thomas Wolfe* (New York: Simon and Schuster, 1967), 184.

45. Holman and Ross, *Letters of Thomas Wolfe to His Mother,* 234–35.

46. Ibid., 199.

47. "The gallant" Pelham was killed at Kelly's Ford in 1863; Stuart was mortally wounded at Yellow Tavern in 1864.

48. Turnbull, *Thomas Wolfe,* 202.

49. Ibid., 232–33.

50. Donald, *Look Homeward,* 414.

51. Nowell, *Letters of Thomas Wolfe,* 625.

52. Donald, *Look Homeward*, 414.

53. Richard S. Kennedy, ed., *Beyond Love and Loyalty: The Letters of Thomas Wolfe and Elizabeth Nowell* (Chapel Hill: University of North Carolina Press, 1983), 65.

54. Nowell, *Letters of Thomas Wolfe*, 625–26.

55. Edward C. Aswell, "A Note on Thomas Wolfe," in Thomas Wolfe, *The Hills Beyond* (New York: Harper and Brothers, 1941), 379.

56. Reeves, *Thomas Wolfe: The Critical Reception*, 171; J. Donald Adams, "Thomas Wolfe's Last Book," review of "Chickamauga," *New York Times Book Review*, Oct. 26, 1941, 1.

57. Thomas Wolfe, "Chickamauga," in *The Hills Beyond*, 88.

58. For a description and analysis of the entire book, see Meindl, "Thomas Wolfe's *The Hills Beyond*."

59. Nowell, *Letters of Thomas Wolfe*, 386.

60. Kennedy, *The Window of Memory*, 301.

61. Nowell, *Letters of Thomas Wolfe*, 462.

62. Ibid., 655.

63. Holman, *Loneliness at the Core*, 4.

64. Reeves, *Thomas Wolfe: The Critical Reception*, 169.

65. Ibid., 167–78.

66. Ibid., 168, 170.

67. Ibid., 171–73.

68. Bella Kussy, "The Vitalist Trend and Thomas Wolfe," in *The World of Thomas Wolfe*, ed. C. Hugh Holman (New York: Scribner's, 1962); Herbert J. Muller, *Thomas Wolfe* (Norfolk, Conn.: New Directions, 1947), 20, 156.

69. Meindl, "Thomas Wolfe's *The Hills Beyond*," 28, 30.

70. Kennedy, *The Window of Memory*, 411.

71. A. Wigfall Green, "First Lectures at a University," in *William Faulkner of Oxford*, ed. James W. Webb and A. Wigfall Green (Baton Rouge: Louisiana State University Press, 1965), 135.

1

From *O LOST*

... A STONE, A LEAF, an unfound door; of a stone, a leaf, a door. And of all the forgotten faces.

Naked and alone we came into exile. In her dark womb we did not know our mother's face: from the prison of her flesh have we come into the unspeakable and incommunicable prison of this earth.

Which of us has known his brother? Which of us has looked into his father's heart? Which of us has not remained forever prison-pent? Which of us is not forever a stranger and alone?

O waste of loss, in the hot mazes, lost, among bright stars on this most weary unbright cinder, lost! Remembering speechlessly we seek the great forgotten language, the lost lane-end into heaven, a stone, a leaf, an unfound door. Where? When?

O lost, and by the wind grieved, ghost, come back again.

One morning at the beginning of July, sixty-five years ago, two boys were standing by a Pennsylvania roadside on the outskirts of the little farming village of York Springs, watching a detachment of the Confederate Army as it tramped past on its way to the town of Gettysburg, about twelve miles away to the south.

The older of the two boys was fifteen, the younger was thirteen: they lived near by on a tidy little farm which they helped their mother, a widow, to run. The widow was a rugged woman of forty-three years: she was of Dutch stock, a little under six feet tall, spare, brown, with big high bones—she was as big and strong as a man. She had been born in that region: her people had come over more than a century before in the great migration.

The widow had lost her husband six years before. He was an Englishman: his name was Gilbert Gaunt, which he had later changed to Gant—a concession possibly to Yankee phonetics.

Gaunt, or Gant, had come to America in the autumn of 1837 in a cotton ship bound from Bristol to Baltimore: he had lived in Baltimore for more than two years, buying at first a partnership in a small public house, which he soon lost after his profits began to roll down an improvident gullet, and descending thereafter to the office of bartender, and finally to no office at all.

Still bearing upon his tarnished finery the elegant stamp of a London tailor, he drifted westward into Pennsylvania, always ready, when able, to lay a bet on a horse or a dog, or to spur the feet of a fighting cock: he eked out a dangerous living matching these fowls against the crested champions of country barnyards.

Sometimes he escaped, leaving his champion dead on the battlefield, sometimes he escaped with the bruise of a farmer's big knuckles upon his reckless face, sometimes he escaped, without the clink of a coin in his pocket, after a night in a village jail. But he escaped, and coming at length among the Dutch during the harvest season, he found so fat a pasture for his easy talents that he dropped anchor for a prolonged visit.

Gilbert Gaunt was a tall thin man, and he looked fondly at

the meaty plenty of that rich land. The houses were small and cozy and were tucked warmly away in the shadows of great barns. The Dutch were a clean and thrifty people who loved abundance: they worked hard, scrubbed their houses bright, and ate heartily. All of this Gilbert Gaunt noted with pleasure. He liked people who fed well. He liked to see clean and cozy houses. He liked to look at people who worked hard. He could frequently look at them all day without showing a sign of fatigue.

And the Dutch liked Gilbert Gaunt. He was tall and tan and handsome: he had large black eyes, sunken deep in his head, hollow thirsty-looking cheeks, and a fine sweeping flourish of black hair. He wore bright fancy waistcoats and a watch-fob with several big seals. And he had a rich sonorous voice of great range and power.

It was a grand sight to see him do Hamlet in the manner of the great Edmund Kean—long legs wide apart, hands clasped behind him, thirsty brooding face bowed down into his collar, voice low and deliberate as he began "O that this too too solid flesh would melt," and rising strongly thereafter, while his long body straightened impressively, coming out loudly with a lifted face on "O God! O God!" falling to weary disgust at "Fie on't! O fie!" rising, rising to a crazy yell at "Heaven and earth! Must I remember—" and sinking to sad finality at "Frailty, thy name is woman!"

I remember an old Dutch farmer past eighty who told about one of these recitals when I was ten years old. He said that he had heard Gil Gant do Shakespeare once, and that, although he was only a boy of sixteen at the time, he had never forgotten it. The old man said that Gil Gant was "a born actor" and could have gone far if he had chosen to be one.

"He had the greatest flow of language of any feller I ever knew," the old man said.

The old fellow grinned reminiscently all over his brown

Dutch face: his broad craggy features split up into weathered seams, his little eyes closed, and he showed big yellow nubs of horseteeth.

"He was a great feller," he said, "a great talker. He could tell one story right after another without a stop, and all with a choice of words it would do you good to hear. He was never cut out for farming—he should have been an actor."

After a moment, the old man added with cryptic significance: "Well, we all have our faults, I guess. But Gil was a good feller. We all liked him."

They had liked him so well, in fact, that for several months after his arrival he had been an assiduous diner out. Many a fat hog was slaughtered in honor of the fascinating stranger. Many a keg of cider was broached to oil his hypnotic tongue. And he found shelter for the night under the low eave of many a farmhouse. And meanwhile this easy gentleman spoke vaguely of grand affairs. He spoke with affection of Nature and hinted that he might buy a farm and "settle down."

"For, damn it, gentlemen," he would say, with a fine gesture of his hand among his hair, "I begin to weary of the Ways of Men. I am tired of the Falseness and Corruption of Mankind—the frown of the Tyrant, the fawning of the Slave, the sneer of the Courtier, the trickery of the Knave and the gullibility of the Fool. By heaven, sir," he exclaimed, as he took another long draught of his host's cider, "I had rather my life had run its course here among simple men, where honesty's the only warrant to friendship, than in the Marts of Gold, where a man's worth is measured by the guinea stamp." This was really how he talked.

But after several months, even the lavish hospitality of the Dutch began to wear a little thin. Their smile was still broad, but a little detached. Men did not stay so long to hear him talk. And the Dutch, in low asides at first, begin thriftily to ask when Gil Gant was going to get to work. Then, just when his welcome was wearing threadbare, Gil married a rugged young Dutch woman of twenty-four who had been left the year before by the death of her husband, a farmer, the owner of a cozy little farm.

Gilbert came back into his own. He was a landed gentleman now, a man of substance. And although his Dutch wife bore the brunt of running the farm, and gained for herself a grudging sympathy, her harsh and honest tongue won few supporters. It was said that she led him a dog's life—but she also did most of the work. Meanwhile, Gil's facile tongue kept wagging, he enchanted the farmers with unending stories of the golden world, he continued to dine out. And whatever his deficiencies as a farmer may have been, many a canny Dutchman discovered to his grief that the Englishman's ignorance did not extend to horseflesh.

The unhastened years prowled in on leopard feet. The thin Englishman was still hollow in the cheeks, but he now carried a comfortable paunch. The thick black shock of hair was salted with coarse grey; the thirsty eyes grew dull and bogged; he walked with a gouty limp.

One morning when she went to his room to nag him out of sleep, his wife found him dead of an apoplexy. His thin dark face, with its bladelike nose, was thrust sharply upward as if trying to escape strangulation. And his strange bright eyes stared open, holding in them the secret her harsh tongue had never fathomed, a passionate and obscure hunger for voyages.

So, this Englishman, whose cold brain held from its race the twilight intuitions of the ashen stave, the forged byrnies, and the red rush of the Spear-Danes, and from itself the memory of Bow Bells and Paternoster Row, and the ripe green fields of England, with the hedges, the squire, and the low grey skies, all close and small, came to his death in the ample Dutch country, in a little farmhouse under the shadow of great barns. A destiny that leads the English to the Dutch is strange enough, but one that leads from Epsom into Pennsylvania over the proud coral cry of the cock, is touched by that dark miracle of chance which makes new magic in a dusty world.

The Englishman left a mortgage and five children. The oldest, a girl, he named Augusta. The other four were boys: Gilbert, Oliver, Emerson, and John.

And it was the two oldest of these boys, Gilbert and Oliver, who stood, one summer morning six years after his death, by a roadside well, watching the Confederates on their way in to Gettysburg.

Young Gilbert, who was fifteen and the older of the two boys, was shorter and stockier than his brother. He had a tough brown body, lean and long, heavy shoulders, and a big barrel chest. Both of the boys had powerful knobby bones and strong big hands, brown and long. Both had thin angular faces of sallow coloring, but Gilbert's face had more grim Dutch stolidity than his brother's.

Oliver, who was only thirteen, was more than six feet tall. He had very little meat on his great skeleton save long stringy muscles. His hands, roughened by the hard labor of the farm, were extraordinary: they hung from his bony wrists like big brown rocks. They were twice too big and too strong for his skinny arms. They were broad sinewy hands, without an ounce of fat and with huge knuckles, but the thing one noticed immediately was the great length and power of the fingers. They dangled apishly almost to his knees, with a strong brown curve of the paw. But, in spite of their great power, the hands held curious suggestions of delicacy and skill: they were made to lift great weights of stone, and to work cunningly. They were such hands as a sculptor might have had.

And Oliver's thin face, too, had this curious mixture of roughness and delicacy: his nose was a huge angular blade, hooked sharply, very thin and waxen—his nostrils were merely slits. His mouth was thin and marked at one corner with a small round deeply incised scar, which he had received from a fall on the ice. It gave to his face a marking of grim obstinacy, but the mouth was somewhat petulant and hangdog. His eyes were small, cold-grey, and shallow—they glanced about restlessly, furtively, but at moments they darkened with some obscure and passionate hunger. He had thick brows that grew across the base of his skull, a bony sloping forehead, abundant dark-brown hair, and big masculine ears, with tufts of hair in them.

But as they stood there by the roadside, while the dusty rebels tramped past them, Oliver seemed to turn timidly, shyly towards the stubborn unflinching column of his brother's body. Both boys wore overalls: their big brown feet splayed out solidly in the dust. Gilbert stood planted on spread legs, paying the enemy back stare for stare with hard unafraid defiance.

But that scarecrow army was in cheerful humor. It was going to fight; it was going to fight barefooted. In a way, it was going to fight because of those bare feet, and it did not care. For, during the morning, some of the men of Heth's brigade had come in from Lee's base at Cashtown to look for shoes in the town of Gettysburg. On the outskirts of that little town the shoeless rebels had come upon a detachment of Union cavalry—the fight had begun then and there. Along the dozen roads that lead to Gettysburg the armies of both sides were pouring in, and the town no one had wanted to fight in had become the greatest battlefield of the war.

And now, this marauding host, which had swung northeastward across the Rappahannock in a gesture of loot and capture, tramped along the road past the two boys in rags and tatters: it came with naked toes, wearing the stovepipe hat it had looted exultantly from a country store; it came, coatless and shirtless, magnificently shod in greased and stolen boots; it came shoeless, switching ironically the unctuous tails of a black frock coat. It streamed past without rhythm, without step, in noisy hilarity, apparently a dusty rabble, but really an army of seasoned fighting men, lean as snakes, nut-brown, casual and alert, and able to do its twenty miles a day on a handful of parched corn. And as it passed, tumultuously, with loud good-natured jeers, it saluted the two boys.

"Hi, Yank! Ye'd better hit out fer the woods. Jeb Stuart's lookin' fer ye."

"He'll be looking for you this time to-morrow," Gil shouted angrily. The men roared with laughter. Frightened, Oll drew in a little closer to his brother. Gilbert spat briefly into the dust and stared.

A lean young captain rode in towards the boy on a roan mare and reined up with a strong brown smell of sweat and leather. Oliver shrank back, frightened at this close odor of Mars, but Gilbert stood his ground.

"Give me a drink, Yank," said the officer, with a grin of white teeth between his dusty grey lips.

"Get it yourself, Reb," said Gil. He stared bitterly at the officer for a moment; then, with a sudden blaze of anger, he said: "I wouldn't spit down your throat if your guts were on fire."

The men passing jeered their officer happily: he grinned again and turned to Oliver.

"You look like a smart boy," he said.

In a moment Oliver stepped timidly up to the wellhead and drew a cup of water out of the slopping bucket. The man drank with a hot gulp of thirst and gave the cup back to the boy. Then, resting his hands upon the pommel, he stared down at them for a moment.

"You boys got any cattle?" he asked.

Oliver's sallow face went grey. The boys had driven the widow's cows from the farm during the morning, and had hidden them in a copse of wood that flanked the meadow behind them. But Gil looked at the officer with hard unwavering defiance.

"What's it to you?" he said.

"Where are you hiding them, Yank? These fellows could use a little meat," said the officer nodding towards the dusty troops.

"Dead men don't have to eat," said Gil.

The young captain laughed.

"I'll tell Jeb Stuart about you, Yank. That's what I'll do. He has a little Yank served up for breakfast every morning." Then slapping his dusty grey hat against his boot he rode away.

In a moment, a group of dusty men on horseback rode up to the well. Most of them were grave tired-looking men, past middle age, by their abundant whiskerage officers of high rank.

"Give us a drink of water, son," their leader said. Oliver filled and refilled the dripping cup until all had drunk.

"How far are we from Gettysburg?" the leader asked.

"It's about twelve miles, sir," Oliver said.

"It's a damn sight further comin' than goin'," said Gil savagely. "You'll find that out soon enough."

The officers laughed.

"This is a fightin' little Yankee," said one. "Let's give him to Jeb Stuart."

"Ah!" said Gil contemptuously. "I've heard that before. To hell with Jeb Stuart."

They roared with whiskered laughter, and one of them shouted: "Damn if he ain't a good one!" Then they rode on.

Then a ragged soldier came up and drank—a young man with lank hair, a little silk goatee, and the thin reckless face of a Southerner.

"Know who that feller was?" he drawled.

"What fellow?" said Oliver.

"The one you gave the drink to first."

Oliver shook his head.

"That's General Fitzhugh Lee," said the soldier. "He's old Bob's nephew."

They were silent a moment, awed by the thunder of great names. Then Gil said:

"That won't do him no good where he's goin'."

Then they stood as before watching the ragged rebels as they tramped past. The hot sun made a blue glister on the gun-barrels. There was a halt. The men leaned dustily at the roadside on their rifles. And there was one, among the drawling and terrible mountaineers, who sang hymns while he marched, and preached while he waited. He was a young man of twenty-six, red-faced, bearded, with a broad meaty nose, deep flat cheeks, sensual lips, and a smile mixed of pleased complacency and idiot benignity. He was dressed in shapeless rags; his large odorous feet were bandaged with wound sacking; he gave off from his thick hairy body a powerful decayed stench. In moments of piety, his comrades called him Stinking Jesus, but his real name was Bacchus Pentland.

"Hit's a-comin'! As sure as you're livin', hit's a-comin'," he shouted cheerfully. And, seeing the two boys, he shouted his strange message happily to them, smiling kindly with pleased idiocy.

"Hit's a-comin', boys. Tell yore folks. Armageddon's here."

"You don't need to tell 'em Stinkin' Jesus is here," a mountaineer shouted. "They can smell him already."

Bacchus Pentland answered their roar of laughter with a good-humored smile. Then, where he could be heard again he said: "Hit's a-comin'! The kingdom of Christ upon the earth approacheth. He'll be here a-judgin' an' dividin' by eight o'clock to-morrow morning. I've got it all figgered out accordin' to 'Zekiel."

He drew a roll of paper from the hairy bush of his chest, and opened up a soiled chart with elaborate Biblical notations.

"Hell, Back," drawled a mountaineer, "you had it all figgered out accordin' to Ebenezer at Chancellorsville, an' all I got out of it was a slug of canister in my tail."

"That was the beginnin' of it," said Bacchus, with a smart undaunted wink. He tapped his chart. "Hit all comes out right accordin' to this. Hit's a-comin' as sure as you live. Christ's kingdom is at hand."

"I hope He gits here before the Yanks begin to shoot," said another, spitting drolly.

And another, as he stoppered up his dripping canteen at the well, said: "What air you goin' to be, Back, Brigadier or Vice-President? I wish you'd git me a job on yore staff."

And other men came to the well, and drank, jeering at their strange fellow. He bore their mockery patiently, with his benign smile, touched with its tranquil idiocy, with something inner and unearthly like the strange grin of a primitive Apollo. And he held the chart invitingly in his hands, turning from one to another, eager to debate, to persuade, to explain, when their laughter should dwindle away.

Then they were ordered to resume their march, and they moved on into battle, jesting at God and sudden death. But before he had passed from their hearing, Bacchus Pentland turned and shouted at the staring boys once more his triumphant prophecy of eternal life.

"Hit's a-comin', boys. Tell yore folks hit's a-comin'."

The boy Oliver stared down the road, the hard Dutch order of his life touched by the scarecrow gallantry of the ragged men, with a grey darkening of his small cold eyes as there arose in him the obscure and passionate hunger for voyages that had led from Fenchurch Street to Philadelphia. And as his gaze followed the burly figure of the prophet, he was touched by something strange and fleeting, far more remote than Armageddon. He had been touched by the dark finger of Chance, but he did not know it.

This Bacchus Pentland was of Southern mountain stock which derived some of its vitality, it was said, from the loins of

David Crockett. Bacchus had carried a gun and a chart from the outbreak of the war: he had enlisted in order to be present at Armageddon, and he had announced the coming of that final day at Manassas, Fredericksburg, and the Wilderness. Each of his failures as a prophet only increased his belief in his infallibility and enforced, after a little reflection, his conviction that the ending was only beginning. His comrades bore with him because he amused them, his power of invention was enormous, and his heart kind and simple. And his officers bore with him very cheerfully because they were able to find little fault with a marksman who could pick the fingers off a Yankee's hand at ninety yards and send his enemies into eternity with a Christian sense of having awarded them the honors of Paradise. For there is no commission which so increases a soldier's effectiveness as one which he believes he has received from God.

Wherever he went Bacchus Pentland carried his Bible and his chart. He had been captured at Antietam by a detachment of Joe Hooker's men, and before his escape three weeks later—an escape which his captors did little to prevent—he had shouted his news of Armageddon along the length of McClellan's line. During the two weeks of his three-hundred-mile detour into Virginia, he fed sparingly on parched corn and the roadside carcass of an army mule, which the Divine Providence had bountifully left in his way. And wherever he went he carried his idiot smile, his chart, and his strange message of the end of earth and the beginning of life.

Perhaps, as that ragged horde tramped up the way that led bloodily from Virginia into Maryland, and across the Potomac into Pennsylvania, this prophecy of a day of wrath and judgment, of red tramplings in the vineyard, and an end to pain and labor, touched wearily in them some deep and obscure joy.

So they marched on into the slaughter of July, bearing with them the cracked prophet who had shown the Dutch farmboy the first of that strange clan with which his life was to be mixed.

When all the troops had gone by, the boys stood, listening to the sudden noise of silence, the sleepy buzz of summer. There was a freshening of warm wind among the blades of corn, the drone of a bee as it reeled home drunk with pollen, the fading creak of a gun-carriage down the road.

Then from a little white farmhouse set up on an elevation under some trees at a considerable distance from the road, they heard the bronze clangor of a bell, broken by the wind. They walked rapidly away towards the house, each lost and silent in the blazing pageantry of his thought.

A woman stood in the front doorway sheltered from the sun on a little stoop. She held the bell in one hand, and shaded her eyes with the other, with the powerful gesture of a man. When they were still some distance away, she called out to them in a harsh, rasping, and impatient voice.

"You boys hurry up! You've idled the whole morning away watching those good-for-nothing rebels. You don't care if your mother, a pore old widow woman, works herself to death as long as you fill your bellies. Now, I give you fair warning. I'm not going to put up with it any longer: you're both of you big strapping men, and you've got to earn your keep."

They accepted this tirade casually, without perturbation. When they came up to the door, she said more quietly:

"Did you get the cattle put away?"

"Yes," said Gil. "It's all right. They're in the wood."

"Did any of them ask you where they were?"

"Yes," said Gil.

"What did you tell them?"

"I told them," said Gil, "to go to hell."

"Well," said the widow matter-of-factly, "you boys go and wash up. You're not coming in this house with those filthy hands. Hurry, now! You've kept dinner waiting half an hour."

She turned and went back into the house. Gilbert and Oliver went around to the back door. They filled a battered tin pan with water, pumping for each other, and lathering their big hands with gritty soap.

Then they went into the kitchen for dinner. The kitchen was a big room with a low ceiling. There were rows of pots and pans upon the walls, scrubbed to a silver and copper glitter. There were a great oaken cupboard, a flour bin, and shelves loaded with preserves. In the pantry there were a barrel of apples, a flitch of bacon, and four or five fat smoked hams, which hung by hooks.

The two boys sat down at a table covered by a clean blue linen cloth patterned with stripes and squares of black. The hired man, a bronzed Dutchman of middle age, sat across the table from them, horsily gulping his food. He looked up from his scoured plate after a moment, and said ironically:

"You boys are kinda late, aint you? Did you enjoy your vacation?"

"I'm not going to have any more of it," said the widow Gant, opening the oven door. "You've all got to earn your keep or get out."

"I earn my keep," said Gil calmly. "And more, too."

The hired man rose, wiping his mouth dry of cider.

"Did you see the rebs, Gil?" he asked.

"Yes," said Gil sourly, "and smelled them too."

"There'll be hell a-poppin'," said the hired man. "A Gettysburg man came over this morning. He said the troops are camped all over the country. The rebs have been at Cashtown since yesterday."

"Well," said Gil, "I wish they'd shoot a few on our place. We need the fertilizer."

The grinning Dutchman went out to his work.

Oliver and Gilbert sat together on one side of the long table and waited for their food. Their younger brother Emerson, a boy of eleven, sat opposite them. Emerson had their mean features: his nose, his small grey eyes, and his tight stingy mouth all came slyly to a focal point.

The youngest child, John, a sensitive and delicate-looking boy of eight years with a shock of brown hair, sat next to Emerson, at the head of the table near his mother. Augusta, the only girl, and the oldest, helped her mother put food on the table. She was twenty-three years old, big brown and bony like her mother, with a broad highboned face, a big nose, a wide straight mouth, and coarse black hair parted in the centre and drawn tightly down. But, in spite of her rugged Dutch likeness to the widow, there was a strange tenderness and docility in Augusta.

She had great brown eyes, as big and gentle as a cow's: they gave to her gaunt face an expression of brooding tenderness and fidelity. Her movements were clumsy and deliberate: she had none of her mother's harshness of voice or gesture. She spoke little: she had been formed for obedience.

The widow, opening the oven door again, thrust in her aproned hand and drew out a roasting pan with a smoking quarter of beef, tenderly crisped in its fat and oozing succulently a rich gravy. Augusta cut up smoking squares of brown cracklin bread and put it on the table.

"God knows," said the widow, as she ladled the pan gravy over the roast, "what's going to become of us this winter. They're predictin' it will be bitter cold, and there's no one on the place who'll do any work. I'm an old widow woman, and there's nothing left for me but the porehouse. They'll sell the roof over my head for taxes."

"Now, Mother," said Gilbert, pouring out a glass of cider from a pitcher on the table, "don't start on that. I'm tired of hearing it. I do my work and so does Oll."

"We'll starve before the winter's out," she said gloomily, putting the roast on the table. Then she went to the cupboard and returned with a great platter of cold jellied smearcase.

Augusta meanwhile piled a bowl with meaty smoking ears of yellow corn, and filled other dishes with hot string beans, spinach, sliced tomatoes, and mashed potatoes, whipped to a creamy froth. She put these on the table and returned a moment later with a covered boat of thick gravy. The two women then sat down at opposite ends of the table and began to eat.

Gilbert grasped a carving knife and a steel in his great hands, and after setting up a briefly appetizing clangor, speared the roast to its heart with the long tines of a meatfork and carved off rich savory slabs of the rare beef. Then he served the women, John, Oliver, and himself, pausing finally to stare grimly at Emerson's mean greedy eyes.

"You aint helped me yet," Emerson whined nasally.

He stretched his skinny hand forth for the meatfork. Gilbert rapped him smartly across his knuckles with the steel. He yelped in angry pain.

"Those who don't work," said Gilbert, "don't eat."

"You leave that child alone, Gil," said the widow. She speared a slice of beef and put it on the boy's plate.

"Your brother's right about you," she said harshly. "You're not worth your salt."

"What've I done?" whined Emerson.

"Nothing," said Gilbert. "That's what you've done—nothing. You haven't done any of your chores, and if I had my way you wouldn't eat."

There was the silence of confession for a moment. Then Gil concluded with emphasis: "I do my work. I eat. Oll does his work. He eats. You don't do your work. You don't eat."

"Now that's enough, Gil," said the widow. "Don't tease the child any more."

"Mother," said Oliver nervously and eagerly, "I talked to the rebels. I gave General Fitzhugh Lee a drink of water."

"You were a fool to do it," growled Gilbert. "I'd have seen them in hell first."

"Pore fellows," said the widow, "I suppose they're worn out. God knows, there's enough trouble in the world without tramping all the way from Virginia looking for more."

As he heard the strange name of Virginia, Oliver's cold furtive eyes darkened again with their obscure hunger.

"They were a seedy-looking lot," said Gil. "They looked as if they hadn't eaten for the last month."

"I hope they leave us alone," the widow said. "I've trouble enough making ends meet as it is, and if the rebels roost upon me we'll be eaten out of house and home."

"Mother," said Oliver, with the same eager nervousness, "one of the rebels had his feet wrapped up in old rags, and he kept shouting to us that the end of the world is here. He said that Armageddon is coming to-morrow and to tell everyone to get ready."

"He was crazy," said Gil definitely, "and you're a fool for listening to such talk. I don't pay no attention to it."

"He may not be far wrong," said the widow Gant. "It will be the end of the world sure enough for many a pore soldier, and maybe for some of the rest of us if the fighting comes this way."

But, as they sat there listening to the sleepy drone of July jarred only faintly by the guns, it was hard to believe that the ends of the earth had met in so quiet a land.

Gilbert took a long draught of cider and put his glass down reflectively.

"Mother," he said at length, "I've decided to go away. I'm going to Baltimore to learn a trade."

Oliver turned quickly to him with stopped breath. Augusta stared quietly with her great faithful eyes. The widow made no answer for a moment.

She leaned thoughtfully forward on her bony elbows.

"Well, Gil," she said quietly at last, "if you want to go I won't try to stop you. You're getting big enough to support yourself. We're pore folks and I've never been able to do much for you. But you're a good boy, and a hard worker, and I know you'll get along."

"Mother," said Oliver huskily. "Mother. Let me go with Gil."

She started violently, and turned upon him.

"No!" she cried fiercely, in strong fear. "No!"

Her bony fingers trembled. In a moment she spoke more calmly, with a kind of prayer in her voice.

"Why, Ollie," she said, "my little Ollie. You don't want to go and leave me yet, do you? You don't want to leave your pore old mother all alone, do you?"

"Please, Mother!" said Oliver dryly, desperately. "I want to go with Gil."

She looked, with pain, with an old familiar terror, into his eyes, darkening now with her old enemy—a strange Norse hunger for voyages that she could not understand, darkening with the ghost of the Stranger that she had lost, and that stood spectre-wise here now in his son, that she could not bear to lose.

"Why, Ollie," she coaxed desperately, "Ollie. You're only a child, son. You mustn't leave me yet."

She seized his big hands in her bony grip, and dry-lipped, grey-faced, he answered her desperate stare.

"No. You stay here with Mother for a while, Oll," said Gilbert decisively. "You're not old enough to leave home yet. I'll send for you when the time comes."

His downright bluntness released their tension. Oliver slumped dejectedly in his chair. The women rose and began to clear the table.

Then, over the drowsy heat of the day, there came to them faint broken sounds from the road—of men who sang old songs as their bodies swung wearily in saddles, of hoofbeats dumb with dust, a faint creak of leather, a clink of bit and sabre, but all so drowsed in the sleepy day that they seemed to come from a remote and elfin world.

The widow went to the door and looked out with shaded eyes. Gilbert looked up inquiringly.

"What is it?" he asked.

"Cavalry going by, pore fellows," she said.

Oliver got up suddenly and went to the door.

"I can see the light upon their bridles," he said. "But it all sounds so far away."

He turned to Gilbert with a strange calm excitement, brooding and suppressed.

"Gil! Gil! How long will they go by?"

"How should I know?" said Gilbert surlily. "Do you expect them to parade every day for your benefit?" he asked ironically. "They can't go by forever, you know."

Oliver turned towards the road again, with the old hunger darkening in his eyes.

If they only could! (he thought) If they only could!

The next day they heard the blasting thunder of great guns. During the night Lee had come through on his white horse, with the rest of his 70,000 ragged men.

Save for the tremor of the guns nothing disturbed the hot blue peace of the countryside. The boys brought the cows back to the fields, studded with the hot dry legions of the daisies. And they went stubbornly about their manful work, rising in the dark before dawn to go to the milking, doing half a day's hard labor before the armies began to fight.

The rumors of blood and battle rolled back to them: Gil spat grimly when he heard of the first day's work and the retreat of Meade's army to Cemetery Hill. Then, after a quiet night and forenoon, while the troops dug in, the terrible fighting of the second day began.

Bacchus Pentland toiled up the grim slope of Little Round Top, shooting his enemies dead among the savage rocks of the place, and crying his news of Armageddon as he came in among them clubbing with a brainred gunstock. He was shot through the groin, and ripped up the leg with a bayonet, but he managed to get back to the Wheat Field, where he fought, painting the grain with blood until his blistered hands stuck to the gun barrel. Then night came, and delirium, and he was carried back beyond the road to a field hospital, oblivious alike of the coming of the Lord and the cursing mercy of the surgeons who had no time for wounds that did not need the terrible execution of the meatsaw and the cleaver.

Then morning came and the end of rebellion, as the ragged men charged straight across the fields against that hill of death and union. They melted, formed again, toiled to the cannon's barrel, and were erased. The drawling mountaineer, the tenant farmer had fought to the end for the slaves they had never owned—had left one more myth of chivalry and knighthood for the exploitation of those three assiduous and innumerable quacks: the Major, the Senator, and the Lady.

It was over. Lee drew his broken army together and on the night of the Fourth, with superb manipulations, fell back through the hills towards Maryland while, in torrential rain, stabbed with flashes of lightning, Jeb Stuart's battered horsemen fought to hold the pass at Monterey, and gave bloodily to the retreating army its hour of precious escape.

No more. No more.

On Sunday, which was the fifth, Gil hitched up the rig and drove the family over the mired roads to the little village which had gained its eternity in three days. The farmers stood ruefully in among the ruined grain that was soaked in the blood of an army that had come to devour it.

The victorious army breathed wearily, collecting itself slowly, and, unable to follow its beaten enemy, sent out a brigade of cavalry to harry it. Over the fields the stretcher bearers moved with the wounded, taking them from the sopping canvas of field hospitals to drier quarters.

And from the humid earth there rose the green carrion stench of rotting limbs which the surgeons had piled up in heaps, and the corrupt smell of the dead men, weltering into the mud with putrid deliquescence. The unburied rebels still lay upon the field: they sprawled thick and grey in the casual postures of violent death among the rocks of Little Round Top and Culp's Hill, they lay upon the Wheat Field and in the Peach Orchard, and across that open shot-mown land where Pickett's men had charged they lay, rotting into the earth. Wheeling low above the field with flapping screech, the red-necked vultures plunged downward to their feast.

Gilbert stared at the friendless bodies with satisfaction. But Oliver strode across the fields peering into the corrupt blur of the faces, searching for one that he had seen listening to the language of the lost world, the forgotten faces. He did not find it.

Over the field of Armageddon lay the trampled corn, the broken walls, the yellow pollution of death.

There were new lands. Where? When?

During the next winter, when Oliver was fourteen, he joined Gilbert at Harrisburg. They got employment as muleboys in the quartermaster's camp. The teamsters and hostlers were older than the two boys: they were a profane and violent lot, but Gilbert, who was only sixteen, was the match of any of them in physical strength, and their superior in the surly ferocity of his temper. Oliver turned as ever to his brother for protection.

They slept at night in triple bunks in a room choked with the foul stench of the men. As they lay there in the dark they heard the wooden drumming of mule hooves on the boards. Oliver thought of the cleanly beasts.

In the spring Gilbert went on to Baltimore, where he wanted to learn a trade. Oliver returned to the farm in time for the spring plowing. For another year he helped the widow run the farm. Then, in April, after the news of Appomattox had come, he too departed for Baltimore.

As he walked down a street in Baltimore, Oliver passed the shop of a stonemason. There was a little yard around the shop powdered with stonedust. In the yard were scattered pieces of stone, blocks of grey Vermont granite, Georgia marble, and several bases of sandstone. There was also a monument from Carrara in Italy: it was of a marble angel, with bright carved wings. The angel held a lily delicately upwards between its cold elegant fingers.

Oliver walked on, returned, and peered through the dirty windows of the little shop. Within he saw smooth marble slabs of death, a stone lamb couchant on a granite marker, a cherub volant on a plump foot, a scrollwork, and two joined armless hands. He also saw two more angels with simpering marble faces, and furled wings.

A bearded brawny man wearing a work apron was standing in the yard above a wooden trestle. He held a great wooden mallet and a chisel in his hands and he was chipping with tense craft at a design that had been penciled upon the surface of a marble slab.

As Oliver looked at the man and the big angel with its carved stripe of lilystalk, a cold and nameless excitement possessed him. The long fingers of his big hands curled. He felt that he wanted to carve delicately with a chisel more than anything in the world. He wanted to wreak something dark and unspeakable in him into cold stone. He wanted to carve an angel's head.

Oliver entered the yard and asked the man for a job. The man put down his mallet and looked at him.

"Son," he said kindly, "it is hard work and I can not pay you much while you learn."

"I don't care," said Oliver. "I want to learn the business."

He became the stonecutter's apprentice. He worked in that dusty yard for five years. He became a stonecutter. When his apprenticeship was over, he had become a man.

Gilbert and Oliver lived together. Gilbert was learning the plasterer's trade: he was an apprentice. The two boys lived at a cheap hotel frequented by traveling peddlers, farmers come to market, and laboring men. The hotel was in the district near the market and was run by a great tunbellied man named Jeff Streeter.

Jeff Streeter was a man out of Rabelais or Peter Breughel—he was a man mountain, coarse, loud, obscene, and generous, who could do nothing small or quiet. He was one of those men who leave a heavy stamp on the memory because their lives are expressed in the brutal repetition of two or three movements. Thus, when he wanted to express his disapproval of any act or opinion, of any utterance that smacked too much of affected daintiness, he would lift one huge buttock from his creaking chair, and let out a ripping fart, which he seemed to have corked up for instant use. Then he would move his great jowled head slowly from side to side, looking about him solemnly with an air of innocent surprise. Finally, in a tone of slow wonder, he would exclaim: "Why, God *damn*." Then he would hurl himself back violently in his chair roaring with laughter. All his life was included in these two gestures of flatulence and profanity. He was an epic figure among his guests, and his table was famous for its glut of plenty.

At mealtime Jeff Streeter led the procession to the dining room and settled his huge bulk slowly, with ponderous ceremony, into a creaking barrelshaped chair at the head of the table. Then, after a loud preliminary clangor with the carving steel, he fell upon a huge roast or fowl before his plate, and carved it into enormous portions. As quickly as one roast was carved it was passed down the line of hungry men and another was placed before him. When he had finished, he loaded his own plate. Then with knife and fork gripped in his mighty fists, he rested his hands on the table, and looked slowly and fiercely up and down the feeding lines, with a ponderous rhythm of his massy hog jowls. And if he saw anyone who was too dainty or too nice with his food, or pecked birdily at it, his unvarying command, delivered in a hoarse bull-bellow, was: "Dig down, you son-of-a-bitch! Dig down!"

And under the booming laughter of the feeders, and the ivory grins of the Negro waiters, the laggard dug down.

Gilbert and Oliver shared a hot little back room under the eaves. Each week for their food and lodging they paid $2.50 apiece. At the beginning Oliver earned five dollars a week, and Gilbert seven or eight.

The boys had reached manhood ahead of their years. The hard discipline of the farm, the regular apportionment of labor in the widow's house, and the punctual schedule of their army work had given to each a love of order and custom he was never to lose. And they had a Dutch love of abundance. The groaning table of Sreeter's hotel filled them with delight. They fed with stupendous and discriminating hunger.

But Gilbert found greater satisfaction in the life of Streeter's than did Oliver. Gilbert's desires were strong, few, and simple. He wanted to become a plasterer, to earn good wages, and to have plenty of work. He wanted to go on a roaring spree now and then and to go to bed with a pretty woman.

"And I don't want none of your little skinny ones, Oll," he said. "Give me a big woman," he added with relish, "a big woman with plenty of meat on her."

At night, when he came from work Gilbert turned confidently and happily to the coarse society of the teamsters and laborers. By the time he was eighteen he was as strong and as capable as a man: his big hands were grained and warted by the trowel. He could curse as loud and hard as any of them, and with more eloquence, and he could drink them under the tables. He spent the evenings until bedtime in the smoky bedlam of Streeter's bar: he liked the life and all the people.

But Oliver had greater ambitions. The unbroken brutality of the life about him touched him with disgust. His strong appetites liked the coarseness, the abundance, and the vulgarity, but its sensual monotony—its idiot repetition of food, women, and drunkenness stirred in him a weary contempt.

"I tell you what, Gil," he muttered, "they're a pretty bad lot."

Oliver wanted to cut a figure in the world. He wanted a solid and respectable position. He wanted plenty of money in the bank—although he had a curious distrust of all landed property—and he wanted to carry a well-filled purse. He wanted to go before the world grandly, to live spaciously, to travel—but always from a fixed point, a haven of home and position, of a loaded table and roaring fires. Oliver wanted to be admired and to be loved: he wanted the love of elegant and voluptuous women. Finally, he wanted to be his own master. His strong egotism hated the idea of working for anyone. He wanted to have his own shop.

At twenty Oliver was a strange and interesting-looking person. He was six feet and five inches tall: his great-boned frame had little meat on it, but he gave an impression of powerful physical strength. He had dark brown hair, thick and lank; his head was somewhat small for his big body, but well-shaped; he had a thin sallow face, with thirsty flanks, a great waxen beak of nose, incredibly broad and narrow mouth, and darting unhappy eyes, grey and furtive.

He walked at a lunging violent stride, muttering to himself a denunciation of mankind, accompanying the rhetorical rise and fall of his voice with rapid gestures of his wonderful sinewy hands. From his mother he seemed to have inherited a chronic pessimism, and from his father the temper of an actor. His usual state was one of gaunt tension waiting eagerly for release in torrential invective. And, no matter how trifling the provocative, there was no extravagance of anathema he would not resort to. Sometimes Gil deliberately tormented him in order that the grinning loungers in the bar might hear the miracle of his speech.

Thus, as Oliver lunged in from his day's work with ominous mutterings, the older one might say:

"The washwoman was here, Oll. She says she can't find your boiled shirt."

"What!" Oliver's voice rose to a piercing howl. "Do you mean my good white shirt I wear on Sunday? Surely to God you don't mean she's lost it? I beg of you, I entreat you to tell me the truth. Hey?" The great length of his body bent forward while he turned his tortured face upon his brother in an attitude of comic supplication.

"Yep," said Gil, "I'm afraid it's gone. She says she can't find it."

"Merciful God!" screamed Oliver. "I'm ruined! That it should come to this!" He began to stride up and down the room like a wild man. "They have done me to death, as sure as there's a God in heaven. Fiends that they are, they sit fattening now upon my heartsblood. Ah, me! It was a bitter and accursed day for me when I first left the farm in Pennsylvania and came, a friendless orphan boy, into this cruel and murderous city."

Then, aware suddenly of the grinning teamsters, he fell upon them with bitter contempt.

"You may sneer. But the time may come when you'll laugh out of the other side of your mouth. Low and murderous reprobates that you are, you deserve not even the name of men, so far have you retrograded backwards."

Old Jeff Streeter listened attentively, leaning forward in his chair with one great fist gripped upon his knee. His mouth hung raptly ajar, his red hog jowls quivered expectantly. Then he called out loudly to some newly arrived guests:

"Beat that if you can. By God, I'll bet on that boy to out-talk the world."

All the men said that Oliver should be a lawyer.

But he had hungry love for the theatre. He went constantly, sitting in the cheapest seats of the highest galleries, devouring every gesture, every intonation of the actors. He saw the great Edmund Booth in *Hamlet* several times: he went to see his mad kinsman, Junius Brutus Booth, again and again, and four times in succession he saw Salirni in *Othello*, foiled by the fat glut of the Italian, but memorizing every grand gesture, possessing every accent of the noble rant.

The combination of Shakespeare and Booth had a devastating effect upon Oliver's prose style—his rhetoric was checked from absurdity by no restraint. His howling pentameter curse was mixed with the coarse gustiness of his humor: sometimes after a telling redundancy a faint crafty smile tickled the corners of his thin mouth, and he glanced about slyly at his listeners.

Oliver was known as "a good talker"; he was proud of his gift of gab. He valued the spectacular, the dramatic, more than anything on earth, and almost all of his heroes were soldiers or politicians. He read a great deal—particularly military memoirs and poetry, for which he had a prodigious memory. When he began to get drunk he would recite for the patrons of Streeter's bar: with telling rant he gave them Marc Antony's funeral oration; "I remember, I remember, the house where I was born"; "The Charge of the Light Brigade"; "We are lost, the captain shouted, as he staggered down the stairs"; "Oh why should the spirit of mortal be proud!" (Lincoln's favorite, he feelingly remarked); "Blessings on thee, little man, barefoot boy with cheek of tan"; Gray's "Elegy"; "Man Was Made to Mourn"; and Lincoln's Gettysburg Address.

He loved poetry that spoke of the emptiness of wealth, fame, and power, and of the triumph of death; he loved poetry that extolled fireside contentment and obscure happiness over the hollow rewards of great position; above all he loved poetry that contrasted the innocent joy and trivial miseries of childhood to the carking grief of manhood. Sometimes when he recited "The Barefoot Boy," or "Backward, turn backward, O time in thy flight," he would begin to weep loud sniffling sobs, evoking sympathetic tears as large as henseggs from the lachrymal ducts of the spellbound boozers.

And when he called for his mother, rolling his eyes aloft in desperate supplication as if he saw her printed on the ceiling, even the bleared peepers of old Jeff Streeter distilled their crystal jewelry.

"Boys," reared the jowled leviathan, "I'm God-damned if Oll aint right: she's the best damned friend any of us has got."

"Ah, me!" sighed Oliver, in strong self-pity. "And well do I know it now that it's too late to my bitter sorrow." He began to weep. "Little did I reck when I came into this hell-hole that it would come to this. Fiends that they are, more savage, more cruel, more bloody than the beasts of the field, and they gloat upon my death rattle. They have driven me over the brink of destruction, and they will not rest until I lie cold and buried in my grave. O Mother! Mother! Come down and succor me, I beg of you, I implore you, I entreat you, or I perish."

He cast a wild glance of entreaty upon the ceiling.

"Mother's not up there, Oll," said Gilbert rudely. "She's in Pennsylvania."

2

From *The Web of Earth*

AND YES, NOW! WHAT ABOUT IT? Don't I remember that winter when the deer come boundin' down the hill across the path and stopped and looked at me not ten feet away, and I screamed because I saw its antlers? Lord! I didn't know what to make of it, I'd never heard of such an animal, and how it bounded away into the woods again and how when I told Mother she said, "Yes, you saw a deer. That was a deer you saw all right. The hunters ran it down here off the mountain" and—why, yes! wasn't it only the next spring after that when I was a big girl four years old and remembered everything—that the Yankees began to come through there, and didn't I hear them, didn't I see them with my own eyes, the villains—those two fellers tearing along the road on two horses they had stolen, as hard as they could, as if all hell had cut loose after them—why! it's as plain in my mind to-day as it was then, the way they looked, two ragged-lookin' troopers bent down and whippin' those horses for all that they were worth, with bandanna handkerchiefs tied around their necks and the ends of them whipping back as stiff and straight as if they'd been starched and ironed—now that will give you some idea of how fast they were goin'—and couldn't I hear the people shoutin' and hollerin' all along the road that they were comin', and how the women-folks took on, and made the men go out and hide themselves? "Oh, Lord," says Mother, wringin' her hands, "there they come!" and didn't Addie Patton come running up the hill to tell us, the poor child frightened out of her wits, you know screaming, "Oh, they've come, they've come! And Grandfather's down there all alone," she says. "They'll kill him, they'll kill him!"

Of course we didn't know then that these two Yankee stragglers were alone, we thought they were the advance guard of a whole brigade of Sherman's troopers. But Law! the rest of them never got there for a week, here these two thieving devils had broken away, and I reckon were just trying to see how much they could steal by themselves. Why, yes! Didn't all the men begin to shoot at them then as they went by and when they saw they didn't have the army with them, and didn't they jump off their horses and light out for the mountains on foot as hard as they could, then, and leave the horses? And didn't some people from way over in Bedford County come to claim the horses when the war was over? They identified them, you know, and said those same two fellers were the ones that took 'em. And Lord! didn't they tell it how Amanda Stevens set fire to the Bridge with her own hands on the other side of Sevier so that those that were comin' in from Tennessee were held up for a week before they got across—yes! and stood there laughin' at them, you know; of course they used to tell it on her that she said ("Lord!" I said, "you know she wouldn't say a thing like that!") but of course Amanda was an awful coarse talker, she didn't care what she said, and they all claimed later that's just the way she put it—"Why," she hollers to them, "you don't need a bridge to get across a little stream like that, do you? Well, you must be a pretty worthless lot, after all," she said. "Why, down here," she says, "we'd call it a pretty poor sort of man who couldn't — across it," and, of course, the Yankees had to laugh then, that's the story that they told.

And yes! Didn't they tell it at the time how the day the Yankees marched into town they captured old man Mackery? I reckon they wanted to have some fun with him more than anything else, a great fat thing, you know, with that swarthy yeller complexion and that kinky hair, of course, the story went that he had nigger blood in him and—what about it! he admitted it, sir, he claimed it then and there in front of all the Yankees, I reckon hoping they would let him off. "All right," the Yankees, said, "if you can prove that you're a nigger we'll let you go." Well, he said that he could prove it, then. "Well, how're you going to prove it?" they asked him. "I'll tell you how," this Yankee captain says, calls to one of his troopers, you know, "Run him up and down the street a few times, Jim," he says, and so they started, this soldier and old man Mackery, running up and down in that hot sun as hard as they could go. Well, when they got back, he was wringin' wet with perspiration, Mackery, you know, and the story goes the Yankee went over to him and took one good smell and then called out, "Yes, by God, he told the truth, boys. He's a nigger. Let him go!" Well, that's the way they told it, anyhow.

And yes! Don't I remember it all, yes! With the men comin' by and marchin' along that river road on their way into town to be mustered out and all of us ganged together there in the front yard of Uncle John's place to see them pass, Father and Mother and all the children and all of the Patton and Alexander and Pentland tribes and these two black African niggers that I told you John Patton owned, Willy and Lucindy Patton, and your great grandfather, boy, old Bill Pentland that they called Bill the Hatter because he could make them of the finest felt—learned how to treat the wool with chamber lye, oh! the finest hats you ever saw, why don't I remember an old

farmer coming to our house in my childhood to give a hat to
Uncle Sam to be reblocked, says, "Sam, old Bill Pentland made
that hat for me just twenty years ago and it's as good," he says,
"as it ever was, all it needs is to be blocked and cleaned," and
let me tell you, every one that knew him said that Billy Pentland was certainly a man with a remarkable mind.

3

From *Mannerhouse:*
Prologue and Act 4

Prologue

Scene: Upon a hillside in the South a hundred years ago.

A primitive landscape is in the process of conversion. Here, on top, where the hill is round, and before it slopes away to the east, a clearing has been made in the dense undergrowth of young pine, oak, chestnut, and laurel. It is clearly summer, but in that warm lush wooded place, the brown and fragrant needles of the pines yet carpet the earth.

In the foreground are the stumps of trees white and bleeding fresh. In the background, black-barred against a red and smoky sun which is sloping swiftly into the west, is a forest of great pines.

Beside the pines, upon the very brink of the hill, before it drops, a house is rearing its white and comely sides. From within comes the sound of hammering, and the shearing of boards, and a low steady sustained and savage chant sung by deep barbaric voices.

To the left, a wide path has been cut straight down the flank of the hill through the dense growth: in that green place it bleeds like a wound.

From below there are cries and confused noises, and the sound of men crashing through the thickets.

Near the path, and slant-wise cross the clearing, a great white column of the house lies at its length upon the ground.

Behind the column, and above the entrance to the path, a man is standing on guard. His attitude is at once casual and alert; he bears loosely but handily in the crook of his arm a long-barreled rifle, and when he moves his long brown sinewy figure even slightly, he is alive with the slow yet rapid stealth of a cat.

He wears a shirt of a coarse white stuff, open at his corded neck; his clothes are a rough spun substance, brown.

His face is the face of a gentleman who has gone out to subdue a kingdom for himself, its gentleness and sweetness has been replaced by sternness, inflexibility, resolve. The forehead is high and narrow; the head is a small lean box, carried fiercely and swiftly and beautifully above his straight body; the eyes are sunken well below thick brows; mouth and nose are straight and thin; and there is upon the man very little flesh; there is nothing which is not carried gauntly and magnificently.

Before this man, up and down the path, into the house and back again, bearing in upon their bodies heavy baskets holding bricks, or beams, or pieces of timber, coming out with bodies bent by labor, huge, sinister, gorillalike, is passing and repassing an endless chain of savage black men. They are naked save for short trousers which extend to the knee; their great bodies gleam with sweat; their faces are contorted by the shrill brute agony of their labors. For the most part they are silent, although occasionally they jabber a few words to one another in an outlandish tongue. Their leader, evidently, is a huge man, stronger, fiercer, more savage looking than the rest, but with the pride and chrysm of majesty upon him. He bears the heaviest loads—he bears them with fierce contemptuous ease— and occasionally he shouts and snarls at them in tones of heavy command.

A small NEGRO, a mulatto, a little man with a sharp, furtive, weazened face, and apparently an overseer, for he wears shoes and

*a hat, walks back and forth, eyeing the men and occasionally di-
recting them about the disposition of the heaviest pieces of timber.*

*And the WHITE MAN never ceases to watch them with his
quick, fierce eyes. There is a stirring in the path; a LITTLE MAN
in ministerial garb, with the bones and quick movements of a bird,
and with the agony of salvation on his pinched small face, comes up,
clasping the gospels in his hand.*

There is a wind in the tall pines.

MINISTER *(To the man on guard).* You are Mr. Ramsay?

RAMSAY *(Looking but not moving).* That is my name, sir.

MINISTER. I am the minister in the village.

(A pause)

RAMSAY *(Inflexibly).* Yes. There is a village, I suppose.

MINISTER *(Doubtfully).* I have come to bid you welcome.

RAMSAY *(Coldly, a little fiercely).* Thank you, sir.

MINISTER. I am glad to know you, sir.

*(He extends his hand. RAMSAY takes it briefly, crushes it, and
discards it)*

MINISTER. You are not alone, I believe. That was your
son, perhaps, that I saw directing the workmen at the foot of
the hill.

RAMSAY. That is my son Robert.

MINISTER. And the rest of your family—where are they?

RAMSAY. My wife and the girls will come from Virginia—
when my house is built.

MINISTER. We shall be glad to welcome them when they
come. You will find us a friendly and neighborly folk—a God-
fearing folk.

RAMSAY. Thank you. My wife enjoys neighbors: she likes
to go to church.

(A pause)

MINISTER. And you as well, I hope, sir.

(A pause)

RAMSAY *(Coldly, implacably)*. I must build my house.

MINISTER *(Awkwardly)*. You set great store by your house, Mr. Ramsay.

RAMSAY. Some houses are like people; if you should cut them, they would bleed.

MINISTER. Oh, justly so, justly so. It is a beautiful and enduring structure.

RAMSAY *(In a low, fierce, exultant voice which rises toward the end)*. My house will be more strong than death; it will possess and make its own the lives of valiant men and women when I and my son are gone. I have built him here on this high hill, where he may catch the sun at night and dawn, when all the world is dark. And on this column of my house you will find our motto engraved in bronze.

(The MINISTER *approaches and reads)*

MINISTER. Nil Separabit.

RAMSAY. "Nothing shall part us"—not while the house may stand and take us in its arms to give us rest and shelter. So may it comfort me. So, I pray God, may it comfort my son and his sons. And if the time should come when it must go—for even houses must grow old and die—I pray this earth on which it rests may keep its ghost, and bear again another like it in all respects. I say, God keep such houses, and all who rest in them!

MINISTER. Amen, amen—Your house is like a live thing to you.

RAMSAY. Some houses are like people—if you should cut them they would bleed.

MINISTER. My Father's House is like that, Mr. Ramsay. Ah, you should be thankful to the goodness of Him who has so blessed you.

RAMSAY *(A little ironically)*. Yes?

MINISTER. For He has given you wealth, a fine family; and finally He has shown His trust in you by delivering these heathen into your keeping.

RAMSAY. Ah, but that is friendly of Him, isn't it? *(With genuine pride in his voice)* But they are a likely set, aren't they? I got them, by the way, in the Port of Charleston in South Carolina, from one of the Lord's servants.

MINISTER. Oh—a missionary.

RAMSAY. No; a ship's captain from Salem in Massachusetts.

(The MINISTER *turns and begins to harangue the passing* BLACKS. *They understand from his tone and manner that he is addressing them, and they stare curiously at the tight-faced little man who thus harangues them).*

MINISTER. Servants, be obedient to thy masters, not only to the good and gentle, but also to the forward. First Timothy II, 18. Thou shalt seek for bondmen of the heathen that are round about ye: of them shall ye have bondmen and bondmaids. Ephesians II, 6. Woe unto ye, servants, in an evil hour, that shall say no unto thy masters. Ezekiel IV, 13. The faithful servant shall be given peaceful labors; I shall wither the wicked in my wrath. I Corinthians XI, 14. Both thy bondsmen and thy bondmaids, which thou shalt have, shall be of the heathen that are round about you; of them shall ye buy bondmen and bondmaids.

(They stare curiously at the tight-faced little man who thus harangues them, and they turn to each other with broad grins, and jabber in their strange tongue, gesticulating and pointing toward him)

(He shows some irritation at their conduct, but continues, growing more and more solemn as he goes on)

Let as many servants as are under the yoke count their own masters worthily of all honor. I Timothy VI, i. Exhort servants to be obedient unto their masters. Titus II, 9. Servants, be obedient to them that are your masters according to the flesh, with fear and trembling. Ephesians VI, 5. Servants, be subject to your masters with all fear; not only to the good and gentle, but also to the forward. I Peter II, 18.

(By this time, the blacks, tickled at his rapid gesticulations, and his earnest, vehement tones, are chuckling and laughing openly. Somewhat enraged at their conduct, and not understanding the reason, he continues with great bitterness)

Aye, laugh if ye will, in your heathenish fashion, but I draw my warrant from the scriptures of the old and new Testament— the sole, the only revealed word of God. So, Hear ye and take warning. He that knoweth his master's will and doeth it not, shall be beaten with many stripes. Luke XII, 47.

RAMSAY *(Quietly, with irony)*. I am afraid they don't understand you.

MINISTER *(Incredulously)*. Don't understand me!

RAMSAY. Not a word, I'm afraid. You see, God has neglected to teach them English.

MINISTER *(Appalled)*. But how awful, how awful this is. Do you mean to tell me these poor ignorant wretches have lived their lives in ignorance of scripture and the Blood of the Lamb?

RAMSAY. I'm afraid they have.

MINISTER *(Solemnly)*. It's a sign from Jehovah—we could not go to them—He has sent them to us. Our duty is plain.

RAMSAY. I shall be glad to help you, of course. But you see how they are now. If you could only say to them then, what you have just said—*(He makes an expressive gesture of his hands)* It would do a great deal of good, I am sure. They are savage and ignorant, and stand in need of your teaching.

MINISTER *(In an ecstasy)*. No, now, now. Did not Christ's disciples go out among the highways and byways of the world converting strange peoples? I should be unworthy of my cloth if I refused to do the same now.

RAMSAY. Yes, minister. And so?

MINISTER. And so, let us invoke God's mercy for the salvation of these souls which have lived so long in darkness. Let us pray.

RAMSAY *(With the same strange irony)*. Thy will be done. Shall they kneel?

MINISTER. That would be best.

(RAMSAY *stops his men with a single gesture, and by motions indicates that he desires them to kneel. They do not understand. Finally, he goes to each in turn, forces him down upon his knees and raises his arms in an attitude of supplication. All obey, except the giant* BLACK *who alone seems to have grasped the significance of the business. He backs away angrily and rebelliously, talking fiercely and peremptorily to his subjects, commanding them to rise. Some get up, others look doubtfully from the* WHITE MAN *to the* BLACK. *The question is now much more important than that of religious conversion: it is a question of obedience and supremacy.* RAMSAY *sternly motions the* REBEL *to assume a kneeling posture. He refuses, withdrawing fiercely and proudly. The* WHITE MAN *settles the matter by approaching the* REBEL *and knocking him to the ground with a blow of his fist. All then kneel.* RAMSAY *returns and takes up his old watchful position slightly behind the* MINISTER)

RAMSAY *(Grimly, coldly, quietly)*. I think you may begin now, Mr. Campbell.

(The MINISTER *bows his head and prays)*

MINISTER. Almighty God, our gracious Heavenly Father, we come to Thee today on bended knees, invoking Thy tender love and guidance, and asking of Thee, like Solomon, no greater boon than wisdom. Oh God, we beseech Thee, be merciful to us, and to those with us, and to those about us, and to these wretched heathen whom Thou hast delivered unto our care; vouchsafe that we may be kind and just and temperate in our dealings with them, and that we may lead them, with Thy love, from the dark forest. And give us wisdom and resolve,

Almighty God, to know Thy way and to follow it, for our road is a weary road, and our sinful, worldly sight is baffled by Thy brightness, and we see Thee not, tho Thou standest where all may see. Thou hast made men, O God—likewise hast Thou made masters—Thou hast put Thy mark and Thy injunction on both. Thou has said unto us, "Servants, do unto your masters as you would be done by them: masters, do unto your servants, as you would if you were servant"—for thus, God, do we interpret Thy word with the wisdom which Thou bast given us. All, all, O God, were conceived in sin, begotten in darkness, and live in error, but to some, more than to others, hast Thou given to be less sinful, less wicked, less swayed by error. For some, in time past, O God, were good and dutiful servants, and Thou blessed them, but the wicked and rebellious made a tower 'gainst Thee, and Thou smote them hip and thigh, and burnt their skins black, and put the confusion of strange and savage tongues upon them as a mark whereby all men might know them, so that they were afraid before Thy wrath, and fled away into the strange, unknown places. And these Thou hast delivered unto us. Hear us and answer us, O God, so that in time these souls which have lived in error may be brought to light, that through Christ's love and blood and sacrifice upon the Cross, the souls of these savages may all at length be saved.

> Our Father which art in heaven,
> Hallowed be Thy name,
> Thy kingdom come,
> Thy will be done,
> On earth as it is in heaven.
> Give us this day
> Our daily bread.
> And forgive us our trespasses
> As we forgive those Who trespass against us.
> And lead us not into temptation,

But deliver us from evil,
For Thine is the Kingdom,
And the power and the glory
Forever and ever,
Amen.

(The MINISTER *is joined in the last part of the prayer by* RAMSAY. *When they are done, they pause and are silent for a moment in the quiet hush of the evening. During all this time, the* BLACKS, *holding their arms stiffly and solemnly erect, have listened with growing awe and wonder to the great cadences of the voices and the prayer. They have been very deeply stirred by the solemn rhythm of the man—by his fierce intensity. Now, at a sign from* RAMSAY, *they rise again, and go about their work with a sort of wonder, passing and repassing silently into the house, listening dumbly to the low fierce, bitter harangue of their fallen chief. The* MINISTER's *face is alight with happiness, ecstasy)*

MINISTER. God will find a way! He will! He will! Did you see those black faces shine?

RAMSAY *(Quietly).* Yes, I think they were very much impressed.

MINISTER. God has found a way! Already his light has entered into them—the light of our God, the true God, the Christian God!

RAMSAY. It was a very fine prayer, sir. You must come again.

MINISTER. Ah friend, my work is just begun. I shall not rest until the idols are all overthrown.

RAMSAY. Then we shall see you soon!

MINISTER. I shall come daily until my work is done.

RAMSAY. Then, for the present, goodbye, my friend.

MINISTER. God bless you, friend.

(They clasp hands, warmly this time, and the little man reels off into the path as if drunken)

(And as he goes, he sings with all the passion of his heart, a great

hymn about the Passion and the Blood of Christ. The NEGROES, *never halting in their even stride, follow him with many glances of the eye as he goes, giving him a wide and respectful leeway)*

RAMSAY *(A straight, gray figure in the shadows as before, but with a baffled look in his eyes—in a low voice)*. If it were true! If it were true!

(The NEGROES *resume their great low chant)*

(It grows darker. The sun has set. Twilight. Dusk comes quickly and the great black beasts go padding in and out more swiftly)

(RAMSAY *stands again, a gray, swift, silent figure, in the shadows back of the column. There is a stirring in the brush behind him. He gives no sign that he has heard. The great* SAVAGE CHIEFTAIN *comes from darkness like a cat and stands behind the* WHITE MAN, *poised upon his toes. In a moment he raises his huge right arm and brandishes lightly there a short-handled, brightly gleaming axe. The* LITTLE MULATTO, *stationed just in front of his master, has seen the whole occurrence. With eyes that are glazed with horror, he squeaks twice like a frightened rat, and the* WHITE MAN *hurls himself face downward to the earth, as the axe whirls over and above him, and sinks itself, quivering, in the wood of the column. The* SAVAGE *springs like a cat upon the prostrate body of his master, but is knocked senseless by a blow from* RAMSAY's *gun stock. The* WHITE MAN *leaps to his feet and confronts the threatening* BLACKS *who have rushed to the spot and stand in a baleful circle. With his rifle, he forces them back into the path, and along their processional, holding them at bay, while he dispatches the* MULATTO *for his son)*

RAMSAY *(Curtly)*. Go tell my son Robert to come here.

(The MULATTO *runs off into the path and returns presently with the son—a slender, fair-skinned, blond young man of twenty-three or -four years. He also is armed)*

(Sharply) Go behind me, Robert.

ROBERT *(Trembling)*. What is it?

RAMSAY. The big one tried to kill me with an axe. Now

we must watch them. They are ugly. (ROBERT *shudders but takes up his position behind his father)* Turn your back to me so that you'll be facing the other way. (ROBERT *does so*) Now we're ready for whatever happens!

(The BLACK BODY *on the ground moves)*

ROBERT *(Hoarsely).* Father!

RAMSAY. Yes?

ROBERT. He's not dead! He moved!

RAMSAY *(Grimly).* It is well. He was strong before; now he will be faithful.

(The great BLACK BODY *begins to drag itself slowly and painfully towards the path)*

ROBERT. Father! He's going!

RAMSAY. Let him go! I have put my mark upon him!

(Suddenly the BLACK *gets to his feet, turns suddenly, and advances toward the* WHITE MAN)

(RAMSAY *makes a threatening movement with his rifle. With a gesture in which there is majesty and dignity, without any servility, the* SAVAGE *falls to his knees and acknowledges obedience to his new king by kissing his hand. Then he arises, lurches drunkenly into the path, and disappears)*

RAMSAY *(In a low tone filled with terrible satisfaction).* It is the first time a king has kissed my hand. What he has done the others must do. I will be king in my own right.

(The great BLACK FIGURES, *bearing in their heavy burdens, coming out with bodies bent, huge, sinister, gorillalike, pad swiftly and softly past. And ever as they go, the* WHITE MAN *watches them warily and warns them back into their trodden path, and turns lightly on his feet in a half circle, so that always is he facing them, in the manner of a circus man in a cage with animals. And as they go now in the dark, faster and faster as it seems, a mad barbaric chant comes low and fierce from their deep throats. Silence and darkness. The even sustained noises of little night*

things—crickets and whippoorwills. The LITTLE MULATTO *no longer trusts himself away from the feet of his master: he crouches, tense, stricken, moaning softly to himself)*

(In a low, still voice, at length) My God! Is this, then, how a prayer is answered? *(With a cry)* Oh then, our cause is one, God.

(A wind blows through the pines and A THIN FAR VOICE *has whispered in its laughter, "Conversion." All the million-noted little creatures of the night have come to life and are singing now in a vast, low chorus: a weird ululation which seems to continue and prolong the deep chant of the* SAVAGE; *which seems to hold in it the myriad voices of their demons. The young man shudders convulsively and slips down weakly until he sits upon the column, his rifle at rest beside him)*

(RAMSAY *continues to stand gauntly above the figures of the* MULATTO *and his son. His face is at once stern, slightly contemptuous, yet strangely tender. The pines are bent by the wind again)*

A THIN FAR VOICE *(With evil mockery, rushing away on the wind).* Conversion, Conversion!

(The great BLACK FIGURES *continue to pad swiftly and softly past. A church bell rings slowly and sweetly, far away)*

Curtain

Act 4

Late on a night when the ruinous years have passed: a clear cold Autumn night, prided keen and bright with frosty stars, and with a horned moon, at rest above the dim forest in the distance.

Old doors swing painfully within the house, perhaps dim faces glimmer in the dark; faint footfalls, half aware of sound, pad dreamily above; and a tall tree out of sight prints swinging shadows on the moonlit floor.

The great doors at the back sag heavily on creaking hinges—but they are open to the moon.

With frosty clearness, a great bell booms three times, and a tall MAN, meanly clothed, and weary of the road, climbs slowly to the porch, and comes in past the rotted column of the house.

There is a gentle scurry of undiscovered feet; and thin gay mocking laughter in the distance.

SOFT VOICES *(Laughing)*. Eugene. Eugene!
(The ghostly echoings of ancient music)
EUGENE *(In a low voice)*. Old house! My God, old house, old house! *(The soft dim feet are moving now to the even rhythm of the waltz. With a cry)* Oh, I will join you, even if I cannot dance.
(Gay, thin, gentle laughter)
VOICES *(very faint)*. Ah, Eugene, Eugene.
EUGENE *(Moving around the room)*. Where are you, then? Where are you?
VOICES *(Laughing softly)*. Where are *you*, 'Gene. Where are you?
EUGENE. My heart is emptied of its song, but I will see you dance. Oh, little feet, where are you?
VOICES *(Now here, now there—laughing gently)*. Here, 'Gene. Here. *(Shadows of those who dance are printed on the moonlit walls where the tall tree prints the shadow of its limbs)*
EUGENE *(As the elfin music swells)*. Now loosen your hair, Margaret, and I shall see its smoky shadow on the wall.
VOICES *(Laughing softly)*. You may not see her, 'Gene.
(The music fills the house with elfin bigness, dominant, omnipresent, and remote)
EUGENE. Where are you, my ghost? Where are you?
VOICES *(Softly)*. Not here—not here—not here, Eugene.
EUGENE. Shadows, oh just and everlasting shadows, let me see her shadow on the wall—among you. Let me see her

dark long hair uncoil like smoke before the moon—oh, shadows, let me see the shadow of your hands; of hers, for they are curative and just; for I am one with you, dim shadows—your comrade and your slave forevermore—life like an echo breaks upon the solid shores of earth. Too far, too far and faint. Oh, shadows, have I come again to you, my shadows, and [my] pilgrimage is done; and you will never die, dear shadows.

(A cloud is driven on the moon, the walls are darkened, and the shadows disappear)

VOICES *(Laughing gently as they go, and as the music fades).* And we shall never die, Eugene.

EUGENE *(With a great cry).* Oh, Christ, I am forsaken by my shadows even!

A VOICE *(Softly).* Not by *your* shadows, shadow.

(EUGENE falls slowly to a chair. Silence and darkness, save for the punctual fall of the merciless drop of water. An old door opens slowly in the house, and there is a swift pad as of a mighty cat who comes. The negro TOD, like something swift and deathless enters, bearing high aloft a dim and smoky lantern. He bends swiftly above the sleeping form of EUGENE and raises him gently in his great arms, and bears him swiftly from the room)

(An old wind comes upon the house, filled with faint and evil mockery. The FAITHFUL DOG pads through the room and sits upon its haunch in moonlight)

(The scene is darkened wholly. The curtain falls for a moment)

Curtain

When the curtain rises, late afternoon has come, a small sun, dim and smoky red, is low above the dark trees of the forest.

From within the house from every quarter, there is a steady din of hammering, and the sounds of boards, wrenched with a heavy rasp from their moorings in the wall.

Backward, forward, coming in with empty hands, going out again bent low under heavy burdens of old wood an endless chain of BLACK MEN, *but this time in stained and dirty clothes, are entering and leaving the house.*

Within the room two white CARPENTERS *are beating old boards from the wall and floor with heavy hammers.*

FIRST CARPENTER. Well, sir, she took hold of That Thing an' she give it one look an' she said, "Gr-e-e-at God, Almighty."

SECOND CARPENTER. Mister, yore wife'll whup you, ef she knows whar you're spendin' yore spare time. A feller over on Hominy Creek got to goin' with a gal an' he bigged her. Now he spends all his time hidin' out in the woods a-munchin' nuts like a goddam squirrel.

FIRST CARPENTER. What fer?

SECOND CARPENTER. He cain't go home. He tried to once an' his old woman met him at the dore with a shotgun. She got him in the seat o' the pants jest as he was goin' out o' the gate.

FIRST CARPENTER *(Laughing coarsely).* Go-o-d Almighty! I reckon he ain't sat down yet.

SECOND CARPENTER. Last I heard tell o' him he was still in the woods, a-pickin' buckshot out o' his tail with a screw-driver.

(They laugh with coarse big hilarity, slapping their thighs)

FIRST CARPENTER *(Pounding a board).* Ole man's wust I ever seen. He'd save skin off'n a sausage. What's he want with these ole boards.

SECOND CARPENTER. Good timber heah yet.

(EUGENE *comes in*)

FIRST CARPENTER *(Roughly).* Did ye finish at the mill?

EUGENE. Yes.

FIRST CARPENTER. They'll be needin' ye upstairs, I reckon.

(EUGENE *goes out*)

SECOND CARPENTER. Th' ole man'll hire any tramp

that comes along. Gits 'em fer next to nothin'. Don't like workin' with 'em, neither. Lazy an' shif'less.

FIRST CARPENTER. This 'un worked hard today. No foolin'.

SECOND CARPENTER. Ole man was watching.

(PORTER *comes in flensing his hand. He has been drinking. They become studiously busy*)

PORTER. Got yore pay, didn't ye?

FIRST CARPENTER. Yes, Sir.

PORTER. Allus got it prompt, ain't ye?

FIRST CARPENTER. Yes, Sir.

PORTER. Tend to yore damn business.

SECOND CARPENTER *(Muttering)*. Ain't hired to wo'k with a tramp.

PORTER. Go t'hell.

(He goes out)

(EUGENE *returns*)

EUGENE. Has anyone seen my good little master?

FIRST CARPENTER *(Muttering—making as if to leave)*. Won't stay on the job with a damn drunk tramp.

SECOND CARPENTER. He's crazy. Let him be.

(CARPENTER *goes back to work*)

(PORTER *comes in flensing his terrible hand*)

PORTER *(With his twisted grin)*. Lookin' fer me?

EUGENE *(Clapping his hands together)*. Oh, I know who it is! It's my dear kind little master!

PORTER *(Scaling his horrible hand and grinning)*. An' to-morrow ye git shaved.

EUGENE. Oh yes, my dear master.

PORTER *(Putting his good hand on* EUGENE's *arm)*. Now, we'll have one together.

EUGENE. Yes, master. But put your other hand upon me.

(PORTER *moves around him, and seizes him with his terrible hand*)

(Shuddering) Thank you, my dear master. But you should have a beak to go with your claw.

PORTER *(Pushing him toward the door, with his terrible smile)*. An' tomorrow ye git shaved!

EUGENE. Yes, master. Did you know that someone has spilled blood in your eyes?

PORTER. An' tomorrow ye git shaved!

EUGENE. Yes, master.

PORTER. Let's have a drink.

(They go)

(MARGARET *enters wearing a hat*)

MARGARET *(To* CARPENTER). You do not mind if I look around, do you?

FIRST CARPENTER. No, ma'am.

(They regard her curiously, and whisper among themselves)

(PORTER *returns*)

MARGARET. How do you do, Mr. Porter.

PORTER *(Flensing his hand)*. Miss Patton, ain't hit?

MARGARET. Yes.

(EUGENE *enters and works quietly in a corner. It grows darker)*

PORTER. Didn't know ye with yore hat on.

MARGARET *(Pleasantly)*. No? Shall I take it off, Mr. Porter?

PORTER *(Winking and nodding toward* EUGENE). New Hand! He'll show ye about. Funny feller. Like funny fellers, don't ye?

(He goes out)

(EUGENE *bends low in a corner)*

MARGARET. You are a new man, aren't you?

EUGENE. Yes, lady.

MARGARET. A stranger here?

EUGENE. Yes, lady.

MARGARET. There are a great many new people here, I believe.

EUGENE. Yes, lady. I believe so.

(A pause)

MARGARET. Do you always talk to people with your back turned?

EUGENE. Yes, lady. Whenever I can.

MARGARET. It is becoming quite dark, and I cannot see you very well. Will you turn around?

EUGENE *(In a low voice)*. Yes, lady.

(He faces her slowly, and they look at each other for a long level moment)

MARGARET *(In a low voice)*. You see I was right. It is becoming quite dark.

EUGENE. Yes, lady.

MARGARET. And you do not see me very well, do you?

EUGENE. Not very well.

MARGARET. But a little—you see me a little?

EUGENE. I see your eyes, lady—I could see them very well even if I were far off.

MARGARET. And in the dark?

EUGENE. Yes. In the dark.

MARGARET. And in the light you could not tell that I have grown old?

EUGENE. No, lady. In this light I could not tell that you were anything but young, and deathless, and forever lovely.

MARGARET. What a beautiful thing is darkness, then.

EUGENE. Yes, lady. More true than dawn; more hopeful than the sun.

MARGARET. And on what road did you learn that?

EUGENE. There are no answers, lady; there are no questions.

MARGARET. And is that all?

EUGENE. That is all! There is only the distance and all the pain.

MARGARET. It was for that you sought the world!

EUGENE. It was for that. The ends of the earth are met in darkness—I shall not go beyond it.

MARGARET *(With a sudden cry).* My God, my God, Eugene—but they have hurt you!

EUGENE *(With a touch of mockery).* Have you not heard? The brothers kill each other in the dark.

MARGARET. You will not go again.

EUGENE. I shall not go again, ghost. Put your hands upon me in the dark—for I am desolate and sick. Your touch may heal me.

MARGARET. Eugene! Eugene!

(He kisses her)

EUGENE. Go away, go away, my ghost. I will come when my work is over.

MARGARET *(Going).* I shall heal you and make you well, Eugene.

EUGENE. Go away, little ghost, go away.

(Soft laughter through the room)

(She goes)

(A whistle is blown. The CARPENTERS, *bearing their kits of tools, go through the room towards the entrance)*

FIRST CARPENTER *(Sharply).* What ye hangin round fer? Heah the whistle?

EUGENE. Yes, centurion. I am going.

FIRST CARPENTER *(Angrily).* What'd you call me?

EUGENE. Je voudrai faire le pipi.

SECOND CARPENTER. Leave him alone. You can't expect no different from a tramp. *(To* EUGENE, *roughly)* Go 'long now an' don't go callin' decent people names.

EUGENE. Be quiet, carpenter. I can see plainly that you have ancestors.

SECOND CARPENTER *(Furiously, moving forward).* Did ye hear that, hey?

PORTER *(Entering, flensing his hand)*. Go 'long, go 'long! Ye heard the whistle.

FIRST CARPENTER. Ain't paid t'be insulted by—

PORTER. Git out.

(They go. In the gathering dusk the BLACKS tramp heavily out in a solid arid implacable wedge)

EUGENE. And the day is done for me as well, my good kind master?

PORTER. Fer you! Why, ye must learn tonight how houses are torn down.

EUGENE. And you will teach me, master?

PORTER. I'll teach ye sure enough—you've never handled tools 'fore this.

EUGENE. No.

(The gentle voices and the music are heard, far off)

And do you hear the music in the house, good master?

PORTER *(Grizzly)*. I can tell the best jokes now, my son.

EUGENE. You do not hear? Then the mark is not upon you yet, good master.

PORTER *(Approaching)*. You sure you ain't never handled tools before, have ye?

EUGENE *(Using the hammer clumsily)*. No.

PORTER *(With a contorted smile, flensing his hand)*. Never learned when you growed up, I reckon.

EUGENE. No.

PORTER. I'll show ye how hit's done. Give me the hammer. (EUGENE *gives it to him)* Hold hit like this—d'ye see?

EUGENE *(Nodding)*. Yes.

PORTER *(With his contorted smile)*. Now, I reckon we'll have to have somethin' to use hit on, won't we?

EUGENE. Yes.

PORTER *(Coming closer)*. Mebbe you'd better pick somethin' out—an' I'll show ye how hit's done.

EUGENE. I think you had better pick it out.

(PORTER *seats himself in the* GENERAL'S *chair*)

(Quickly) You had better sit here, hadn't you? *(He indicates another chair)*

PORTER *(Flensing his hand, grinning).* What fer?

EUGENE. It's an old chair—this one is better for you.

PORTER *(Reflectively, striking the arm of the chair).* An old chair? Pshaw! Hit's good as th' day hit was made. *(As if struck by a sudden idea)* Look heah! I'll show ye how good hit is. *(He gets up quickly)* Whar's the hammer?

EUGENE. Here it is. *(He gives it to him)*

PORTER. Ye hold, but like this—*(He indicates)*—an ye hit it like this.

(He deals a savage blow which demolishes one arm of the chair)

EUGENE *(Hoarsely).* You mustn't do that, do you hear?

PORTER *(With a smile of malevolent innocence) (Flensing his terrible hand).* What fer? Hit's only an' ole chair. You were right about hit. Hit ain't as good as I thought hit was. *(Laughing shrilly)* By God, hit ain't as good as I thought hit was. *(Shrilling with insane laughter)* Hit—ain't—as good—as I thought—hit was. Looky that! *(He deals another savage and demolishing blow)*

EUGENE *(Reeling on his feet).* No, no! You mustn't do that!

PORTER *(Becoming quiet).* What's that? Mustn't do hit! *(As if comprehending suddenly)*

Oh, I see! Ye don't want me to smash hit up! Ye want me to keep hit fer myself. *(He seats himself)* Why, you're all right, you bastard. A smart feller! I'll jest do that. Hit jest fits me, don't hit?

EUGENE *(In a low voice).* Yes. It fits you very well, master.

PORTER. The ole man hisse'f, eh? *(Rising)* Now, you do hit. I'll jest look on. This table—mebbe—er the mantel—see how easy hit is. *(He strikes the mantel with the hammer)* You try hit now. *(He gives* EUGENE *the hammer)*

EUGENE *(In a low voice, advancing on him)*. Yes. Upon your dirty skull, my good master.

PORTER *(In a sudden shrill voice)*. All right, out thar! Help!

(EUGENE *hurls himself upon the man and throttles him. The* CARPENTERS *run in, and overcome him)*

(Gasping) Throw the bastard out.

EUGENE. But remember that there are endings for us both, good master.

FIRST CARPENTER. No, you don't, you damn tramp!

SECOND CARPENTER. Come along, now.

(He is led out. The CARPENTERS *return)*

PORTER *(Flensing his terrible hand)*. See that he gits his pay. (EUGENE *leans wearily, against the column)* Git along, thar, now. *(To* CARPENTERS*)* Clean up the mess. He tried to smash things up.

MARGARET'S VOICE *(Far up, in the house)*. Eugene!

EUGENE. Oh, I am coming, ghost.

VOICES *(Softly)*. Oh, come, oh come, Eugene.

(Within the house, a board is wrenched from its ancient moorings, and comes away with an audible rasping)

EUGENE *(With one hand on the column)*. I am a part of all that I have touched.

VOICES *(Whispering)*. Then come, Eugene.

(The sun, streaked with red filaments of smoke, gives a dim and fading light to those within the house)

EUGENE *(Tracing the wording of the ancient scroll)*. Nil separabit. *(With a cry)* Oh, my fathers were valiant men!

(He wraps his gaunt arms fiercely round the column, where its bulk has rotted to a slender pulp. There is a convulsive movement of his ruined frame, and he snaps the column in two pieces on his breast. It falls upon him slowly, and he is borne to the earth, and lies at length athwart the shallow steps, his gaunt face still turned upward to the sun)

(Far off within the house there is a mighty thrill, a great, grow-ing vibration, which trembles through the walls. A heavy timber is heard to bend and buckle. PORTER *and the* CARPENTERS *run toward the door)*

EUGENE *(Calling faintly from below the column).* Tod! Tod! Oh, I have failed! Tod! Here was a house. It was by you begun; by you it must be ended. Tod! Tod!

(The negro TOD *leaps like a cat into the room, and thrusts his great body before the door)*

(They spring upon him, and he throws them back. PORTER *rushes upon the* NEGRO *with a drawn knife and stabs him re-peatedly in the breast.*

(The NEGRO, *with a smile of savage triumph, which reveals his yellow fangs, makes no resistance, but when the man is done, sinks slowly forward upon him, and breaks him in his mighty grip.*

*(*TOD *falls slowly forward upon the floor. The* CARPEN-TERS *attempt to rush to safety, past his body, and the broken frame of* PORTER.

(A timber falls slant-wise cross the door, and they are held. The FAITHFUL DOG *trots in and guards the door.*

(The men are flattened to the walls in terror; they fix their eye aloft on some nameless and unfathomable horror which we do not see—a tiny spurt of white dust sifts down their faces, their heads, then clothes.

(The great vibrations lengthen to a thunder.

*(*PORTER, *dying, lies half against the door sill, his eyes fixed on something which is plunging down on him from above, his mouth twisted in its queer terrible, contorted smile, his stubby fingers flensing, as before, his unspeakable hand)*

The curtain drops quickly.

(There is heard immediately a terrific crash and the sounds of heavy timbers, which buckle and settle. There is a lesser reverbera-

tion followed by silence, save for the soft musical laughter of the triumphant little voices: save for the faint far ending of a waltz which dies upon the wind; save for a merciless little drop of water which somewhere swells, develops, and falls at length with punctual, unvarying monotony)

A THIN VOICE *(Faint and far)*. Snap your fingers, gentlemen.

The End

4

From *Of Time and the River*

AT DAY-BREAK SUDDENLY, HE AWOKE. The first light of the day, faint, gray-white, shone through the windows of his berth. The faint gray light fell on the stiff white linen, feverishly scuffed and rumpled in the distressful visions of the night, on the hot pillows and on the long cramped figure of the boy, where dim reflection already could be seen on the polished surface of the berth above his head. Outside, that smokegray light had stolen almost imperceptibly through the darkness. The air now shone gray-blue and faintly luminous with day, and the old brown earth was just beginning to emerge in that faint light. Slowly, the old brown earth was coming from the darkness with that strange and awful stillness which the first light of the day has always brought.

The earth emerged with all its ancient and eternal quality: stately and solemn and lonely-looking in that first light, it filled men's hearts with all its ancient wonder. It seemed to have been there forever, and, though they had never seen it before, to be more familiar to them than their mother's face. And at the same time it seemed they had discovered it once more, and if they had been the first men who ever saw the earth, the solemn joy of this discovery could not have seemed more strange or more familiar. Seeing it, they felt nothing but silence and wonder in their hearts, and were naked and alone and stripped down to their bare selves, as near to truth as men can ever come. They knew that they would die and that the earth would last forever. And with that feeling of joy, wonder, and sorrow in their hearts, they knew that another day had gone, another day had come, and they knew how brief and lonely are man's days.

The old earth went floating past then in that first gaunt light of the morning, and it seemed to be the face of time itself, and the noise the train made was the noise of silence. They were fixed there in that classic design of time and silence. The engine smoke went striding out upon the air, the old earth, field and wood and hill and stream and wood and field and hill—went stroking, floating past with a kind of everlasting repetitiveness, and the train kept making on its steady noise that was like silence and forever—until it almost seemed that they were poised there in that image of eternity forever, in moveless movement, unsilent silence, spaceless flight.

All of the noises, rhythms, sounds and variations of the train seemed to belong to all the visions, images, wild cries and oaths and songs and haunting memories of the night before, and now the train itself seemed united to this infinite mono-tone of silence, and the boy felt that this land now possessed his life, that he had known it forever, and could now think only with a feeling of unbelief and wonder that yesterday—just yesterday—he had left his home in the far mountains and now was stroking eastward, northward towards the sea.

And against the borders of the East, pure, radiant, for the first time seen in the unbelievable wonder of its new discovery, bringing to all of us, as it had always done, the first life that was ever known on this earth, the golden banner of the day appeared.

VI

In morning sunlight on a hospital porch, five flights above the ground, an old dying spectre of a man was sitting, looking mournfully out across the sun-hazed sweep of the city he had known in his youth. He sat there, a rusty, creaking hinge, an almost severed thread of life, a shockingly wasted integument of skin and bone, of which every fibre and sinew was almost utterly rotted out, consumed and honey-combed by the great plant of the cancer which flowered from his entrails and had now spread its fibrous roots to every tissue of his life. Everything was gone: everything was wasted from him: the face was drawn tight and bony as a beak, the skin was clean, tinged with a fatal cancerous yellow, and almost delicately transparent. The great thin blade of nose cut down across the face with knife-like sharpness and in the bony, slanting, almost reptilian cage-formation of the skull, the smallish cold-graygreen eyes were set wearily, with a wretched and enfeebled dullness, out across the great space of the city which swept away and melted at length into the sun-hazed vistas of October.

Nothing was left but his hands. The rest of the man was dead. But the great hands of the stonecutter, on whose sinewy and bony substance there was so little that disease or death could waste, looked as powerful and living as ever. Although one of his hands—the right one—had been stiffened years before by an attack of rheumatism, they had lost none of their character of power and massive shapeliness.

In the huge shapely knuckles, in the length and sinewy thickness of the great fingers—which were twice the size of an ordinary man's—and in the whole length and sinewy contour of the hand, there was a quality of sculptural design which was as solid and proportionate as any of the marble hands of love and grace which the stonecutter had so often carved upon the surface of a grave-yard monument.

Thus, as he sat there now, staring dully out across the city, an emaciated and phantasmal shadow of a man, there was, in the appearance of these great living hands of power (one of which lay with an enormous passive grace and dignity across the arm of his chair and the other extended and clasped down upon the handle of a walking stick), something weirdly incongruous, as if the great strong hands had been unnaturally attached to the puny lifeless figure of a scarecrow.

Now, wearily, desperately, the old enfeebled mind was trying to grope with the strange and bitter miracle of life, to get some meaning out of that black, senseless fusion of pain and joy and agony, that web that had known all the hope and joy and wonder of a boy, the fury, passion, drunkenness, and wild desire of youth, the rich adventure and fulfillment of a man, and that had led him to this fatal and abominable end.

But that fading, pain-sick mind, that darkened memory could draw no meaning and no comfort from its tragic meditation.

The old man's land of youth was far away in time, yet now only the magic lonely hills of his life's journey, his wife's people, seemed sorrowful, lonely, lost, and strange to him. Now he remembered all places, things, and people in his land of youth as if he had known them instantly and forever!

Oh, what a land, a life, a time was that—that world of youth and no return. What colors of green-gold, magic, rich plantations, and shining cities were in it! For now when this dying man thought about this vanished life that tragic quality of sorrow and loneliness had vanished instantly. All that he had read in books about old wars seemed far and lost and in another time, but when he thought about these things that he had known as a boy, he saw them instantly, knew them, breathed them, heard them, felt them, was there beside them, living them with his own life. He remembered now his wife's people!— tramping in along the Carlisle Pike on that hot first morning in July, as they marched in towards Gettysburg. He had been standing there with his next older brother Gil, beside the dusty road, as they came by.

And he could see them now, not as shadowy, lost, phantasmal figures of dark time, the way they were in books; he saw them, heard them, knew them again as they had been in their shapeless rags of uniforms, their bare feet wound in rags, their lank disordered hair, sometimes topped by stove-pipe hats which they had looted out of stores.

"God!" the old man thought, wetting his great thumb briefly, grinning thinly, as he shook his head, "What a scare-crow crew that was! In all my days I never saw the like of it! A bum-looking lot, if ever there was one!—And the bravest of the brave, the finest troops that ever lived!"—his mind swung upward to its tide of rhetoric—"Veterans all of them, who had been through the bloodiest battles of the war, they did not know the meaning of the word 'fear,' and they would have gone into the valley of death, the jaws of hell, at a word from their Commander!" His mind was alive again, in full swing now, the old voice rose and muttered on the tides of rhetoric, the great hand gestured, the cold-gray, restless eyes glared feverishly about—and all of it began to live for him again.

He remembered how he and Gil had been standing there beside the road, two barefoot farmer boys, aged thirteen and fifteen, and he remembered how the rebels would halt upon their march, and shout jesting remarks at the two boys standing at the road. One shouted out to Gil:

"Hi, there, Yank! You'd better hide! Jeb Stuart's on the way an' he's been lookin' fer you!"

And Gil, older, bolder, more assured than he, quick-tempered, stubborn, fiercely partisan, had come back like a flash:

"He'll be lookin' fer *you* when we get through with you!" said Gil and the rebels had slapped their ragged thighs and howled with laughter, shouting at their crestfallen, grinning comrade.

"'Y, God! I reckon you'll be quiet now! He shore God put it on ye that time!"

And he was there beside his brother, seeing, hearing, living it again, as he remembered his strange first meeting with the Pentland tribe, the haunting miracle of that chance meeting. For among that ragged crew he had first seen his wife's uncle, the prophet, Bacchus Pentland, and he had seen him, heard him that hot morning, and had never been able to forget him, although it would be twenty years, after many strange turnings of the roads of destiny and wandering, before he was to see the man again, and know his name, and join together the two halves of fated meeting.

Yes, there had been one among the drawling and terrible mountaineers that day who passed there on that dusty road, and paused, and talked, and waited in the heat, one whose face he had never been able to forget, one whose full, ruddy face and tranquil eyes were lighted always by a smile of idiot and beatific saintliness, whose powerful fleshy body gave off a stench that would have put a goat to shame, and who on this account was called by his jesting comrades, "Stinking Jesus." Yes, he had been there that morning, Bacchus Pentland, the fated and chosen of God, the supernatural appearer on roads at nightfall, the harbinger of death, the prophet, chanting even then his promises of Armageddon and the Coming of the Lord, speaking for the first time to the fascinated ears of those two boys, the full, drawling, unctuous accents of the fated, time-triumphant Pentlands.

They came, they halted in the dust before the two young brothers, the lewd tongues mocked and jested, but that man of God, the prophet Bacchus Pentland, was beautifully unmoved by their unfaith, and chanted, with a smile of idiot beatitude, his glorious assurances of an end of death and battle, everlasting peace:

"Hit's a comin'!" cried the prophet with the sweet purity of his saintly smile. "Hit's a comin'! Accordin' to my figgers the

Great Day is almost here! Oh, hit's a comin', boys!" he sweetly, cheerfully intoned, "Christ's kingdom on this airth's at hand! We're marchin' in to Armageddon now!"

"Hell, Back!" drawled one, with a slow grin of disbelief. "You said the same thing afore Chancellorsville, an' all I got from it was a slug of canister in my tail!"—and the others slapped their ragged thighs and shouted.

"Hit's a comin'!" Bacchus cried, with a brisk wink, and his seraphic smile, unmoved, untouched, by their derision. "He'll be here a-judgin' an' decreein' afore the week is over, settin' up His Kingdom, an' sortin' us all out the way it was foretold—the sheep upon His right hand an' the goats upon His left."

"An' which side are you goin' to be on, Back, when all this sortin' starts?" one drawled with evil innocence. "Are you goin' to be upon the sheep-side or the goat-side?" he demanded.

"Oh," cried Bacchus cheerfully, with his seraphic smile, "I'll be upon the sheep-side, brother, with the Chosen of the Lord."

"Then, Back," the other slowly answered, "you'd shore God better begin to smell a whole lot better than you do right now, for if the Lord starts sortin' in the dark, Back, He's goin' to put you where you don't belong—He'll have you over thar among the goats!"—and the hot brooding air had rung then with their roars of laughter. Then a word was spoken, an order given, the ragged files trudged on again, and they were gone.

Now this was lost, a fume of smoke, the moment's image of a fading memory, and he could not say it, speak it, find a word for it—but he could see that boy of his lost youth as he sat round the kitchen table with the rest of them. He could see his cold-gray, restless, unhappy eyes, the strange, gaunt, almost reptilian conformation of his staring face, his incredibly thin, blade-like nose, as he waited there in silence, looking uneasily at the others with his cold-gray, shallow, most unhappy eyes. And the old man seemed to be the spy of destiny, to look at once below the roofs of a million little houses everywhere and on the star-shone, death-flung mystery of the silent battlefield.

He seemed to be a witness of the secret weavings of dark chance that threads our million lives into strange purposes that we do not know. He thought of those dead and wounded men upon the battlefield whose lives would touch his own so nearly, the wounded brother that he knew, the wounded stranger he had seen that day by magic chance, whom he could not forget, and whose life, whose tribe, in the huge abyss and secret purpose of dark time would one day interweave into his own.

Oh, he could not find a word, a phrase to utter it, but he seemed to have the lives not only of those people in him, but the lives of millions of others whose dark fate is thus determined, interwove, and beyond their vision or their knowledge, foredone and made inevitable in the dark destiny of unfathomed time. And suddenly it seemed to him that all of it was his, even as his father's blood and earth was his, the lives and deaths and destinies of all his people. He had been a nameless atom in the great family of earth, a single, unknown thread in the huge warp of fate and chance that weaves our lives together and because of this he had been the richest man that ever lived; the power, grandeur, glory of this earth and all its lives of men were his.

And for a moment he forgot that he was old and dying, and pride, joy, pain, triumphant ecstasy that had no tongue to utter it rose like a wordless swelling pæan in his throat, because it seemed to him that this great familiar earth on which his people lived and wrought was his, that all the mystery, grandeur and beauty in the lives of men were his, and that he must find a word, a tongue, a door to utter what was his, or die!

How could he say it! How could he ever find a word to speak the joy, the pain, the grandeur bursting in the great vine of his heart, swelling like a huge grape in his throat—mad, sweet, wild, intolerable with all the mystery, loneliness, wild secret joy, and death, the ever-returning and renewing fruitfulness of the earth!

A cloud-shadow passed and left no light but loneliness on the massed green of the wilderness! A bird was calling in a secret wood! And there was something going, coming, fading there across the sun, oh, there was something lonely and most sorrowful, his mother's voice, the voices of lost men long, long ago, the flowing of a little river in the month of April—and all, all of it was his!

A man had passed at sunset on a lonely road and vanished unknown years ago! A soldier had toiled up a hill at evening and was gone! A man was lying dead that day upon a bloody field!—and all, all, all of it was his!

He had stood beside a dusty road, feet bare, his gaunt boy's face cold-eyed, staring, restless, and afraid. The ragged jesting rebels passed before him in the dusty heat, the huge drowse and cricketing stitch of noon was rising from the sweet woods and nobly swelling, fertile fields of Pennsylvania and all, all, all of it was his!

A prophet passed before him in the road that day with the familiar haunting unction of an unmet, unheard tribe; a wounded prophet lay that night below the stars and chanted glory, peace, and Armageddon; the boy's brother lay beside the prophet bleeding from the lungs; the boy's people grimly waited all night long in a little house not fourteen miles away; and all, all, all of it was his!

Over the wild and secret earth, the lonely, everlasting, and unchanging earth, under the huge tent of the all-engulfing night, amid the fury, chaos, blind confusions of a hundred million lives, something wild and secret had been weaving through the generations, a dark terrific weaving of the threads of time and destiny.

But it had come to this: an old man dying on a porch, staring through the sun-hazed vistas of October towards the lost country of his youth.

This was the end of man, then, end of life, of fury, hope, and passion, glory, all the strange and bitter miracle of chance, of history, fate, and destiny which even a stonecutter's life could include. This was the end, then:—an old man, feeble, foul, complaining and disease-consumed who sat looking from the high porch of a hospital at the city of his youth. This was the sickening and abominable end of flesh, which infected time and all man's living memory of morning, youth, and magic with the death-putrescence of its cancerous taint, and made us doubt that we had ever lived, or had a father, known joy: this was the end, and the end was horrible in ugliness. At the end it was not well.

5

The Four Lost Men

SUDDENLY, AT THE GREEN HEART of June, I heard my father's voice again. That year I was sixteen; the week before I had come home from my first year at college, and the huge thrill and menace of war, which we had entered just two months before, had filled our hearts. And war gives life to men as well as death. It fills the hearts of young men with wild song and jubilation. It wells up in their throats in great-starred night the savage goat-cry of their pain and joy. And it fills them with a wild and wordless prophecy not of death, but life, for it speaks to them of new lands, triumph, and discovery, of heroic deeds, the fame and fellowship of heroes, and the love of glorious unknown women—of shining triumph and a grand success in a heroic world, and of a life more fortunate and happy than they have ever known.

So it was with us all that year. Over the immense and waiting earth, the single pulse and promise of the war impended. One felt it in the little towns at dawn, with all their quiet, casual, utterly familiar acts of life beginning. One felt it in the route-boy deftly flinging the folded block of paper on a porch, a man in shirt-sleeves coming out upon the porch and bending for the paper, the slow-clopping hoofs of the milk horse in a quiet street, the bottle-clinking wagon, and the sudden pause, the rapid footsteps of the milkman and the clinking bottles, then clopping hoof and wheel, and morning, stillness, the purity of light, and the dew-sweet bird-song rising in the street again.

In all these ancient, ever-new, unchanging, always magic acts of life and light and morning one felt the huge impending presence of the war. And one felt it in the brooding hush of noon, in the warm, dusty stir and flutter of the feathery clucking of the sun-warm hens at noon. One felt it in the ring of the ice-tongs in the street, the cool whine of the ice-saws droning through the smoking block. One felt it poignantly somehow, in the solid lonely liquid leather shuffle of men in shirt-sleeves coming home to lunch in one direction in the brooding hush and time-enchanted spell of noon, and in the screens that slammed and sudden silence. And one felt it in the humid warmth and hungry fragrance of the cooking turnip greens, in leaf and blade and flower, in smell of tar, and the sudden haunting green-gold summer absence of street-car after it had gone.

In all these ancient, most familiar things and acts and colors of our lives, one felt, with numbing ecstasy, the impending presence of the war. The war had got in everything: it was in things that moved, and in things that were still, in the animate red silence of an old brick wall as well as in the thronging life and traffic of the streets. It was in the faces of the people passing and in the thousand familiar moments of man's daily life and business.

And lonely, wild, and haunting, calling us on forever with the winding of its far lost horn, it had got into the time-enchanted loneliness of the magic hills around us, in all the sudden, wild, and lonely lights that came and passed and vanished on the massed green of the wilderness.

The war was in far cries and broken sounds and cow bells tinkling in the gusty wind, and in the far, wild, wailing joy and sorrow of a departing train, as it rushed eastward, seaward, war-ward through a valley of the South in the green spell and golden magic of full June. The war was in the ancient red-gold light of fading day that fell without violence or heat upon the streets of life, the houses where men lived, the brief flame and fire of sheeted window panes.

And it was in field and gulch and hollow, in the sweet green mountain valleys, fading into dusk, and in the hill-flanks reddened with the ancient light and slanting fast into steep cool shade and lilac silence. It was in the whole earth breathing the last heat and weariness of day out in the huge hush and joy and sorrow of oncoming night.

Finally, the war had gotten into all sounds and secrecies, the sorrow, longing, and delight, the mystery, hunger, and wild joy that came from the deep-breasted heart of fragrant, all-engulfing night. It was in the sweet and secret rustling of the leaves in summer streets, in footsteps coming quiet, slow, and lonely along the darkness of a leafy street, in screen doors slammed, and silence, the distant barking of a dog, far voices, laughter, faint pulsing music at a dance, and in all the casual voices of the night, far, strangely near, most intimate and familiar, remote as time, as haunting as the briefness of our days.

And suddenly, as I sat there under the proud and secret mystery of huge-starred, velvet-breasted night, hearing my father's great voice sounding from the porch again, the war, with a wild and intolerable loneliness of ecstasy and desire, came to me in the sudden throbbing of a racing motor, far-away silence, an image of the cool sweet darkness of the mountainside, the white flesh and yielding tenderness of women. And even as I thought of this, I heard the low, rich, sensual welling of a woman's voice, voluptuous, low, and tender, from the darkness of a summer porch across the street.

What had the war changed? What had it done to us? What miracle of transformation had it wrought upon our lives? It had changed nothing; it had heightened, intensified, and made glorious all the ancient and familiar things of life. It had added hope to hope, joy to joy, and life to life; and from that vital wizardry it had rescued all our lives from hopelessness and despair, and made us live again who thought that we were lost.

The war seemed to have collected in a single image of joy, and power, and proud compacted might all of the thousand images of joy and power and all-exulting life which we had always had, and for which we had never had a word before. Over the fields of silent and mysterious night it seemed that we could hear the nation marching, that we could hear, soft and thunderous in the night, the million-footed unison of marching men. And that single, glorious image of all-collected joy and unity and might had given new life and hope to all of us.

My father was old, he was sick with a cancer that flowered and fed forever at his entrails, eating from day to day the gaunt sinew of his life away beyond a hope or remedy, and we knew that he was dying. Yet under the magic life and hope the war had brought to us, his life seemed to have revived again out of its grief and pain, its death of joy, its sorrow of irrevocable memory.

For a moment he seemed to live again in his full prime. And instantly we were all released from the black horror of death and time that had menaced us for years. Instantly we were freed from the evil spell of sorrowful time and memory that had made his living death more horrible than his real one could ever be.

And instantly the good life, the golden and jubilant life of childhood, in whose full magic we had been sustained by the power of his life, and which had seemed so lost and irrevocable that it had a dreamlike strangeness when we thought of it, had under this sudden flare of life and joy and war returned in all its various and triumphant colors. And for a moment we believed that all would be again for us as it had been, that he

never could grow old and die, but that he must live forever, and
that the summertime, the orchard and bright morning, would
be ours again, could never die.

I could hear him talking now about old wars and ancient
troubles, hurling against the present and its leaders the full indictment of his soaring rhetoric that howled, rose, fell, swept
out into the night, piercing all quarters of the darkness with
the naked penetration which his voice had in the old days
when he sat talking on the porch in summer darkness, and the
neighborhood attended and was still.

Now as my father talked, I could hear the boarders on the
porch attending in the same way, the stealthy creak of a rocker
now and then, a low word spoke, a question, protest, or agree-
ment, and then their hungry, feeding, and attentive silence as
my father talked. He spoke of all the wars and troubles he had
known, told how he had stood, "a bare-foot country boy,"
beside a dusty road twelve miles from Gettysburg and had
watched the ragged rebels march past upon the road that led
to death and battle and the shipwreck of their hopes.

He spoke of the faint and ominous trembling of the guns
across the hot brooding silence of the countryside, and how
silence, wonder, and unspoken questions filled the hearts of all
the people, and how they had gone about their work on the
farm as usual. He spoke of the years that had followed on the
war when he was a stone-cutter's apprentice in Baltimore, and
he spoke of ancient joys and labors, forgotten acts and histories, and he spoke then with familiar memory of the lost
Americans—the strange, lost, time-far, dead Americans, the
remote, voiceless, and bewhiskered faces of the great Americans, who were more lost to me than Egypt, more far from me
than the Tartarian coasts, more haunting strange than Cipango
or the lost faces of the first dynastic kings that built the Pyramids, and whom he had seen, heard, known, found familiar in
the full pulse, and passion, and proud glory of his youth: the

lost, time-far, voiceless faces of Buchanan, Johnson, Doug-
las, Blaine—the proud, vacant, time-strange and bewhiskered
faces of Garfield, Arthur, Harrison, and Hayes.

"Ah, Lord!" he said—his voice rang out in darkness like
a gong, "Ah, Lord!—I've known all of 'em since James Buchanan's time—for I was a boy of six when he took office!"
Here he paused a moment, lunged forward violently in his
rocking chair, and spat cleanly out a spurt of strong tobacco
juice across the porch-rail into the loamy earth, the night-
sweet fragrance of the geranium beds. "Yes, sir," he said gravely,
lunging back again, while the attentive, hungry boarders waited
in the living darkness and were still, "I remember all of them
since James Buchanan's time, and I've seen most of them that
came since Lincoln!—Ah, Lord!" he paused briefly for another
waiting moment, shaking his grave head sadly in the dark.
"Well do I remember the day when I stood on a street in
Baltimore—poor friendless orphan that I was!" my father went
on sorrowfully, but somewhat illogically, since at this time his
mother was alive and in good health, upon her little farm in
Pennsylvania, and would continue so for almost fifty years—"A
poor friendless country boy of sixteen years, alone in the great
city where I had come to learn my trade as an apprentice—
and heard Andrew Johnson, then the President of this *great*
nation," said my father, "speak from the platform of a horse-
car—and he was so drunk—so *drunk*," he howled, "the President of this country was so *drunk* that they had to stand on
each side of him and hold him as he spoke—or he'd a-gone
head over heels into the gutter!" Here he paused, wet his great
thumb briefly, cleared his throat with considerable satisfaction,
lunged forward violently again in his rocking chair, and spat
strongly a wad of bright tobacco juice into the loamy fragrance
of the dark geranium bed.

"The first vote I ever cast for President," my father continued presently, as he lunged back again, "I cast in 1872, in Bal-

timore, for that *great* man—that brave and noble soldier—U.S. Grant! And I have voted for every Republican nominee for President ever since. I voted for Rutherford Hayes of Ohio in 1876—that was the year, as you well know, of the great Hayes-Tilden controversy, in 1880 for James Abram Garfield—that *great* good man," he said passionately, "who was so foully and brutally done to death by the cowardly assault of a murderous assassin." He paused, wet his thumb, breathing heavily, lunged forward in his rocking chair, and spat again. "In 1884, I cast my vote for James G. Blaine in the year that Grover Cleveland defeated him," he said shortly, "for Benjamin Harrison in 1888, and for Harrison again in 1892, the time that Cleveland got in for his second term, a time that we will all remember to our dying days," my father said grimly, "for the Democrats were in and we had soup kitchens. And, you can mark my words," he howled, "you'll have them again, before these next four years are over—your guts will grease your backbone as sure as there's a God in heaven before that fearful, that awful, that cruel, in-human, and bloodthirsty Monster who kept us out of war," my father jeered derisively, "is done with you—for hell, ruin, mis-ery, and damnation commence every time the Democrats get in. You can rest assured of that!" he said shortly, cleared his throat, wet his thumb, lunged forward violently, and spat again. And for a moment there was silence, and the boarders waited.

"Ah, Lord!" my father said at length sadly, gravely, in a low, almost inaudible tone. And suddenly, all the old life and howl-ing fury of his rhetoric had gone from him: he was an old man again, sick, indifferent, dying, and his voice had grown old, worn, weary, sad.

"Ah, Lord!" he muttered, shaking his head sadly, thinly, wearily in the dark. "I've seen them all. . . . I've seen them come and go . . . Garfield, Arthur, Harrison, and Hayes . . . and all . . . all . . . all of them are dead. . . . I'm the only one that's left," he said illogically, "and soon I'll be gone, too." And for a moment he was silent. "It's pretty strange when you come to think of it," he muttered. "By God it is!" And he was silent, and darkness, and mystery, and night were all about us.

Garfield, Arthur, Harrison, and Hayes—time of my father's time, blood of his blood, life of his life, had been living, real, and actual people in all the passion, power, and feeling of my father's youth. And for me they were the lost Americans: their gravely vacant and bewhiskered faces mixed, melted, swam together in the sea-depths of a past intangible, immeasurable, and unknowable as the buried city of Persepolis.

And they were lost.

For who was Garfield, martyred man, and who had seen him in the streets of life? Who could believe his footfalls ever sounded on a lonely pavement? Who had heard the casual and familiar tones of Chester Arthur? And where was Harrison? Where was Hayes? Which had the whiskers, which the burnsides: which was which?

Were they not lost?

Into their ears, as ours, the tumults of forgotten crowds, upon their brains the million printings of lost time, and suddenly upon their dying sight the brief, bitter pain and joy of a few death-bright, fixed, and fading memories: the twisting of a leaf upon a bough, the grinding felloe-rim against the curb, the long, and distant retreating thunder of a train upon the rails.

Garfield, Hayes, and Harrison were Ohio men; but only the name of Garfield has been brightened by his blood. But at night had they not heard the howlings of demented wind, the sharp, clean, windy raining to the earth of acorns? Had all of them not walked down lonely roads at night in winter and seen a light and known it was theirs?

Had they not known the smell of old bound calf and well-worn leathers, the Yankee lawyer's smell of strong tobacco spit and court-house urinals, the smell of horses, harness, hay, and sweating country men, of jury rooms and court rooms—the strong male smell of justice at the county seat, and heard a tap along dark corridors where a drop fell in darkness with a punctual crescent monotone of time, dark time?

Had not Garfield, Hayes, and Harrison studied law in offices with a dark brown smell? Had not the horses trotted past below their windows in wreaths of dust along a straggling street of shacks and buildings with false fronts? Had they not heard below them the voices of men talking, loitering up in drawling heat? Had they not heard the casual, rich-fibered, faintly howling country voices, and heard the rustling of a woman's skirt, and waiting silence, slyly lowered tones of bawdry and then huge guffaws, slapped meaty thighs, and high, fat, choking laughter? And in the dusty dozing heat, while time buzzed slowly, like a fly, had not Garfield, Arthur, Harrison, and Hayes then smelled the river, the humid, subtly fresh, half-rotten river, and thought of the white flesh of the women then beside the river, and felt a slow, impending passion in their entrails, a heavy rending power in their hands?

Then Garfield, Arthur, Harrison, and Hayes had gone to war, and each became a brigadier or major general. All were bearded men: they saw a spattering of bright blood upon the leaves, and they heard the soldiers talking in the dark of food and women. They held the bridge-head in bright dust at places with such names as Wilson's Mill and Spangler's Run, and their men smashed cautiously through dense undergrowth. And they heard the surgeons cursing after battle and the little rasp of saws. They had seen boys standing awkwardly holding their entrails in their hands, and pleading pitifully with fear-bright eyes: "Is it bad, General? Do you think it's bad?"

When the canister came through, it made a ragged hole. It smashed through tangled leaves and boughs; sometimes it plunked solidly into the fiber of a tree. Sometimes when it struck a man, it tore away the roof of his brain, the wall of his skull, raggedly, so that his brains seethed out upon a foot of wilderness, and the blood blackened and congealed, and he lay there in his thick clumsy uniform, with a smell of urine in the wool, in the casual, awkward, and uncompleted attitude of sudden death. And when Garfield, Arthur, Harrison, and Hayes saw these things, they saw that it was not like the picture they had had as children; it was not like the works of Walter Scott and William Gilmore Simms. They saw that the hole was not clean and small and in the central front, and the field was not green nor fenced, nor mown. Over the vast and immemorable earth the quivering heated light of afternoon was shining, a field swept rudely upward to a lift of rugged wood, and field by field, gully by gulch by fold, the earth advanced in rude, sweet, limitless convolutions.

Then Garfield, Arthur, Harrison, and Hayes had paused by the bridge-head for a moment and were still, seeing the bright blood at noon upon the trampled wheat, feeling the brooding hush of six o'clock across the fields where all the storming feet had passed at dawn, seeing the way the rough field hedge leaned out across the dusty road, the casual intrusions of the coarse field grasses and the hot, dry daisies to the edges of the road, seeing the rock-bright shallows of the creek, the sweet cool shade and lean of river trees across the water.

They paused then by the bridge-head, looking at the water. They saw the stark blank flatness of the old red mill that somehow was like sunset, coolness, sorrow, and delight, and looking at the faces of the dead boys among the wheat, the most-oh-most familiar plain, the death-strange faces of the dead Americans, they stood there for a moment, thinking, feeling, thinking, with strong wordless wonder in their hearts:

"As we leaned on the sills of evening, as we stood in the

frames of the marvelous doors, as we were received into silence, the flanks of the slope and the slanted light, as we saw
the strange hushed shapes upon the land, the muted distances,
knowing all things then—what could we say except that our
comrades were spread quietly around us and that noon was far?

"What can we say now of the lonely land—what can we say
now of the deathless shapes and substances—what can we say
who have lived here with our lives, bone, blood, and brain, and
all our tongueless languages, hearing on many a casual road the
plain familiar voices of Americans, and tomorrow will be buried in the earth, knowing the fields will steep to silence after
us, the slant light deepen on the slopes, and peace and evening
will come back again, at one now with the million shapes and
single substance of our land, at one with evening, peace, the
huge stride of the undulant oncoming night, at one, also, with
morning?

"Silence receive us and the field of peace, hush of the mea-
sureless land, the unabated distances, shape of the one and
single substance and the million forms, replenish us, restore us,
and unite us with your vast images of quietness and joy. Stride
of the undulant night, come swiftly now, engulf us, silence, in
your great-starred secrecy; speak to our hearts of stillness, for
we have, save this, no speech.

"There is the bridge we crossed, the mill we slept in, and the
creek. There is a field of wheat, a hedge, a dusty road, an apple
orchard, and the sweet wild tangle of a wood upon that hill.
And there is six o'clock across the fields again, now and always
as it was and will be to the world's end forever. And some of
us have died this morning coming through the field, and that
was time—time—time. We shall not come again, we never
shall come back again as we did once at morning—so, brothers, let us look again before we go . . . There is the mill, and
there the hedge, and there the shallows of the rock-bright waters of the creek, and there the sweet and most familiar cool-

ness of the trees—and surely we have been this way before!"
they cried.

"Oh, surely, brothers, we have sat upon the bridge, before
the mill, and sung together by the rock-bright waters of the
creek at evening, and come across the wheat field in the morning and heard the dew-sweet bird-song rising from the hedge
before! You plain, oh-most-familiar and most homely earth,
proud earth of this huge land unutterable, proud nobly swelling earth, in all your delicacy, wildness, savagery, and terror—
grand earth in all your loneliness, beauty and wild joy, terrific
earth in all your limitless fecundities, swelling with infinite
fold and convolution into the reaches of the west forever—
American earth!—bridge, hedge, and creek and dusty road—
you plain tremendous poetry of Wilson's Mill where boys died
in the wheat this morning, you unutterable far-near, strange-
familiar, homely earth of magic, for which a word would do if
we could find it, for which a word would do if we could call it
by its name, for which a word would do which never can be
spoken, that can never be forgotten, and that will never be
revealed—oh, proud, familiar, nobly swelling earth, it seems
we must have known you before! It seems that we must have
known you forever, but all we know for certain is that we came
along this road one time at morning, and now our blood is
painted on the wheat, and you are ours now, we are yours forever, and there is something here we never shall remember,
there is something here we never shall forget!"

Had Garfield, Arthur, Harrison, and Hayes been young? Or
had they been born with flowing whiskers, sideburns, and
wing-collars, speaking gravely from the cradle of their mother's arms the noble vacant sonorities of far-seeing statesman-
ship? It could not be. Had they not been young men in the
Thirties, the Forties, and the Fifties? Did they not, as we, cry
out at night along deserted roads into demented winds? Did

they not, as we, cry out the fierce goat-cry of ecstasy and exultancy, as the full measure of their hunger, their potent and inchoate hope, went out into that single wordless cry?

Did they not, as we, when young, prowl softly up and down past brothels in the dark hours of the night, seeing the gas lamps flare and flutter on the corner, falling with livid light upon the corners of old cobbled streets of brownstone houses? Had they not heard the lonely clopping of a horse, the jounting wheels of a hansom cab, upon those barren cobbles? And had they not waited, trembling in the darkness till the horse and cab had passed, had vanished with the lonely recession of shod hoofs, and then were heard no more?

And then had Garfield, Arthur, Harrison, and Hayes not waited, waited in the silence of the night, prowling up and down the lonely cobbled street, with trembling lips, numb entrails, pounding hearts? Had they not set their jaws, made sudden indecisive movements, felt terror, joy, a numb impending ecstasy, and waited, waited then—for what? Had they not waited, hearing sounds of shifting engines in the yards at night, hearing the hoarse, gaseous breath of little engines through the grimy fan-flare of their funnels, the racketing clack of wheels upon the light, ill-laid, ill-joined rails? Had they not waited in that dark street with the fierce lone hunger of a boy, feeling around them the immense and moving quietness of sleep, the heartbeats of ten thousand sleeping men, as they waited, waited, waited in the night?

Had they not, as we, then turned their eyes up and seen the huge starred visage of the night, the immense and lilac darkness of America in April? Had they not heard the sudden, shrill, and piping whistle of a departing engine? Had they not waited, thinking, feeling, seeing then the immense mysterious content of night, the wild and lyric earth, so casual, sweet and strange-familiar, in all its space and savagery and terror, its mystery and joy, its limitless sweep and rudeness, its delicate and savage fecundity? Had they not had a vision of the plains, the mountains, and the rivers flowing in the darkness, the huge patter of the everlasting earth and the all-engulfing wilderness of America?

Had they not felt, as we have felt, as they waited in the night, the huge lonely earth of night time and America, on which ten thousand lonely sleeping little towns were strewn? Had they not seen the fragile network of the light, racketing, ill-joined little rails across the land, over which the lonely little trains rushed on in darkness, flinging a handful of lost echoes at the river's edge, leaving an echo in the cut's resounding cliff, and being engulfed then in huge lonely night, in all-brooding, all-engulfing night? Had they not known, as we have known, the wild secret joy and mystery of the everlasting earth, the lilac dark, the savage, silent, all-possessing wilderness that gather in around ten thousand lonely little towns, ten million lost and lonely sleepers, and waited and abode forever, and was still?

Had not Garfield, Arthur, Harrison, and Hayes then waited, feeling the goat-cry swelling in their throats, feeling wild joy and sorrow in their hearts, and a savage hunger and desire—a flame, a fire, a fury—burning fierce and lean and lonely in the night, burning forever while the sleepers slept? Were they not burning, burning, burning, even as the rest of us have burned? Were Garfield, Arthur, Harrison, and Hayes not burning in the night? Were they not burning forever in the silence of the little towns with all the fierce hunger, savage passion, limitless desire that young men in this land have known in the darkness?

Were they not burning with the wild and wordless hope, the incredible belief that all young men have known before the promise of that huge mirage, the deathless dupe and invincible illusion of this savage, all-exultant land where all things are impending and where young men starve? Were they

not burning in the enfabled magic, mystery, and joy of the lilac
dark, the lonely, savage, secret, everlasting earth on which we
lived, and wrought, and perished, mad with hunger, unfed,
famished, furious, unassuaged? Were they not burning, burning where a million doors of glory, love, unutterable fulfillment, impended, waited in the dark for us, were here, were
here around us in the dark forever, were ready to our touch
forever, and that duped us, mocked forever at our hunger, mad-
dened our hearts and brains with searching, took our youth,
our strength, our love, our life, and killed us, and were never
found?

Had Garfield, Arthur, Harrison, and Hayes not waited
then, as we have waited, with numb lips and pounding hearts
and fear, delight, strong joy, and terror stirring in their entrails
as they waited in the silent street before a house, proud, evil,
lavish, lighted, certain, secret, and alone? And as they heard
the hoof, the wheel, the sudden whistle, and the immense and
sleeping silence of the town, the lonely, wild, and secret earth,
the lilac dark, the huge starred visage of the night—did they
not wait there in the dark, thinking:

"Oh, there are new lands, morning, and a shining city. Soon,
soon, soon!"

And then as Garfield, Arthur, Harrison, and Hayes prowled
softly up and down in the dark cobbled streets, hearing the
sudden shrill departure of the whistle in the night, the great
wheels pounding at the river's edge, feeling the lilac dark, the
heart-beats of the sleeping men, and the attentive silence, the
terror, savagery, and joy, the huge mystery and promise of
the immense and silent earth, thinking, feeling, thinking, with
wild silent joy, intolerable desire, did they not say:

"Oh, there are women in the West, and we shall find them.
They will be waiting for us, calm, tranquil, corn-haired, un-
surprised, looking across the wall of level grain with level eyes,
looking into the flaming domains of the red, the setting sun, at

the great wall and the soaring vistas of the western ranges. Oh, there are lavish corn-haired women in the West with tranquil eyes," cried Garfield, Arthur, Harrison, and Hayes, "and we shall find them waiting in their doors for us at evening!

"And there are women in the South," they said, "with dark eyes and the white magnolia faces. They are moving beneath the droop of tree-barred levels of the South. Now they are moving on the sweep of ancient lawns, beside the great slow-flowing rivers in the night! Their step is light and soundless as the dark, they drift the white ghost-glimmer of their beauty under ancient trees, their words are soft and slow and hushed, and sweeter far than honey, and suddenly their low and tender laugh, slow, rich, and sensual, comes welling from the great vat of the dark. The perfume of their slow white flesh is flower-sweet, magnolia strange, and filled with all the sweet languors of desire! Oh, there are secret women in the South," they cried, "who move by darkness under drooping trees the white ghost-glimmer of magnolia loveliness, and we shall find them!

"And there are women in the North," cried Garfield, Arthur, Harrison, and Hayes, "who wait for us with Viking eyes, the deep breasts and the great limbs of the Amazons. There are powerful and lovely women in the North," they said, "whose eyes are blue and depthless as a mountain lake. Their glorious hair is braided into ropes of ripened grain, and their names are Lundquist, Nielsen, Svenson, Jorgenson, and Brandt. They are waiting for us in the wheat fields of the North, they are waiting for us at the edges of the plains, they are waiting for us in the forests of great trees. Their eyes are true and level, and their great hearts are the purest and most faithful on the earth, and they will wait for us until we come to them.

"There are ten thousand lonely little towns at night," cried Garfield, Arthur, Harrison, and Hayes, "ten thousand lonely little towns of sleeping men, and we shall come to them forever in the night. We shall come to them like storm and fury, with a demonic impulse of wild joy, dark chance, dropping suddenly upon them from the fast express at night—leaving the train in darkness, in the dark mid-watches of the night, and being left then to the sudden silence, mystery, and promise of an unknown little town. Oh, we shall come to them forever in the night," they cried, "in winter among howling winds and swirling snow. Then we shall make our tracks along the sheeted fleecy whiteness of an empty silent little street, and find our door at length, and know the instant that we come to it that it is ours.

"Coming by storm and darkness to the lonely, chance, and secret towns," they said, "we shall find the well-loved face, the longed-for step, the well-known voice, there in the darkness while storm beats about the house and the white mounting drifts of swirling snow engulf us. Then we shall know the flower-whiteness of a face below us, the night-time darkness of a cloud of hair across our arm, and know all the mystery, tenderness, and surrender, of a white-dark beauty, the fragrant whiteness, the slow bounty of a velvet undulance, the earth-deep fruitfulness of love. And we shall stay there while storm howls about the house," they said, "and huge drifts rise about us. We shall leave forever in the whitened silence of the morning, and always know the chance, the secret, and the well-beloved will be there waiting for us when storms howl at night, and we come again through swirling snow, leaving our footprints on the whitened, empty, silent streets of unknown little towns, lost at the heart of storm and darkness upon the lonely, wild, all-secret mystery of the earth."

And finally did not Garfield, Arthur, Harrison, and Hayes, those fierce and jubilant young men, who waited there, as we have waited, in the silent barren street with trembling lips, numb hands, with terror, savage joy, fierce rapture alive and stirring in their entrails—did they not feel, as we have felt, when they heard the shrill departing warning of the whistle in the dark, the sound of great wheels pounding at the river's edge? Did they not feel, as we have felt, as they awaited there in the intolerable sweetness, wildness, mystery and terror of the great earth in the month of April, and knew themselves alone, alive and young and mad and secret with desire and hunger in the great sleep-silence of the night, the impending, cruel, all-promise of this land? Were they not torn, as we have been, by sharp pain and wordless lust, the asp of time, the thorn of spring, the sharp, the tongueless cry? Did they not say:

"Oh, there are women in the East—and new lands, morning, and a shining city! There are forgotten fume-flaws of bright smoke above Manhattan, the forest of masts about the crowded isle, the proud cleavages of departing ships, the soaring web, the wing-like swoop and joy of the great bridge, and men with derby hats who come across the bridge to greet us—come, brothers, let us go to find them all! For the huge murmur of the city's million-footed life, far, bee-like, drowsy, strange as time, has come to haunt our ears with all its golden prophecy of joy and triumph, fortune, happiness, and love such as no men before have ever known. Oh, brothers, in the city, in the far-shining, glorious, time-enchanted spell of that enfabled city we shall find great men and lovely women, and unceasingly ten thousand new delights, a thousand magical adventures! We shall wake at morning in our rooms of lavish brown to hear the hoof and wheel upon the city street again, and smell the harbor, fresh, half-rotten, with its bracelet of bright tides, its traffic of proud sea-borne ships, its purity and joy of dancing morning gold—and feel, with an unspeakable sorrow and delight, that there are ships there, there are ships—and something in our hearts we cannot utter.

"And we shall smell the excellent sultry fragrance of boiling coffee and think of silken luxury of great walnut chambers in whose shuttered amber morning-light proud beauties slowly stir in sensual warmth their lavish limbs. Then we shall smell, with the sharp relish of young hunger, the grand breakfast smells: the pungent bacon, crisping to a turn, the grilled kidneys, eggs, and sausages, and the fragrant stacks of gold-brown wheat cakes smoking hot. And we shall move, alive and strong and full of hope, through all the swarming lanes of morning and know the good green smell of money, the heavy leathers and the walnut of great merchants, the power, the joy, the certitude and ease of proud success.

"We shall come at furious noon to slake our thirst with drinks of rare and subtle potency in sumptuous bars of swart mahogany in the good fellowship of men, the spicy fragrance of the lemon rind and angostura bitters. Then, hunger whetted, pulse aglow, and leaping with the sharp spur of our awakened appetite, we shall eat from the snowy linen of the greatest restaurants in the world. We shall be suavely served and tenderly cared for by the pious unction of devoted waiters. We shall be quenched with old wine and fed with rare and priceless honesty, the maddening succulence of grand familiar food and noble cooking, fit to match the peerless relish of our hunger!

"Street of the day, with the unceasing promise of your million-footed life, we come to you!" they cried. "Streets of the thunderous wheels at noon, streets of the great parades of marching men, the band's bright oncoming blare, the brave stick-candy whippings of a flag, street of the cries and shouts, the swarming feet, the man-swarm ever passing in its million-footed weft—street of the jounting cabs, the ringing hooves, the horse-cars and the jingling bells, the in-horse ever bending its sad nodding head toward its lean and patient comrade on the right—great street of furious life and movement, noon, and joyful labors, your image blazes in our hearts forever, and we come!

"Street of the morning, street of hope!" they cried. "Street of coolness, slanted light, the frontal cliff and gulch of steep blue shade, street of the dancing morning-gold of waters on the flashing tides, street of the rusty weathered slips, the blunt-nosed ferry foaming in with its packed wall of small white staring faces, all silent and intent, all turned toward *you*—proud street! Street of the pungent sultry smells of new-ground coffee, the good green smell of money, the fresh half-rotten harbor smells with all its evocation of your mast-bound harbor and its tide of ships, great street! Street of the old buildings grimed richly with the warm and mellow dinginess of trade—street of the million morning feet forever hurrying onward in the same direction, proud street of hope and joy and morning, in your steep canyon we shall win the wealth, the fame, the power, and the esteem which our lives and talent merit!

"Street of the night!" they cried. "Great street of mystery and suspense, terror and delight, eagerness and hope, street edged forever with the dark menace of impending joy, and unknown happiness and fulfillment, street of gaiety, warmth, and evil, street of the great hotels, the lavish bars and restaurants, and the softly golden glow, the fading lights and empetaled whiteness of a thousand hushed white thirsty faces in the crowded theaters, street of the tidal flood of faces, lighted with your million lights and all thronging, tireless, and unquenched in their insatiate searching after pleasure, street of the lovers coming along with slow steps, their faces turned toward each other, lost in the oblivion of love among the everlasting web and weaving of the crowd, street of the white face, the painted mouth, the shining and inviting eye—oh, street of night, with your mystery, joy, and terror—we have thought of you, proud street.

"And we shall move at evening in the noiseless depths of sumptuous carpets through all the gaiety, warmth, and brilliant happiness of great lighted chambers of the night, filled with the mellow thrum and languor of the violins, and where

the loveliest and most desirable women in the world—the be-
loved daughters of great merchants, bankers, millionaires, or
rich young widows, beautiful, loving, and alone—are moving
with a slow proud undulance, a look of depthless tenderness in
their fragile lovely faces. And the loveliest of them all," they
cried, "is ours, is ours forever, if we want her! For brothers, in
the city, in the far-shining, magic, golden city we shall move
among great men and glorious women and know nothing but
strong joy and happiness forever, winning by our courage, talent, and deserving the highest and most honored place in the
most fortunate and happy life that men have known, if only
we will make it ours!"

So thinking, feeling, waiting, as we have waited, in the
sleeping silence of the night in silent streets, hearing, as we
have heard, the sharp blast of the warning whistle, the thunder
of great wheels upon the river's edge, feeling, as we have felt,
the mystery of night time and of April, the huge impending
presence, the wild and secret promise, of the savage, lonely,
everlasting earth, finding, as we have found, no doors to enter,
and being torn, as we were torn, by the thorn of spring, the
sharp, the wordless cry, did they not carry these young men
of the past, Garfield, Arthur, Harrison, and Hayes—even as
we have carried, within their little tenements of bone, blood,
sinew, sweat, and agony, the intolerable burden of all the pain,
joy, hope, and savage hunger that a man can suffer, that the
world can know?

Were they not lost? Were they not lost, as all of us have
been, who have known youth and hunger in this land, and who
have waited lean and mad and lonely in the night, and who
have found no goal, no wall, no dwelling, and no door?

The years flow by like water, and one day it is spring again.
Shall we ever ride out of the gates of the East again, as we did
once at morning, and seek again, as we did then, new lands, the

promise of the war, and glory, joy, and triumph, and a shining city?

O youth, still wounded, living, feeling with a woe unutterable, still grieving with a grief intolerable, still thirsting with a thirst unquenchable—where are we to seek? For the wild tempest breaks above us, the wild fury beats about us, the wild hunger feeds upon us—and we are houseless, doorless, unassuaged, and driven on forever; and our brains are mad, our hearts are wild and wordless, and we cannot speak.

6

From *The Good Child's River*

MY FATHER, JOSEPH BARRETT, was a Gentile: he came from a family which had been well known in New England for many generations. He was born in the town of Brantford, Connecticut, where his father owned a general store. It was one of those wonderful country stores in which everything could be bought from oil lamps to yellow cheese, from calico to coffee, from a boiled shirt to a tub of butter. Upon the long wooden counters every variety of thing was piled, and one was aware of the clean smells of boiled cloth—of cotton, wool, silk, and linen; of the coarse sweet leather of thick brogans and creaking harnesses; and rows of rakes, hoes, shovels, forks, and nails. My grandfather, Samuel Barrett, was a man of considerable wealth for those times, but his feeling against slavery was so intense and bitter that it outweighed any material consideration: at the outbreak of the Civil War he sold his store as soon as he could, and helped organize the first regiment of volunteer troops to go to the war from Connecticut.

At this time my father was a child of six or seven years. He was the youngest of three children: he had a sister who was twelve and a brother who was nine. During the war they all lived on a farm outside of town which belonged to his uncle. The uncle could not go to the war because he was too fat, he weighed over three hundred pounds: he stayed on the farm and took care of all of them. He was very good to them: he was a wonderful man, and later I shall tell of him and of his two sons, John and Frederick Barrett.

When the war was over, my grandfather returned in such poor health he could not go back into business: he had some money left and he took his family to New York to live. At this time my father was eleven years old.

Three years after the family moved to New York my father's brother died of typhoid fever. My grandfather died four years later: the manner of his death was so horrible that it cast a shadow over my father's entire youth. During the war my grandfather had been wounded in the knee at the battle of Antietam: the army surgeons who removed the shot did their work badly and apparently never got all of it out. The wound never healed, a festering kind of gangrene set in, and for years my grandfather literally died by inches. First his right leg was amputated in an effort to save his life. But, apparently none of the surgeons of that time knew how to check the advance of this poison which ate its way into his vitals. Perhaps they know no more about it now. My grandfather was literally cut to pieces: year by year he endured a series of terrible amputations on the stump of his leg. The family lived constantly below this menace of death and horror. Their lives were absorbed by it. They watched the progress of the disease with the terrible fascination with which trapped prisoners might watch the progress of a train of fire toward an explosion which they are powerless to touch. And in the midst of all his horrible suffering, daily watching the death of his own body, able almost to reckon to the month the time of his death, my grandfather looked on life with love and joy; his great laugh filled the house.

My father did not often talk to me about him. I think his memory of his father's suffering and death was so painful he did not like to speak of it. But I know that he loved him dearly. Whenever he spoke of his father, even with the most casual reference, I noticed a remarkable change in his expression: my father had the most luminous and penetrating eyes of anyone I have ever known. They were a living and powerful grey; one instantly noticed their magnetic and vital quality: Whenever my father felt deeply about anything, the pupils of his eyes would widen and darken until they were smoke-black. This always happened when he spoke of his father. He told me his father was the bravest man he had ever known. He told me that even before one of these terrible operations his father would make jokes with the surgeons. He told me that once his father had said to them:

"Well, what's it going to be this time? Another cut off the joint?"

When the doctor said it would be, my grandfather replied:

"You know, doc, I don't mind these cuts off the joint so much, but when you begin carving off rump steaks I'm going to holler."

He died in unspeakable agony. In the four days before his death, the surgeons operated twice, the last time without an anesthetic. My grandfather would not cry out: his effort was so great his teeth bit completely through his lower lip. After his death they had to pry his teeth apart.

For months, it seemed, there had been little of the man to keep alive except his magnificent spirit. His body was leprous from head to foot. Almost immediately after his death there was a powerful odor of decomposition. The doctors urged immediate burial. In spite of this, my grandmother, who was a fanatic Methodist, refused. She refused to bury him in New York: she insisted on taking the body back to Connecticut for burial. Furthermore she insisted on services in both places, on the terrible death-watch and barbarous prolongation of Christian burial. Finally, she refused to allow embalming. She had an obscene shame and terror of nakedness, even the nakedness of dead bodies: even before her husband she had never unclothed her body, and as a young woman she had given instructions that, in the event of her death, her own body should not be touched by undertakers, and, if possible, should not be fully exposed to anyone. She now insisted that her husband's body be treated the same way.

My father told me the whole story once, but never referred to it again. At the time of his father's death, he said, he was eighteen years old. And at this time all of the bitter accumulation of years of dislike and misunderstanding came to a head. He felt that his mother could have done much more than she did to ease and comfort the last years of his father's life. He said she had never in her life uttered a word of love and tenderness for anyone: apparently she had always been convinced that life was evil, that men were bad, and that her husband was what she called a "sinner." My father said she felt this way about him because, like all his family, he liked good food and drink, and the gaiety and joy of living. He had never shared in her church-going activity—in her fierce devotion to what she called "The work of the Lord." After he returned from the war, and the family came to New York to live, he never went to church at all. During this time he was, of course, dying by inches, and his indifference to the church infuriated her: she exhorted him upon his evil-doing, besieged him with ministers and church people who tried to prevail on him to "come back to the fold," and she never lost a chance to remind him he was dying and must lose no time if he wanted to repent and save his soul.

"I think she liked to see people suffer," my father told me. "Nothing else seemed to give her any pleasure."

My grandfather loved music and had a fine voice: my father would sit beside him for hours while he sang the songs he had learned as a soldier—the great marching songs of the Civil

War, the campfire songs, and a great many jolly and rollicking songs that were then popular but have now been forgotten. He would sing them keeping time with the foot of his good leg, until my father knew them all, and they could sing together. The one hymn that he seemed to like best was "The Battle Hymn of the Republic": When he came to the line "Oh! be swift, my soul, to answer Him, be jubilant, my feet!" his eyes would glow with joy, his good leg would fairly dance upon the floor, and his maimed stump would jerk up and down briskly under the impulse of his feeling, and finally his voice would lift triumphantly on the magnificent line, "As he died to make men holy, let us die to make men free." And once he said to my father: "That would really be worth dying for, wouldn't it?—to make men free." When my father asked him if that wasn't what men had died for in the Civil War he laughed, and said: "Yes. Free for the surgeons and the worms." In his youth he had been very bitter against the South because of slavery, but now his bitterness seemed to have vanished completely: he spoke of the ability and courage of the Southern troops and of the campaigns of Lee and Stonewall Jackson with as much pride and tenderness as if they had belonged to his own side. I think this change in feeling must have come during the war, because I still have a remarkable letter which he wrote to his brother, Wesley, the one that was called Uncle Bud, the great fat fellow I have mentioned:

"Most of the boys down here," he wrote, "have had about enough of this war, but I see that the women and preachers back home are determined to fight it out to the bitter end. I never saw such a bloodthirsty lot as these women and preachers are: they just seem to live on fighting and it looks like they're not going to give the rest of us much peace until they've got the rebs all mashed up into jelly. For my part, I never felt so peaceable in my life, I've had enough fighting to do me from now to Kingdom Come, I could be friends right now with almost anyone, I could be friends with a reb or a preacher. I've got a good idea: in the next war why don't they let the women and the preachers do the fighting? It seems to me that they ought to let these people fight who enjoy fighting, and let the rest of us who want to be peaceable stay at home and make the crops. They could put all the women on one side and all the preachers on the other and let them fight it out to their heart's content.

"Bud, I've been having dreams about you. Have you still got that big fat belly? I've been telling some of the boys about it and they say, by God, they don't believe I'm telling them the truth, they say they're coming home with me to see it when the war is over. My own gut is rammed up against my backbone: they're like twins, I don't know if I'll ever get them apart again, but if I do I'm going to see to it they stay strangers as long as I live. Anyway, we're better off than the rebs: I was talking to one we took prisoner the other day and he said they'd been eating so much parched corn on his side some of the fellows had begun to crow like roosters. He said one of them came by him down the road the other day running for all he was worth. When he asked him where he was going this fellow flapped his arms a couple of times and cackled right in his face. When the man got so he could talk he said he'd eaten so much corn the hens thought he was a rooster: he said every hen in Virginia had been after him, he said they wouldn't leave him alone, and with that he let out another cackle, flapped his arms, and let out down the road with six big Donnecker hens right after him. Now, Bud, do you believe that fellow was telling the truth? Well, Bud, you take care of yourself now and that big belly. When I come home I want to look at it and feel it and see if it is real.

"Your brother,

"Sam Barrett"

From this letter, with its reference to "women and preachers," I believe that my grandfather must have been thinking of his wife and her church friends, and my father told me this was true. I think anyone could see from reading this letter that the man who wrote it was brave, kind, and wise: his feeling about war is the feeling that many people have today and that we have come to think of as "modern," but I think that my grandfather and my father must have been very much alike in this respect: they were such men as belong to no particular time, but are able to live for themselves and by themselves. They are able to get wisdom out of living without being very much influenced by the custom of the moment. My father had this power more than anyone I have ever known.

There was another cause for the bitter feeling between my father and his mother. After the family came to New York, he went frequently with his father to the theatre. My grandfather loved the theatre and had committed to memory the entire plays of Shakespeare. By his fourteenth year my father knew more about these plays than most educated people ever know: they read or declaimed the speeches to each other, and they set each other a task of tagging lines the other began. Once my father caught him up in a mistake, and he said it was the proudest moment of his life. During the war my grandfather had become a good friend of an actor in his regiment (of this man I shall speak later), and now, in New York, he knew a great many people in the theatre. He knew the great actor Booth, and he knew Joseph Jefferson. Many of these people came to see him at his house: when they did there was laughter and music and punch in the parlor. My grandmother refused to take any part in these gatherings: she thought that her house was polluted by the presence of such people, and she reviled and insulted her husband for having such friends. At that time, the actor was almost a social outcast: he lived a wretched wandering life on the fringes of society; even the few distinguished artists like Booth and Jefferson never won the full acceptance to which their talents entitled them. To millions of church people like my grandmother, the actor was a depraved and evil man, and the theatre the devil's dwelling place. My grandmother was convinced that this was true, yet, she could boast at the same time that she had never been in a theatre in her life.

A year before her husband's death an incident occurred which enraged her, and helped to hasten the final breach with her son. My father at this time was only seventeen, but for years, from the first time his father had taken him into a theatre, he had felt the complete fascination of its magic and he had already resolved that this was the life he wanted and the life he was going to follow. In this desire his father agreed, and wanted to help him. That year, accordingly, he was given his first chance. His father's war-time friend, of whom I have spoken, was a man named Clark: Mr. Clark was an actor who had played in many parts and had also been a manager of several theatres. Mr. Clark, therefore, got my father a small part in a play that was soon to open: it was a melodrama and in one scene there was a thrilling fight between two groups of hoodlums. My father was given the part of leader of one of these gangs, and he was given a single speech of three short words. My father was supposed to rush out on the stage at the head of his gang, glare fiercely at the other leader when he saw him, throw up his fists in a fighting attitude, and run forward crying: "Now for it!"

As every actor knows, it is often more difficult to play a small part well than to play a big part. When the actor is given only one or two short speeches, he is likely to be oppressed by a feeling that he must make every syllable and situation count, that there cannot be the slightest flaw or slip in his execution. As a consequence he is often strained and unnatural in his delivery of a few words, whereas if the words were only a fragment of a larger part, he could deliver them with perfect ease and naturalness.

During the course of rehearsals my father was repeatedly told to accent the second of his three words—that is, to say "Now *for* it!" Invariably, however, perhaps because he had been warned so often and erred through trying to avoid error, he would deliver his three words with the accent, thus bounding up upon the last: "Now for *it!*" Finally, the director, out of patience, told him curtly he would be discharged if he did not deliver his speech correctly on the night of the dress rehearsal. My father was heartsick and desperate at the prospect: he strode up and down backstage for hours repeating "Now *for* it!" thousands of times, until he thought it was rooted in his brain beyond possibility of error. On the night of the dress rehearsal, however, he failed again. He rushed out on the stage, shouted "Now for *it!*" and then, turning to the director, he burst into tears and begged the man to give him another chance. To his stupefaction everyone roared with laughter, and the director told him to say his speech in any way he pleased. Thereafter, he always got it right: the play ran for several weeks and he performed creditably.

My grandmother had known nothing of this. When Mr. Clark had got the job for him, my father and my grandfather agreed to say nothing to her about it. But my father's absences from home on the evenings aroused her suspicion: when she asked him what he was doing, he told her. She flew into a terrible fit of temper, told him he was on the road to hell, and insisted that he give up his work at once. He refused; she then turned upon her husband, demanded that he compel the boy to stop, but he would not do this: he stood by his son and told her he should do as he wished. After the play had finished its run, my father made no effort to find new employment in the theatre, knowing that it would cause new tirades and invectives and that his father, now enduring the last hours of his agony, would have to bear the brunt of her bitterness and hate. But she never forgave either of them for it: she thought that both of them were damned and lost, and the harsh weight of her tongue was turned upon her husband to the end.

But now that he was dead, and his house was filled with these people his wife brought there from her church, my father could not endure this obscenity of mourning. It did not seem to him as if his father had died: it seemed that life had died, that the house in which they lived had died, that the corrupted body there belonged to death, was itself death, and had never had a union with his father's life. He remembered his father's bright living eye, his great laugh, and the superb purity and courage of his spirit, which had lived life with such fierce joy, and had been trapped to die there in that corrupted flesh whose evil stench had, even in the last months of his life, polluted the air about him. And now that this corrupted carcass should be cherished hideously by this woman to do duty to these rusty mourners in place of the bright spirit they could never know was not to be endured: my father went to her and begged her to have it taken from the house at once and buried. She refused: I think she must have been insane because she told him that this odor of putrefaction came from evil living, and that the road which he was traveling would lead him to the same decay.

My father went almost mad: he went out and walked the streets like a man who has been struck at the base of the brain and has no knowledge of what he is doing. Toward dark, however, he composed himself somewhat and went to see his father's friend, the actor, Clark. When my father had told his story to Mr. Clark, the man got up, took his hat, and told my father to come with him. They went directly to my grandfather's house: when they got there full dark had come, dim lamps were burning, and they could hear the voices of the mourners filled with their lust of pain and darkness. When Mr. Clark went into the house, he asked my grandmother if she would let him speak to her in private: immediately she denounced him and ordered him out of the house. My father protested at this, he told her Clark had been one of his father's best friends and that he had asked him to come there to talk with her: at this, his mother started to revile them both. She said Clark had been responsible for her husband's wickedness and that he was now bent on ruining her son. My father said that this was not true. His mother then appealed to her friends, the mourners: she asked them if they had heard the son say that his mother lied, and they said yes, they had heard, and they had never listened to such infamy. She then screamed at him that she had loved him and tried to save him, she said she had done all a mother could do for him, and that he was an unnatural son. She told him he would have to choose between herself and God and "that actor," meaning Mr. Clark. She said if he did not do as she wished and go with her to Connecticut for the burial, he could get out of her house at once and that she never wanted to see his face again. My father waited until she had finished: then he told her he would go and that she could have her wish. Then my father left the house with Mr. Clark, and from that day he never saw his mother again. She went back to her home in Connecticut, she spent the rest of her life there, but she had not long to live: she died there three years later.

What spirit shaped this woman? Of what unknown elements was she made: Wrought by what troubled brain, what cruel heart? In all the chronicles of my life's rich journey there has been no one to be compared with her: we, with our fruitful cries, our warmth of love, our hate of hate, our depth of passion and of living, had strangeness and mystery enough for unbelief; but I knew the source we came from. But she would live for me like some legendary monster of some tainted earth, had I not proof of her existence: she coined the metal of her soul and flesh into the substance of her oldest child, her daughter, my Aunt Kate, with whom a portion of my youth was spent, and in whom I saw the spirit of this woman rise and walk. And my other proof lies bound up in a handful of yellowed letters which she wrote my father during these last years of her life. I have them yet: the faded scrawl upon those faded pages lives with a fierce eternity of hatred, a corrupt animation which no years nor centuries can wither up.

Whether he ever answered these letters I do not know, nor did I ever ask him. I believe he must have, since hers had been addressed to him at various stages in his wanderings, and I suppose she must have known his address from letters which he wrote to her.

That woman seemed to have all the books of the Old Testament committed to memory, and she used them as an almanac, a prophesy, a constant weather report of human earthquake and catechism: there was not an evil mischance which could befall mankind for which she did not have at once the corresponding warning in the gospel. As she said, "it has all been written down": she could see the hand of God, she could believe in His living presence only in some act of horror in the universe—the sum and confirmation of her fierce belief was suffering and destruction, and wherever she saw stricken men, wherever she saw grief and agony, her triumphant faith cried out that God lived and wrought and that his presence was abroad throughout the earth. As one reads these letters today, with their dense compilation of quoted prophesies, the immense and twisted erudition—with which instantly she could tag with prophetic doom the most trivial events—the death of a horse, the diseases of sheep and cattle, the intervention of lightning in the life of a child or a withered hag—the reader may have at first the sense of unbelief, a comic sense of something grotesque and droll. But as he reads, whatever quality of humor he felt will disappear: the woman emerges with a horrible intensity and reality, like someone we have never known but instantly recognize, a harpy screaming from the rocks of a separate, a stricken, planet, who belongs to no age, untouched by space or time, brought to this earth by what black charm, what evil incantation no one knows.

My father told me the whole story of his life with her only once, and I do not think I heard him speak of her, even casually, over a half dozen times in his life. He told me that he knew instantly when he left her that night that his feeling for her would never change, that he loathed her with all his heart and spirit, and that he would never see her again. At this moment of resolution all the tangled and bewildered dislike and resentment of years became clear and decisive: he knew exactly how he felt, he made a swingeing admission to himself, and thereafter he had no doubt about his feeling. Yet, he told me, for years he was to feel the bitter indecision of self mistrust: he could not change his feeling for her, nor say he had any love or affection for her, but her last words of reproach and indictment haunted him. He wondered if she had been right—if he was an "unnatural" son, if his feeling branded him a monster, if his lack of love for her meant that there was a deformed and twisted isolation in his spirit. He was only a boy of eighteen years, and there was no one to whom he could confide. I think it was during these years that he acquired the certitude and independence of spirit that he had thereafter, but he bought it with the intense and lonely pain of his youth.

This was his final comment: one Sunday afternoon a great many years after this, and at least ten years after his marriage, for I must have been eight years old or more at the time, we had as a caller at Bella's house, one of her friends, an actor named Grantham. Mr. Grantham was from Indiana, but he had not lived there for many years. Grantham's mother had died a week or two before and he had gone back to Indiana for the funeral: he had just returned to New York and now he was telling us about his mother. I think that actors as a rule spend as little time in thinking of their parents or kinfolk as any class of people I know: the reason for this, I think, is that the actor lives in a world that is unduly separated from the one in which he was born, and he constantly becomes more absorbed in one and more remote from the other. Yet, no one can talk more eloquently than an actor about the beauty of mother love: his eyes will fill with tears at the sound of a "mammy song," and he can weep copiously when he speaks of his love for a mother he has made no attempt to see in twenty years. Mr. Grantham was doing this now, and I think we all felt a little ashamed of him: everyone knew he had not been to see his mother for at least fifteen years, yet here he was saying that her death was the greatest sorrow he had ever known, that the thought of her and her teaching had inspired and guided him at every moment of his life, and that mother love was the most wonderful and beautiful thing on earth.

At length my father said: "I think you are very fortunate to feel that way." Mr. Grantham looked at my father in a sharp suspicious manner. I think he was uneasy about his own feeling, and had been trying to convince himself of his devotion and grief by talking of it. At any rate, he thought that there was something critical of him in my father's words.

"Fortunate?" he said. "How so? I only feel the way about my mother that all men feel."

"No," my father said. "I do not think so."

Mr. Grantham became a little excited: he still thought his beautiful emotion was being doubted, and he said:

"I loved my mother more than anyone else in the world. No one can say I didn't."

"I do not doubt you," my father answered. "I only said that all men do not feel as you."

"Oh, yes they do!" said Mr. Grantham.

"Oh, no they don't!" said father.

"Didn't you?" said Grantham, feeling that he had my father trapped.

"No, I didn't," my father said at once.

"Do you mean to say," said Grantham, slowly, "that you did *not—love—really* love—your mother?"

"Yes," my father said, "that is what I mean to say. I did not love my mother. I will go farther than that. I did not even like her. I had the most intense dislike for her that I have ever felt for any person, and I know she felt the same for me."

No one spoke. I think you could have heard their hearts beat in the silence. My own was pounding in my throat. As for Grantham, he was stupefied. At length he said:

"That is the most unnatural thing I have ever heard."

"Is it unnatural because I say it is or because I feel it?" my father asked.

"Because you feel it," Grantham said. "You would not say it unless you felt it, would you?"

My father's eyes had suddenly got black and smoky. He said:

"I would not go so far as that, Grantham. I think *you* must have known people who said things that they did not feel."

Mr. Grantham made no answer for a moment. My father looked at him. His face turned a fiery red. Then he said:

"But you really feel that way about your mother. Anyone can see you do."

"Yes," my father said. "I really feel that way. And I tell you, Grantham, it is not unnatural. I tell you there are many men who feel as I do. Yes! I tell you there are men who even feel the most savage and unmitigated hatred for their mothers, and I do not blame them for it!"

We sat there in a hypnotic silence, and we felt awe and terror. My father's cheeks were burning with two badges of bright red. I saw his fingers tremble. In a moment he spoke again in a voice so low, so charged with some strange deep passion that it did not seem to be his own.

"But I'll tell you what *is* unnatural, Grantham. It is to say we have big feelings when we have not got them. It is to live by words when the words have no real meaning for us: it is to mock at love and mercy we have never felt."

No one said anything for several moments. All of us felt a kind of terror. Yet what he had said had cut like a sharp sword through all the falseness and hypocrisy. We knew that what he had said was the truth, but at that time few people would have dared to utter such an opinion: it was a blasphemy of the accepted and cherished sentiment. Suddenly our smooth Sunday tea had been shattered by an utterance which came up out of a burning depth of pain and wisdom none of us had known. Our spirits had shrunk away a little from him, because what he had said had frightened us, and none of us were willing to stand by him at that moment. I wanted to be near him. I loved him, and yet I was afraid to go up to him. Then, all at once he looked so lonely sitting there among us. I looked at him, and instantly he was revealed to me: I saw how lonely and silent his spirit was, and what dreadful depths it had known. I looked at the dark and potent beauty of the Jews, my mother's quiet and living faithfulness, and Bella's radiant power and opulence, and I saw that he had come to us as a stranger and a wanderer of the earth, and I knew now why he loved us, and I knew why we could never know each other. His secret and withdrawn spirit had a wall around it we could never break: my mother lifted her eyes to him and it seemed to me they looked at each other across a great and inseparable distance, and yet their look had the greatest love and loyalty in it I had ever seen.

As I remember my father now I always remember his lonely and secret spirit. Yet there was no one who loved the companionship of people more, and people always wanted to be near him. They wanted to be near him because it is the secret and lonely people who attract us most: we feel in them an integrity and power which other people do not have, we are drawn by a luminous mystery in them. Perhaps we feel that if we can pluck out the heart of this mystery we will find the wisdom and power we need in our own lives. It seems now that my father was always alone: even in a crowd he was isolated, the other people made a continent of life, they were bound together by great tides and rivers, but he dwelt among them like an island.

7

His Father's Earth

As the boy stood looking at the circus with his brother, there came to him two images, which had haunted his childhood and the life of every boy who ever lived, but were now for the first time seen together with an instant and magic congruence. And these two images were the images of the circus and his father's earth.

He thought then he had joined a circus and started on the great tour of the nation with it. It was spring: the circus had started in New England and worked westward and then southward as the summer and autumn came on. His nominal duties—for, in his vision, every incident, each face and voice and circumstance were blazing real as life itself—were those of ticket seller, but in this tiny show, everyone did several things: the performers helped put up and take down the tents, load and unload the wagons, and the roustabouts and business people worked wherever they were needed.

The boy sold tickets, but he also posted bills and bartered with tradesmen and farmers in new places for fresh food. He became very shrewd and clever at this work, and loved to do it—some old, sharp, buried talent for shrewd trading, that had come to him from his mountain blood, now aided him. He could get the finest, freshest meats and vegetables at the lowest prices. The circus people were tough and hard, they always had a fierce and ravenous hunger, they would not accept bad food and cooking, they fed stupendously, and they always had the best of everything.

Usually the circus would arrive at a new town very early in the morning, before daybreak. He would go into town immediately: he would go to the markets, or with farmers who had come in for the circus. He felt and saw the purity of first light, he heard the sweet and sudden lutings of first birds, and suddenly he was filled with the earth and morning in new towns, among new men: he walked among the farmers' wagons, and he dealt with them on the spot for the prodigal plenty of their wares—the country melons bedded in sweet hay of wagons, the cool sweet prints of butter wrapped in clean wet cloths, with dew and starlight still on them, the enormous battered cans foaming with fresh milk, the new laid eggs which he bought by the gross and hundred dozens, the tender limy pullets by the score, the rude country wagons laden to the rim with heaped abundancies—with delicate bunches of green scallions, the heavy red ripeness of huge tomatoes, the sweet-leaved lettuces crisp as celery, the fresh podded peas and the succulent young beans, as well as the potatoes spotted with the loamy earth, the powerful winey odor of the apples, the peaches, and the cherries, the juicy corn stacked up in shocks of living green, and the heavy blackened rinds of home-cured hams and bacons.

As the market opened, he would begin to trade and dicker with the butchers for their finest cuts of meat: they would hold great roasts up in their gouted fingers, they would roll up tubs of fresh ground sausage, they would smack with their long palms the flanks of beeves and porks: he would drive back to the circus with a wagon full of meat and vegetables.

At the circus ground the people were already in full activity. He could hear the wonderful timed tattoo of sledges on driven stakes, the shouts of men riding animals down to water, the slow clank and pull of mighty horses, the heavy rumble of the wagons as they rolled down off the circus flat cars. By now the eating table would be erected, and as he arrived, he could see the cooks already busy at their ranges, the long tables set up underneath the canvas with their rows of benches, their tin plates and cups, their strong readiness. There would be the amber indescribable pungency of strong coffee, and the smell of buckwheat batter.

And the circus people would come in for their breakfast: hard and tough, for the most part decent and serious people, the performers, the men and women, the acrobats, the riders, the tumblers, the clowns, the jugglers, the contortionists, and the balancers would come in quietly and eat with a savage and inspired intentness.

The food they ate was as masculine and fragrant as the world they dwelt in: it belonged to the stained world of mellow sun-warmed canvas, the clean and healthful odor of the animals, and the mild sweet lyric nature of the land in which they lived as wanderers, and it was there for the asking with a fabulous and stupefying plenty, golden and embrowned: they ate stacks of buckwheat cakes, smoking hot, soaked in hunks of yellow butter which they carved at will with a wide free gesture from the piled prints on the table, and which they garnished (if they pleased) with ropes of heavy black molasses, or with the lighter, freer maple syrup.

They ate big steaks for breakfast, hot from the pan and lashed with onions, they ate whole melons, crammed with the ripeness of the deep pink meat, rashers of bacon, and great platters of fried eggs, or eggs scrambled with calves' brains, they helped themselves from pyramids of fruit piled up at intervals on the table—plums, peaches, apples, cherries, grapes, oranges, and bananas—they had great pitchers of thick cream to pour on everything, and they washed their hunger down with pint mugs of strong deep-savored coffee.

For their mid-day meal they would eat fiercely, hungrily, with wolfish gusts, mightily, with knit brows and convulsive movements of their corded throats. They would eat great roasts of beef with crackled hides, browned in their juices, rare and tender, hot chunks of delicate pork with hems of fragrant fat, delicate young boiled chickens, only a mouthful for these ravenous jaws, twelve-pound pot roasts cooked for hours in an iron pot with new carrots, onions, sprouts, and young potatoes, together with every vegetable that the season yielded: huge roasting ears of corn, smoking hot, stacked like cord wood on two-foot platters, tomatoes cut in slabs with wedges of okra and succotash, and raw onion, mashed potatoes whipped to a creamy smother, boats swimming with pure beef gravy, new carrots, turnips, fresh peas cooked in butter, and fat string beans seasoned with the flavor of big chunks of cooking-pork. In addition, they had every fruit that the place and time afforded: hot crusty apple, peach and cherry pies, encrusted with cinnamon, puddings and cakes of every sort, and blobbering cobblers inches deep.

Thus the circus moved across America, from town to town, from state to state, eating its way from Maine into the great plains of the West, eating its way along the Hudson and the Mississippi rivers, eating its way across the prairies and from the North into the South, eating its way across the flat farm lands of the Pennsylvania Dutch colony, the eastern shore of Maryland and back again across the states of Virginia, North Carolina, Tennessee, and Florida—eating all good things that this enormous, this inevitably bountiful and abundant cornucopia of a continent yielded.

They ate the cod, bass, mackerel, halibut, clams, and oysters of the New England coast, the terrapin of Maryland, the fat beeves, porks, and cereals of the Middle West, and they had, as well, the heavy juicy peaches, watermelons, cantaloupes of Georgia, the fat sweet shad of the Carolina coasts, and the rounded and exotic citrus fruits of the tropics: the oranges, tangerines, bananas, kumquats, lemons, guavas down in Florida, together with a hundred other fruits and meats—the Vermont turkeys, the mountain trout, the bunched heaviness of the Concord grapes, the red winey bulk of the Oregon apples, as well as the clawed, shelled, and crusted dainties, the crabs, the clams, the pink meated lobsters that grope their way along the sea-floors of America.

The boy awoke at morning in three hundred towns with the glimmer of starlight on his face; he was the moon's man; then he saw light quicken in the east, he saw the pale stars drown, he saw the birth of light, he heard the lark's wing, the bird tree, the first liquorous liquefied lutings, the ripe-aired trillings, the plumskinned birdnotes, and he heard the hoof and wheel come down the streets of the nation. He exulted in his work as food-producer for the circus people, and they loved him for it. They said there had never been anyone like him— they banqueted exultantly, with hoarse gulpings and with joy, and they loved him.

Slowly, day by day, the circus worked its way across America, through forty states and through a dozen weathers. It was a little world that moved across the enormous loneliness of the earth, a little world that each day began a new life in new cities, and that left nothing to betray where it had been save a litter of beaten papers, the droppings of the camel and the elephant in Illinois, a patch of trampled grass, and a magical memory.

The circus men knew no other earth but this; the earth came to them with the smell of the canvas and the lion's roar. They saw the world behind the lights of the carnival, and everything beyond these lights was phantasmal and unreal to them; it lived for them within the circle of the tent as men and women who sat on benches, as the posts they came to, and sometimes as the enemy.

Their life was filled with the strong joy of food, with the love of traveling, and with danger and hard labor. Always there was the swift violence of change and movement, of putting up and tearing down, and sometimes there was the misery of rain and sleet, and mud above the ankles, of wind that shook their flimsy residence, that ripped the tent stakes from their moorings in the earth and lifted out the great center pole as if it were a match. Now they must wrestle with the wind and hold their dwelling to the earth; now they must fight the weariness of mud and push their heavy wagons through the slime; now, cold and wet and wretched, they must sleep on piles of canvas, upon the flat cars in a driving rain, and sometimes they must fight the enemy—the drunk, the savage, the violent enemy, the bloody man, who dwelt in every place. Sometimes it was the city thug, sometimes the mill hands of the South, sometimes the miners in a Pennsylvania town—the circus people cried, "Hey, Rube!" and fought them with fist and foot, with pike and stake, and the boy saw and knew it all.

When the men in a little town barricaded the street against their parade, they charged the barricade with their animals, and once the sheriff tried to stop the elephant by saying: "Now, damn ye, if you stick your God-damned trunk another inch, I'll shoot."

The circus moved across America foot by foot, mile by mile. He came to know the land. It was rooted in his blood and his brain forever—its food, its fruit, its fields and forests, its deserts, and its mountains, its savage lawlessness. He saw the crimes and the violence of the people with pity, with mercy, and with tenderness: he thought of them as if they were children. They smashed their neighbors' brains out with an ax, they disemboweled one another with knives, they were murderous and lost upon this earth they dwelt upon as strangers.

The tongueless blood of the murdered men ran down into the earth, and the earth received it. Upon this enormous and indifferent earth the little trains rattled on over ill-joined rails that loosely bound the sprawling little towns together. Lost and lonely, brief sawings of wood and plaster and cheap brick ugliness, the little towns were scattered like encampments through the wilderness. Only the earth remained, which all these people had barely touched, which all these people dwelt upon but could not possess.

Only the earth remained, the savage and lyrical earth with its rude potency, its thousand vistas, its heights and slopes and levels, with all its violence and delicacy, the terrible fecundity, decay, and growth, its fierce colors, its vital bite and sparkle, its exultancy of space and wandering. And the memory of this earth, the memory of all this universe of sight and sense, was rooted in this boy's heart and brain forever. It fed the hungers of desire and wandering, it breached the walls of his secret and withdrawn spirit. And for every memory of place and continent, of enormous coffee-colored rivers and eight hundred miles of bending wheat, of Atlantic coast and midland prairie, of raw red Piedmont and tropic flatness, there was always the small, fecund, perfect memory of his father's land, the dark side of his soul and his heart's desire, which he had never seen, but which he knew with every atom of his life, the strange phantasmal haunting of man's memory. It was a fertile, nobly swelling land, and it was large enough to live in, walled with fulfilled desire.

Abroad in this ocean of earth and vision he thought of his father's land, of its great red barns and nobly swelling earth, its clear familiarity and its haunting strangeness, and its dark and secret heart, its magnificent, its lovely and tragic beauty. He thought of its smell of harbors and its rumors of the seas, the city, and the ships, its wine-red apples and its brown-red soil, its snug weathered houses, and its lyric unutterable ecstasy.

A wonderful thing happened. One morning he awoke suddenly to find himself staring straight up at the pulsing splendor of the stars. At first he did not know where he was, but he knew instantly, even before he looked about him, that he had visited this place before. The circus train had stopped in the heart of the country, for what reason he did not know. He could hear the languid and intermittent breathing of the engine, the strangeness of men's voices in the dark, the casual stamp of the horses in their cars, and all around him the attentive and vital silence of the earth.

Suddenly he raised himself from the pile of canvas on which he slept. It was the moment just before dawn: against the east, the sky had already begun to whiten with the first faint luminosity of day, the invading tides of light crept up the sky, drowning the stars out as they went. The train had halted by a little river which ran swift and deep next to the tracks, and now he knew that what at first had been the sound of silence was the swift and ceaseless music of the river.

There had been rain the night before, and now the river was filled with the sweet clean rain-drenched smell of earthy deposits. He could see the delicate white glimmer of young birch trees leaning from the banks, and on the other side he saw the winding whiteness of the road. Beyond the road, and bordering it, there was an orchard with a wall of lichened stone: a row of apple trees, gnarled and sweet, spread their squat twisted branches out across the road, and in the faint light he saw that they were dense with blossoms: the cool intoxication of their fragrance overpowered him.

As the wan light grew, the earth and all its contours emerged sharply, and he saw again the spare, gaunt loneliness of the earth at dawn, with all its sweet and sudden cries of spring. He saw the worn and ancient design of lichened rocks, the fertile soil of the baked fields, he saw the kept order, the frugal cleanliness, with its springtime overgrowth, the mild tang of opulent greenery. There was an earth with fences, as big as a man's

heart, but not so great as his desire, and after his giant wanderings over the prodigal fecundity of the continent, this earth
was like a room he once had lived in. He returned to it as a
sailor to a small closed harbor, as a man, spent with the hunger
of his wandering, comes home.

Instantly he recognized the scene. He knew that he had
come at last into his father's land. It was a magic that he knew
but could not speak; he stood upon the lip of time, and all of
his life now seemed the mirage of some wizard's spell—the
spell of canvas and the circus ring, the spell of the tented
world which had possessed him. Here was his home, brought
back to him while he slept, like a forgotten dream. Here was
the dark side of his soul, his heart's desire, his father's country,
the earth his spirit dwelt on as a child. He knew every inch of
the landscape, and he knew, past reason, doubt, or argument,
that home was not three miles away.

He got up at once and leaped down to the earth; he knew
where he would go. Along the track there was the slow swing
and dance of the brakemen's lamps, that moving, mournful,
and beautiful cloud of light along the rails of the earth, that he
had seen so many times. Already the train was in motion; its
bell tolled and its heavy trucks rumbled away from him. He
began to walk back along the tracks, for less than a mile away,
he knew, where the stream boiled over the lip of a dam, there
was a bridge. When he reached the bridge, a deeper light had
come: the old red brick of the mill emerged sharply and with
the tone and temper of deep joy fell sheer into bright shining
waters.

He crossed the bridge and turned left along the road: here
it moved away from the river, among fields and through dark
woods—dark woods bordered with stark poignancy of fir and
pine, with the noble spread of maples, shot with the naked
whiteness of birch. Here was the woodland maze: the sweet

density of the brake and growth. Sharp thrummings, woodland flitters broke the silence. His steps grew slow, he sat upon
a wall, he waited.

Now rose the birdsong in first light, and suddenly he heard
each sound the birdsong made. Like a flight of shot the sharp
fast skaps of sound arose. With chittering bicker, fast-fluttering
skirrs of sound, the palmy honeyed bird-cries came. Smooth
drops and nuggets of bright gold they were. Now sang the
birdtrees filled with lutings in bright air: the thrums, the lark's
wing, and tongue-trilling chirrs arose now. The little nameless
cries arose and fell with liquorous liquified lutings, with lir-
ruping chirp, plumbellied smoothness, sweet lucidity.

And now there was the rapid kweet kweet kweet kweet
kweet of homing birds and their pwee pwee pwee: others with
sharp cricketing stitch, a mosquito buzz with thin metallic
tongues, while some with rusty creakings, high shrew's caws,
with eerie rasp, with harsh far calls—all birds that are awake
in the sweet woodland tangles: and above, there passed the
whirr of hidden wings, the strange lost cry of the unknown
birds, in full flight now, in which the sweet confusion of their
cries was mingled.

Then he got up and went along that road where, he knew,
like the prophetic surmise of a dream, the house of his father's
blood and kin lay hidden. At length, he came around a bending
in the road, he left the wooded land, he passed by hedges and
saw the old white house, set in the shoulder of the hill, worn
like care and habit in the earth; clean and cool, it sat below the
clean dark shelter of its trees: a twist of morning smoke coiled
through its chimney.

Then he turned in to the rutted road that led up to the
house, and at this moment the enormous figure of a powerful
old man appeared around the corner prophetically bearing a
smoked ham in one huge hand. And when the boy saw the old

man, a cry of greeting burst from his throat, and the old man answered with a roar of welcome that shook the earth.

Then the old man dropped his ham, and waddled forward to meet the boy: they met half down the road, and the old man crushed him in his hug; they tried to speak but could not; they embraced again and in an instant all the years of wandering, the pain of loneliness and the fierce hungers of desire, were scoured away like a scum of frost from a bright glass.

He was a child again, he was a child that had stood upon the lip and leaf of time and heard the quiet tides that move us to our death, and he knew that the child could not be born again, the book of the days could never be turned back, old errors and confusions never righted. And he wept with sorrow for all that was lost and could never be regained, and with joy for all that had been recovered.

Suddenly he saw his youth as men on hilltops might look at the whole winding course of rivers to the sea, he saw the blind confusions of his wanderings across the earth, the horror of man's little stricken mote of earth against immensity, and he remembered the proud exultancy of his childhood when all the world lay like a coin between his palms, when he could have touched the horned rim of the moon, when heroes and great actions bent before him.

And he wept, not for himself, but out of love and pity for every youth that ever hoped and wandered and was alone. He had become a man, and he had in him unique glory that belongs to men alone, and that makes them great, and from which they shape their mightiest songs and legends. For out of their pain they utter first a cry for wounded self, then, as their vision deepens, widens, the universe of their marvelous sense leaps out and grips the universe; they feel contempt for gods, respect for men alone, and with the indifference of a selfless passion, enact earth out of a lyric cry.

At this moment, also, two young men burst from the house and came running down the road to greet him. They were powerful and heavy young men, already beginning to show signs of that epic and sensual grossness that distinguished their father. Like their father, they recognized the boy instantly, and in a moment he was engulfed in their mighty energies, borne up among them to the house. And they understood all he wanted to say, but could not speak, and they surrounded him with love and lavish heapings of his plate. And the boy knew the strange miracle of return to the dark land of his heart's desire, the father's land which haunts men like a dream they never knew.

Such were the twin images of the circus and his father's land which were to haunt his dreams and waking memory and which now, as he stood there with his brother looking at the circus, fused instantly to a living whole and came to him in a blaze of light.

And in this way, before he had ever set foot upon it, he came for the first time to his father's earth.

8

Chickamauga

ON THE SEVENTH DAY of August, 1861, I was nineteen years
of age. If I live to the seventh day of August this year I'll be
ninety-five years old. And the way I feel this mornin' I intend
to live. Now I guess you'll have to admit that that's goin' a good
ways back.

I was born up at the Forks of the Toe River in 1842. Your
grandpaw, boy, was born at the same place in 1828. His father,
and mine too, Bill Pentland—your great-grandfather, boy—
moved into that region way back right after the Revolutionary
War and settled at the Forks of Toe. The real Indian name fer
hit was Estatoe, but the white men shortened hit to Toe, and
hit's been known as Toe River ever since.

Of course hit was all Indian country in those days. I've
heared that the Cherokees helped Bill Pentland's father build
the first house he lived in, where some of us was born. I've
heared, too, that Bill Pentland's grandfather came from Scot-
land back before the Revolution, and that thar was three brothers. That's all the Pentlands that I ever heared of in this country. If you ever meet a Pentland anywheres you can rest assured
he's descended from one of those three.

Well, now, as I was tellin' you, upon the seventh day of August, 1861, I was nineteen years of age. At seven-thirty in the

mornin' of that day I started out from home and walked the whole way in to Clingman. Jim Weaver had come over from Big Hickory where he lived the night before and stayed with me. And now he went along with me. He was the best friend I had. We had growed up alongside of each other: now we was to march alongside of each other fer many a long and weary mile, how many neither of us knowed that mornin' when we started out.

Hit was a good twenty mile away from where we lived to Clingman, and I reckon young folks nowadays would consider twenty mile a right smart walk. But fer people in those days hit wasn't anything at all. All of us was good walkers. Why Jim Weaver could keep goin' without stoppin' all day long.

Jim was big and I was little, about the way you see me now, except that I've shrunk up a bit, but I could keep up with him anywheres he went. We made hit into Clingman before twelve o'clock—hit was a hot day, too—and by three o'clock that afternoon we had both joined up with the Twenty-ninth. That was my regiment from then on, right on to the end of the war. Anyways, I was an enlisted man that night, the day that I was nineteen years of age, and I didn't see my home again fer four long years.

Your Uncle Bacchus, boy, was already in Virginny: we knowed he was thar because we'd had a letter from him. He joined up right at the start with the Fourteenth. He'd already been at First Manassas and I reckon from then on he didn't miss a big fight in Virginny fer the next four years, except after Antietam where he got wounded and was laid up fer four months.

Even way back in those days your Uncle Bacchus had those queer religious notions that you've heared about. The Pentlands are good people, but everyone who ever knowed 'em knows they can go queer on religion now and then. That's the reputation that they've always had. And that's the way Back was. He was a Russellite even in those days: accordin' to his notions the world was comin' to an end and he was goin' to be right in on hit when hit happened. That was the way he had hit figgered out. He was always prophesyin' and predictin' even back before the war, and when the war came, why Back just knowed that this was hit.

Why law! He wouldn't have missed that war fer anything. Back didn't go to war because he wanted to kill Yankees. He didn't want to kill nobody. He was as tender-hearted as a baby and as brave as a lion. Some fellers told hit on him later how they'd come on him at Gettysburg, shootin' over a stone wall, and his rifle bar'l had got so hot he had to put hit down and rub his hands on the seat of his pants because they got so blistered. He was singin' hymns, they said, with tears a-streamin' down his face—that's the way they told hit, anyway—and every time he fired he'd sing another verse. And I reckon he killed plenty because when Back had a rifle in his hands he didn't miss.

But he was a good man. He didn't want to hurt a fly. And I reckon the reason that he went to war was because he thought he'd be at Armageddon. That's the way he had hit figgered out, you know. When the war came, Back said: "Well, this is hit, and I'm a-goin' to be thar. The hour has come," he said, "when the Lord is goin' to set up His kingdom here on earth and separate the sheep upon the right hand and the goats upon the left—jest like hit was predicted long ago—and I'm a-goin' to be thar when hit happens."

Well, we didn't ask him which side he was goin' to be on, but we all knowed which side without havin' to ask. Back was goin' to be on the sheep side—that's the way he had hit figgered out. And that's the way he had hit figgered out right up to the day of his death ten years ago. He kept prophesyin' and predictin' right up to the end. No matter what happened, no matter what mistakes he made, he kept right on predictin'.

First he said the war was goin' to be the Armageddon day. And when that didn't happen he said hit was goin' to come along in the eighties. And when hit didn't happen then he moved hit up to the nineties. And when the war broke out in 1914 and the whole world had to go, why Bacchus knowed that *that* was hit.

And no matter how hit all turned out, Back never would give in or own up he was wrong. He'd say he'd made a mistake in his figgers somers, but that he'd found out what hit was and that next time he'd be right. And that's the way he was up to the time he died.

I had to laugh when I heared the news of his death, because of course, accordin' to Back's belief, after you die nothin' happens to you fer a thousand years. You jest lay in your grave and sleep until Christ comes and wakes you up. So that's why I had to laugh. I'd a-give anything to've been there the next mornin' when Back woke up and found himself in heaven. I'd've give anything just to've seen the expression on his face. I may have to wait a bit but I'm goin' to have some fun with him when I see him. But I'll bet you even then he won't give in. He'll have some reason fer hit, he'll try to argue he was right but that he made a little mistake about hit somers in his figgers.

But Back was a good man—a better man than Bacchus Pentland never lived. His only failin' was the failin' that so many Pentlands have—he went and got queer religious notions and he wouldn't give them up.

Well, like I say then, Back was in the Fourteenth. Your Uncle Sam and Uncle George was with the Seventeenth, and all three of them was in Lee's army in Virginny. I never seed nor heared from either Back or Sam fer the next four years. I never knowed what had happened to them or whether they was dead or livin' until I got back home in '65. And of course I never heared from George again until they wrote me after Chancellorsville. And then I knowed that he was dead. They told hit later when I came back home that hit took seven men

to take him. They asked him to surrender. And then they had
to kill him because he wouldn't be taken. That's the way he
was. He never would give up. When they got to his dead body
they told how they had to crawl over a whole heap of dead
Yankees before they found him. And then they knowed hit
was George. That's the way he was, all right. He never would
give in.

He is buried in the Confederate cemetery at Richmond,
Virginny. Bacchus went through thar more than twenty years
ago on his way to the big reunion up at Gettysburg. He hunted
up his grave and found out where he was.

That's where Jim and me thought that we'd be too. I mean
with Lee's men, in Virginny. That's where we thought that we
was goin' when we joined. But, like I'm goin' to tell you now,
hit turned out different from the way we thought.

Bob Saunders was our Captain; L. C. McIntyre our Major;
and Leander Briggs the Colonel of our regiment. They kept us
thar at Clingman fer two weeks. Then they marched us into
Altamont and drilled us fer the next two months. Our drillin'
ground was right up and down where Parker Street now is. In
those days thar was nothing thar but open fields. Hit's all built
up now. To look at hit today you'd never know thar'd ever been
an open field thar. But that's where hit was, all right.

Late in October we was ready and they moved us on. The
day they marched us out, Martha Patton came in all the way
from Zebulon to see Jim Weaver before we went away. He'd
known her fer jest two months; he'd met her the very week we
joined up and I was with him when he met her. She came from
out along Cane River. Thar was a camp revival meetin' goin' on
outside of Clingman at the time, and she was visitin' this other
gal in Clingman while the revival lasted; and that was how Jim
Weaver met her. We was walkin' along one evenin' toward sunset and we passed this house where she was stayin' with this
other gal. And both of them was settin' on the porch as we

went past. The other gal was fair, and she was dark: she had black hair and eyes, and she was plump and sort of little, and she had the pertiest complexion, and the pertiest white skin and teeth you ever seed; and when she smiled there was a dimple in her cheeks.

Well, neither of us knowed these gals, and so we couldn't stop and talk to them, but when Jim saw the little 'an he stopped short in his tracks like he was shot, and then he looked at her so hard she had to turn her face. Well, then, we walked on down the road a piece and then Jim stopped and turned and looked again, and when he did, why, sure enough, he caught *her* lookin' at him too. And then her face got red—she looked away again.

Well, that was where she landed him. He didn't say a word, but Lord! I felt him jerk there like a trout upon the line—and I knowed right then and thar she had him hooked. We turned and walked on down the road a ways, and then he stopped and looked at me and said:

"Did you see that gal back thar?"

"Do you mean the light one or the dark one?"

"You know damn good and well which one I mean," said Jim.

"Yes, I seed her, what about her?" I said.

"Well, nothin', only I'm a-goin' to marry her," he said.

I knowed then that she had him hooked. And yet I never believed at first that hit would last. Fer Jim had had so many gals—I'd never had a gal in my whole life up to that time, but Lord! Jim would have him a new gal every other week. We had some fine-lookin' fellers in our company, but Jim Weaver was the handsomest feller that you ever seed. He was tall and lean and built just right, and he carried himself as straight as a rod: he had black hair and coal-black eyes, and when he looked at you he could burn a hole through you. And I reckon he'd burned a hole right through the heart of many a gal before be first saw Martha Patton. He could have had his pick of the whole lot—a born lady-killer if you ever seed one—and that was why I never thought that hit'd last.

And maybe hit was a pity that hit did. Fer Jim Weaver until the day that he met Martha Patton had been the most happy-go-lucky feller that you ever seed. He didn't have a care in the whole world—full of fun—ready fer anything and into every kind of devilment and foolishness. But from that moment on he was a different man. And I've always thought that maybe hit was a pity that hit hit him when hit did—that hit had to come jest at that time. If hit had only come a few years later—if hit could only have waited till the war was over! He'd wanted to go so much, he'd looked at the whole thing as a big lark—but now! Well she had him, and he had her: the day they marched us out of town he had her promise, and in his watch he had her picture and a little lock of her black hair, and as they marched us out, and him beside me, we passed her, and she looked at him, and I felt him jerk again and knowed the look she gave him had gone through him like a knife.

From that time on he was a different man; from that time on he was like a man in hell. Hit's funny how hit all turns out—how none of hit is like what we expect. Hit's funny how war and a little black-haired gal will change a man—but that's the story that I'm goin' to tell you now.

The nearest rail head in those days was eighty mile away at Locust Gap. They marched us out of town right up the Fairfield Road along the river up past Crestville, and right across the Blue Ridge there, and down the mountain. We made Old Stockade the first day's march and camped thar fer the night. Hit was twenty-four miles of marchin' right across the mountain, with the roads the way they was in those days, too. And let me tell you, fer new men with only two months' trainin' that was doin' good.

We made Locust Gap in three days and a half, and I wish you'd seed the welcome that they gave us! People were hollerin'

and shoutin' the whole way. All the women folk and childern were lined up along the road, bands a-playin', boys run-
nin' along beside us, good shoes, new uniforms, the finest-
lookin' set of fellers that you *ever* seed—Lord! you'd a-thought
we was goin' to a picnic from the way hit looked. And I reckon
that was the way most of us felt about hit, too. We thought we
was goin' off to have a lot of fun. If anyone had knowed what
he was in fer or could a-seed the passel o' scarecrows that came
limpin' back barefoot and half naked four years later, I reckon
he'd a-thought twice before he 'listed up.

Lord, when I think of hit! When I try to tell about hit thar
jest ain't words enough to tell what hit was like. And when I
think of the way I was when I joined up—and the way I was
when I came back four years later! When I went away I was an
ignorant country boy, so tender-hearted that I wouldn't harm
a rabbit. And when I came back after the war was over I could
a-stood by and seed a man murdered right before my eyes
with no more feelin' than I'd have had fer a stuck hog. I had
no more feelin' about human life than I had fer the life of a
sparrer. I'd seed a ten-acre field so thick with dead men that
you could have walked all over hit without steppin' on the
ground a single time.

And that was where I made my big mistake. If I'd only
knowed a little more, if I'd only waited jest a little longer after
I got home, things would have been all right. That's been the
big regret of my whole life. I never had no education. I never
had a chance to git one before I went away. And when I came
back I could a-had my schoolin' but I didn't take hit. The reason was I never knowed no better: I'd seed so much fightin' and
killin' that I didn't care fer nothin'. I jest felt dead and numb
like all the brains had been shot out of me. I jest wanted to git
me a little patch of land somewheres and settle down and fergit about the world.

That's where I made my big mistake. I didn't wait long

enough. I got married too soon, and after that the childern came and hit was root, hawg, or die: I had to grub fer hit. But if I'd only waited jest a little while hit would have been all right. In less'n a year hit all cleared up. I got my health back, pulled myself together and got my feet back on the ground, and had more mercy and understandin' in me, jest on account of all the sufferin' I'd seen, than I ever had. And as fer my head, why hit was better than hit ever was: with all I'd seen and knowed I could a-got a schoolin' in no time. But you see I wouldn't wait. I didn't think that hit'd ever come back. I was jest sick of livin'.

But as I say—they marched us down to Locust Gap in less'n four days' time, and then they put us on the cars fer Richmond. We got to Richmond on the mornin' of one day, and up to that very moment we had thought that they was sendin' us to join Lee's army in the north. But the next mornin' we got our orders—and they was sendin' us out west. They had been fightin' in Kentucky: we was in trouble thar; they sent us out to stop the Army of the Cumberland. And that was the last I ever saw of old Virginny. From that time on we fought it out thar in the west and south. That's where we was, the Twenty-ninth, from then on to the end.

We had no real big fights until the spring of '62. And hit takes a fight to make a soldier of a man. Before that, thar was skirmishin' and raids in Tennessee and in Kentucky. That winter we seed hard marchin' in the cold and wind and rain. We learned to know what hunger was, and what hit was to have to draw your belly in to fit your rations. I reckon by that time we knowed hit wasn't goin' to be a picnic like we thought that hit would be. We was a-learnin' all the time, but we wasn't soldiers yet. It takes a good big fight to make a soldier, and we hadn't had one yet. Early in '62 we almost had one. They marched us to the relief of Donelson—but law! They had taken her before we got thar—and I'm goin' to tell you a good story about that.

U.S. Grant was thar to take her, and we was marchin' to
relieve her before old Butcher could git in. We was seven mile
away, and hit was comin' on to sundown—we'd been marchin'
hard. We got the order to fall out and rest. And that was
when I heared the gun and knowed that Donelson had fallen.
Thar was no sound of fightin'. Everything was still as Sunday.
We was settin' thar aside the road and then I heared a cannon boom. Hit boomed five times, real slow like—Boom!—
Boom!—Boom!—Boom!—Boom! And the moment that I
heared hit, I had a premonition. I turned to Jim and I said:
"Well, thar you are! That's Donelson—and she's surrendered!"

Cap'n Bob Saunders heared me, but he wouldn't believe me
and he said: "You're wrong!"

"Well," said Jim, "I hope to God he's right. I wouldn't care
if the whole damn war had fallen through. I'm ready to go
home."

"Well, he's wrong," said Captain Bob, "and I'll bet money on
hit that he is."

Well, I tell you, that jest suited me. That was the way I was
in those days—right from the beginnin' of the war to the very
end. If thar was any fun or devilment goin' on, any card playin'
or gamblin', or any other kind of foolishness, I was right in on
hit. I'd a-bet a man that red was green or that day was night,
and if a gal had looked at me from a persimmon tree, why, law!
I reckon I'd a-clumb the tree to git her. That's jest the way hit
was with me all through the war. I never made a bet or played
a game of cards in my life before the war or after hit was over,
but while the war was goin' on I was ready fer anything.

"How much will you bet?" I said.

"I'll bet you a hundred dollars even money," said Bob Saunders, and no sooner got the words out of his mouth than the
bet was on.

We planked the money down right thar and gave hit to Jim
to hold the stakes. Well, sir, we didn't have to wait half an hour

before a feller on a horse came ridin' up and told us hit was no use goin' any farther—Fort Donelson had fallen.

"What did I tell you?" I said to Cap'n Saunders, and I put the money in my pocket.

Well, the laugh was on him then. I wish you could a-seen the expression on his face—he looked mighty sheepish, I tell you. But he admitted hit, you know, he had to own up.

"You were right," he said. "You won the bet. But—I'll tell you what I'll do!" He put his hand into his pocket and pulled out a roll of bills. I've got a hundred dollars left—and with me hit's all or nothin'! We'll draw cards fer this last hundred, mine against yorn—high card wins!"

Well, I was ready fer him. I pulled out my hundred, and I said, "Git out the deck!"

So they brought the deck out then and Jim Weaver shuffled hit and held hit while we drawed. Bob Saunders drawed first and he drawed the eight of spades. When I turned my card up I had one of the queens.

Well, sir, you should have seen the look upon Bob Saunders' face. I tell you what, the fellers whooped and hollered till he looked like he was ready to crawl through a hole in the floor. We all had some fun with him, and then, of course, I gave the money back. I never kept a penny in my life I made from gamblin'.

But that's the way hit was with me in those days—I was ready fer hit—fer anything. If any kind of devilment or foolishness came up I was right in on hit with the ringleaders.

Well then, Fort Donelson was the funniest fight that I was ever in because hit was all fun fer me without no fightin'. And that jest suited me. And Stone Mountain was the most peculiar fight that I was in because—well, I'll tell you a strange story and you can figger fer yourself if you ever heared about a fight like *that* before.

Did you ever hear of a battle in which one side never fired a shot and yet won the fight and did more damage and more destruction to the other side than all the guns and cannon in the world could do? Well, that was the battle of Stone Mountain. Now, I was in a lot of battles. But the battle of Stone Mountain was the queerest one of the whole war.

I'll tell you how hit was.

We was up on top of the Mountain and the Yankees was below us tryin' to drive us out and take the Mountain. We couldn't git our guns up thar, we didn't try to—we didn't have to git our guns up thar. The only gun I ever seed up thar was a little brass howitzer that we pulled up with ropes, but we never fired a shot with hit. We didn't git a chance to use hit. We no more'n got hit in position before a shell exploded right on top of hit and split that little howitzer plumb in two. Hit jest fell into two parts: you couldn't have made a neater job of hit if you'd cut hit down the middle with a saw. I'll never fergit that little howitzer and the way they split hit plumb in two.

As for the rest of the fightin' on our side, hit was done with rocks and stones. We gathered together a great pile of rocks and stones and boulders all along the top of the Mountain, and when they attacked we waited and let 'em have hit.

The Yankees attacked in three lines, one after the other. We waited until the first line was no more'n thirty feet below us—until we could see the whites of their eyes, as the sayin' goes—and then we let 'em have hit. We jest rolled those boulders down on 'em, and I tell you what, hit was an awful thing to watch. I never saw no worse destruction than *that* with guns and cannon during the whole war.

You could hear 'em screamin' and hollerin' until hit made your blood run cold. They kept comin' on and we mowed 'em down by the hundreds. We mowed 'em down without firin' a single shot. We crashed them, wiped them out—jest by rollin' those big rocks and boulders down on them.

There was bigger battles in the war, but Stone Mountain was the queerest one I ever seed.

Fort Donelson came early in the war, and Stone Mountain came later toward the end. And one was funny and the other was peculiar, but thar was fightin' in between that wasn't neither one. I'm goin' to tell you about that.

Fort Donelson was the first big fight that we was in—and as I say, we wasn't really in hit because we couldn't git to her in time. And after Donelson that spring, in April, thar was Shiloh. Well—all that I can tell you is, we was thar on time at Shiloh. Oh Lord, I reckon that we was! Perhaps we had been country boys before, perhaps some of us still made a joke of hit before—but after Shiloh we wasn't country boys no longer. We didn't make a joke about hit after Shiloh. They wiped the smile off of our faces at Shiloh. And after Shiloh we was boys no longer: we was vet'ran men.

From then on hit was fightin' to the end. That's where we learned what hit was like—at Shiloh. From then on we knowed what hit would be until the end.

Jim got wounded thar at Shiloh. Hit wasn't bad—not bad enough to suit him anyways—fer he wanted to go home fer good. Hit was a flesh wound in the leg, but hit was some time before they could git to him, and he was layin' out thar on the field and I reckon that he lost some blood. Anyways, he was unconscious when they picked him up. They carried him back and dressed his wound right thar upon the field. They cleaned hit out, I reckon, and they bandaged hit—thar was so many of 'em they couldn't do much more than that. Oh, I tell you what, in those days thar wasn't much that they could do. I've seed the surgeons workin' underneath an open shed with meat-saws, choppin' off the arms and legs and throwin' 'em out thar in a pile like they was sticks of wood, sometimes without no chloroform or nothin', and the screamin' and the hollerin' of

the men was enough to make your head turn gray. And that
was as much as anyone could do. Hit was live or die and take
your chance—and thar was so many of 'em wounded so much
worse than Jim that I reckon he was lucky they did anything
fer him at all.

I heared 'em tell about hit later, how he come to, a-layin'
stretched out thar on an old dirty blanket on the bare floor, and
an army surgeon seed him lookin' at his leg all bandaged up
and I reckon, thought he'd cheer him up and said: "Oh, that
ain't nothin'—you'll be up and fightin' Yanks again in two
weeks' time."

Well, with that, they said, Jim got to cursin' and a-takin' on
something terrible. They said the language he used was enough
to make your hair stand up on end. They said he screamed and
raved and reached down thar and jerked that bandage off and
said—"Like hell I will!" They said the blood spouted up thar
like a fountain, and they said that army doctor was so mad he
throwed Jim down upon his back and sat on him and he took
that bandage, all bloody as hit was, and he tied hit back around
his leg again and he said: "Goddam you, if you pull that bandage off again, I'll let you bleed to death."

And Jim, they said, came ragin' back at him until you could
have heared him fer a mile, and said: "Well, by God, I don't
care if I do; I'd rather die than stay here any longer."

They say they had hit back and forth thar until Jim got so
weak he couldn't talk no more. I know that when I come to see
him a day or two later he was settin' up and I asked him: "Jim,
how is your leg? Are you hurt bad?"

And he answered: "Not bad enough. They can take the
whole damn leg off," he said, "as far as I'm concerned, and bury
hit here at Shiloh if they'll only let me go back home and not
come back again. Me and Martha will git along somehow," he
said. "I'd rather be a cripple the rest of my life than have to
come back and fight in this damn war."

Well, I knowed he meant hit too. I looked at him and seed how much he meant hit, and I knowed thar wasn't anything that I could do. When a man begins to talk that way, thar hain't much you can say to him. Well, sure enough, in a week or two, they let him go upon a two months' furlough and he went limpin' away upon a crutch. He was the happiest man I ever seed. "They gave me two months' leave," he said, "but if they jest let me git back home old Bragg'll have to send his whole damn army before he gits me out of thar again."

Well, he was gone two months or more, and I never knowed what happened—whether he got ashamed of himself when his wound healed up all right, or whether Martha talked him out of hit. But he was back with us again by late July—the grimmest, bitterest-lookin' man you ever seed. He wouldn't talk to me about hit, he wouldn't tell me what had happened, but I knowed from that time on he'd never draw his breath in peace until he left the army and got back home fer good.

Well, that was Shiloh, that was the time we didn't miss, that was where we lost our grin, where we knowed at last what hit would be until the end.

I've told you of three battles now, and one was funny, one was strange, and one was—well, one showed us what war and fightin' could be like. But I'll tell you of a fourth one now. And the fourth one was the greatest of the lot.

We seed some big fights in the war. And we was in some bloody battles. But the biggest fight we fought was Chickamauga. The bloodiest fight I ever seed was Chickamauga. Thar was big battles in the war, but thar never was a fight before, thar'll never be a fight again, like Chickamauga. I'm goin' to tell you how hit was at Chickamauga.

All through the spring and summer of that year Old Rosey follered us through Tennessee.

We had him stopped the year before, the time we whupped

him at Stones River at the end of '62. We tard him out so bad
he had to wait. He waited thar six months at Murfreesboro.
But we knowed he was a-comin' all the time. Old Rosey
started at the end of June and drove us out of Shelbyville. We
fell back on Tullahoma in rains the like of which you never
seed. The rains that fell the last week in June that year was
terrible. But Rosey kept a-comin' on.

He drove us out of Tullahoma too. We fell back across the
Cumberland, we pulled back behind the mountain, but he follered us.

I reckon thar was fellers that was quicker when a fight was
on, and when they'd seed just what hit was they had to do. But
when it came to plannin' and a-figgerin', Old Rosey Rosecrans
took the cake. Old Rosey was a fox. Fer sheer natural cunnin'
I never knowed the beat of him.

While Bragg was watchin' him at Chattanooga to keep him
from gittin' across the Tennessee, he sent some fellers forty
mile up stream. And then he'd march 'em back and forth and
round the hill and back in front of us again where we could
look at 'em, until you'd a-thought that every Yankee in the
world was there. But law! All that was just a dodge! He had
fellers a-sawin' and a-hammerin', a-buildin' boats, a-blowin'
bugles and a-beatin' drums, makin' all the noise they could—
you could hear 'em over yonder gittin' ready—and all the time
Old Rosey was fifty mile or more down stream, ten mile *past*
Chattanooga, a-fixin' to git over way down thar. That was the
kind of feller Rosey was.

We reached Chattanooga early in July and waited fer two
months. Old Rosey hadn't caught up with us yet. He still had
to cross the Cumberland, push his men and pull his trains
across the ridges and through the gaps before he got to us. July
went by, we had no news of him. "Oh Lord!" said Jim, "perhaps
he ain't a-comin'!" I knowed he was a-comin', but I let Jim have
his way.

Some of the fellers would git used to hit. A feller'd git into a frame of mind where he wouldn't let hit worry him. He'd let termorrer look out fer hitself. That was the way hit was with me.

With Jim hit was the other way around. Now that he knowed Martha Patton he was a different man. I think he hated the war and army life from the moment that he met her. From that time he was livin' only fer one thing—to go back home and marry that gal. When mail would come and some of us was gittin' letters he'd be the first in line; and if she wrote him why he'd walk away like someone in a dream. And if she failed to write he'd jest go off somers and set down by himself: he'd be in such a state of misery he didn't want to talk to no one. He got the reputation with the fellers fer bein' queer— unsociable—always a-broodin' and a-frettin' about somethin' and a-wantin' to be left alone. And so, after a time, they let him be. He wasn't popular with most of them—but they never knowed what was wrong, they never knowed that he wasn't really the way they thought he was at all. Hit was jest that he was hit so desperate hard, the worst-in-love man that I ever seed. But law! I knowed! I knowed what was the trouble from the start.

Hit's funny how war took a feller. Before the war I was the serious one, and Jim had been the one to play.

I reckon that I'd had to work too hard. We was so poor. Before the war hit almost seemed I never knowed the time I didn't have to work. And when the war came, why I only thought of all the fun and frolic I was goin' to have; and then at last, when I knowed what hit was like, why I was used to hit and didn't care.

I always could git used to things. And I reckon maybe that's the reason that I'm here. I wasn't one to worry much, and no matter how rough the goin' got I always figgered *I* could hold out if the others could. I let termorrer look out fer hitself. I reckon that you'd have to say I was an optimist. If things got bad, well, I always figgered that they could be worse; and if they got so bad they couldn't be no worse, why then I'd figger that they couldn't last this way ferever, they'd have to git some better sometime later on.

I reckon toward the end thar, when they got so bad we didn't think they'd ever git no better, I'd reached the place where I jest didn't care. I could still lay down and go to sleep and not worry over what was goin' to come termorrer, because I never *knowed* what was to come and so I didn't let hit worry me. I reckon you'd have to say that was the Pentland in me—our belief in what we call predestination.

Now, Jim was jest the other way. Before the war he was happy as a lark and thought of nothin' except havin' fun. But then the war came and hit changed him so you wouldn't a-knowed he was the same man.

And, as I say, hit didn't happen all at once. Jim was the happiest man I ever seed that mornin' that we started out from home. I reckon he thought of the war as we all did, as a big frolic. We gave hit jest about six months. We figgered we'd be back by then, and of course all that jest suited Jim. I reckon that suited all of us. It would give us all a chance to wear a uniform and to see the world, to shoot some Yankees and to run 'em north, and then to come back home and lord it over those who hadn't been and be a hero and court the gals.

That was the way hit looked to us when we set out from Zebulon. We never thought about the winter. We never thought about the mud and cold and rain. We never knowed what hit would be to have to march on an empty belly, to have to march barefoot with frozen feet and with no coat upon your back, to have to lay down on bare ground and try to sleep with no coverin' above you, and thankful half the time if you could find dry ground to sleep upon, and too tard the rest of hit to care. We never knowed or thought about such things as these.

We never knowed how hit would be there in the cedar thickets beside Chickamauga Creek. And if we had a-knowed, if
someone had a-told us, why I reckon that none of us would
a-cared. We was too young and ignorant to care. And as fer
knowin'—law! The only trouble about *knowin'* is that you've
got to know what knowin's *like* before you know what knowin'
is. Thar's no one that can tell you. You've got to know hit fer
yourself.

Well, like I say, we'd been fightin' all this time and still thar
was no sign of the war endin'. Old Rosy jest kept a-follerin' us
and—"Lord!" Jim would say, "will it never end?"

I never knowed myself. We'd been fightin' fer two years, and
I'd given over knowin' long ago. With Jim hit was different.
He'd been a-prayin' and a-hopin' from the first that soon hit
would be over and that he could go back and get that gal. And
at first, fer a year or more, I tried to cheer him up. I told him
that it couldn't last ferever. But after a while hit wasn't no use
to tell him that. He wouldn't believe me any longer.

Because Old Rosey kept a-comin' on. We'd whup him and
we'd stop him fer a while, but then he'd git his wind, he'd be
on our trail again, he'd drive us back.—"Oh Lord!" said Jim,
"will hit never stop?"

That summer I been tellin' you about, he drove us down,
through Tennessee. He drove us out of Shelbyville, and we fell
back on Tullahoma, to the passes of the hills. When we pulled
back across the Cumberland I said to Jim: "Now we've got
him. He'll have to cross the mountains now to git at us. And
when he does, we'll have him. That's all that Bragg's been
waitin' fer. We'll whup the daylights out of him this time," I
said, "and after that thar'll be nothin' left of him. We'll be
home by Christmas, Jim—you wait and see."

And Jim just looked at me and shook his head and said:
"Lord, Lord, I don't believe this war'll ever end!"

Hit wasn't that he was afraid—or, if he was, hit made a

wildcat of him in the fightin'. Jim could get fightin' mad like no one else I ever seed. He could do things, take chances no one else I ever knowed would take. But I reckon hit was jest because he was so desperate. He hated hit so much. He couldn't git used to hit the way the others could. He couldn't take hit as hit came. Hit wasn't so much that he was afraid to die. I guess hit was that he was still so full of livin'. He didn't want to die because he wanted to live so much. And he wanted to live so much because he was in love.

. . . So, like I say, Old Rosey finally pushed us back across the Cumberland. We was in Chattanooga in July, and fer a few weeks hit was quiet thar. But all the time I knowed that Rosey would keep comin' on. We got wind of him again along in August. He had started after us again. He pushed his trains across the Cumberland, with the roads so bad, what with the rains, his wagons sunk down to the axle hubs. But he got 'em over, came down in the valley, then across the ridge, and early in September he was on our heels again.

We cleared out of Chattanooga on the eighth. And our tail end was pullin' out at one end of the town as Rosey came in through the other. We dropped down around the mountain south of town and Rosey thought he had us on the run again.

But this time he was fooled. We was ready fer him now, a-pickin' out our spot and layin' low. Old Rosey follered us. He sent McCook around down toward the south to head us off. He thought he had us in retreat but when McCook got thar we wasn't thar at all. We'd come down south of town and taken our positions along Chickamauga Creek. McCook had gone too far. Thomas was follerin' us from the north and when McCook tried to git back to join Thomas, he couldn't pass us, fer we blocked the way. They had to fight us or be cut in two.

We was in position on the Chickamauga on the seventeenth. The Yankees streamed in on the eighteenth, and took their position in the woods facin' us. We had our backs to Lookout

Mountain and the Chickamauga Creek. The Yankees had their line thar in the woods before us on a rise, with Missionary Ridge behind them to the east.

The Battle of Chickamauga was fought in a cedar thicket. That cedar thicket, from what I knowed of hit, was about three miles long and one mile wide. We fought fer two days all up and down that thicket and to and fro across hit. When the fight started that cedar thicket was so thick and dense you could a-took a butcher knife and drove hit in thar anywheres and hit would a-stuck. And when that fight was over that cedar thicket had been so destroyed by shot and shell you could a-looked in thar anywheres with your naked eye and seed a black snake run a hundred yards away. If you'd a-looked at that cedar thicket the day after that fight was over you'd a-wondered how a hummin' bird the size of your thumbnail could a-flown through thar without bein' torn into pieces by the fire. And yet more than half of us who went into that thicket came out of hit alive and told the tale. You wouldn't have thought that hit was possible. But I was thar and seed hit, and hit was.

A little after midnight—hit may have been about two o'clock that mornin', while we lay there waitin' for the fight we knowed was bound to come next day—Jim woke me up. I woke up like a flash, you got used to hit in those days, and though hit was so dark you could hardly see your hand a foot away, I knowed his face at once. He was white as a ghost and he had got thin as a rail in that last year's campaign. In the dark his face looked white as paper. He dug his hand into my arm so hard hit hurt. I roused up sharp-like; then I seed him and knowed who hit was.

"John!" he said—"John!"—and he dug his fingers in my arm so hard he made hit ache—"John! I've seed him! He was here again!"

I tell you what, the way he said hit made my blood run cold. They say we Pentlands are a superstitious people, and perhaps we are. They told hit how they saw my brother George a-comin' up the hill one day at sunset, how they all went out upon the porch and waited fer him, how everyone, the childern and the grown-ups alike, all seed him as he clumb the hill, and how he passed behind a tree and disappeared as if the ground had swallered him—and how they got the news ten days later that he'd been killed at Chancellorsville on that very day and hour. I've heared these stories and I know the others all believe them, but I never put no stock in them myself. And yet, I tell you what! The sight of that white face and those black eyes a-burnin' at me in the dark—the way he said hit and the way hit was—fer I could feel the men around me and hear somethin' movin' in the wood—I heared a trace chain rattle and hit was enough to make your blood run cold! I grabbed hold of him—I shook him by the arm—I didn't want the rest of 'em to hear—I told him to hush up— "John, he was here!" he said.

I never asked him what he meant—I knowed too well to ask. It was the third time he'd seed hit in a month—a man upon a horse. I didn't want to hear no more—I told him that hit was a dream and I told him to go back to sleep.

"I tell you, John, hit was no dream!" he said. "Oh John, I heared hit—and I heared his horse—and I seed him sittin' thar as plain as day—and he never said a word to me—he jest sat thar lookin' down, and then he turned and rode away into the woods. . . . John, John, I heared him and I don't know what hit means!"

Well, whether he seed hit or imagined hit or dreamed hit, I don't know. But the sight of his black eyes a-burnin' holes through me in the dark made me feel almost as if I'd seed hit too. I told him to lay down by me—and still I seed his eyes a-blazin' thar. I know he didn't sleep a wink the rest of that whole night. I closed my eyes and tried to make him think that

I was sleepin' but hit was no use—we lay thar wide awake. And both of us was glad when mornin' came.

The fight began upon our right at ten o'clock. We couldn't find out what was happenin': the woods thar was so close and thick we never knowed fer two days what had happened, and we didn't know fer certain then. We never knowed how many we was fightin' or how many we had lost. I've heared them say that even Old Rosey himself didn't know jest what had happened when he rode back into town next day, and didn't know that Thomas was still standin' like a rock. And if Old Rosey didn't know no more than this about hit, what could a common soldier know? We fought back and forth across that cedar thicket fer two days, and thar was times when you would be right up on top of them before you even knowed that they was thar. And that's the way the fightin' went—the bloodiest fightin' that was ever knowed, until that cedar thicket was soaked red with blood, and thar was hardly a place left in thar where a sparrer could have perched.

And as I say, we heared 'em fightin' out upon our right at ten o'clock, and then the fightin' came our way. I heared later that this fightin' started when the Yanks come down to the Creek and run into a bunch of Forrest's men and drove 'em back. And then they had hit back and forth until they got drove back themselves, and that's the way we had hit all day long. We'd attack and then they'd throw us back, then they'd attack and we'd beat them off. And that was the way hit went from mornin' till night. We piled up there upon their left: they mowed us down with canister and grape until the very grass was soakin' with our blood, but we kept comin' on. We must have charged a dozen times that day—I was in four of 'em myself. We fought back and forth across that wood until there wasn't a piece of hit as big as the palm of your hand we hadn't fought on. We busted through their right at two-thirty in the afternoon and got way over past the Widder Glenn's, where

Rosey had his quarters, and beat 'em back until we got the whole way cross the Lafayette Road and took possession of the road. And then they drove us out again. And we kept comin' on, and both sides were still at hit after darkness fell.

We fought back and forth across that road all day with first one side and then the tother holdin' hit until that road hitself was soaked in blood, They called that road the Bloody Lane, and that was jest the name fer hit.

We kept fightin' fer an hour or more after hit had gotten dark, and you could see the rifles flashin' in the woods, but then hit all died down. I tell you what, that night was somethin' to remember and to marvel at as long as you live. The fight had set the wood afire in places, and you could see the smoke and flames and hear the screamin' and the hollerin' of the wounded until hit made your blood run cold. We got as many as we could—but some we didn't even try to git—we jest let 'em lay. It was an awful thing to hear. I reckon many a wounded man was jest left to die or burn to death because we couldn't git 'em out.

You could see the nurses and the stretcher-bearers movin' through the woods, and each side huntin' fer hits dead. You could see them movin' in the smoke an' flames, an' you could see the dead men layin' there as thick as wheat, with their corpse-like faces an' black powder on their lips, an' a little bit of moonlight comin' through the trees, and all of hit more like a nightmare out of hell than anything I ever knowed before.

But we had other work to do. All through the night we could hear the Yanks a-choppin' and a-thrashin' round, and we knowed that they was fellin' trees to block us when we went fer them next mornin'. Fer we knowed the fight was only jest begun. We figgered that we'd had the best of hit, but we knowed no one had won the battle yet. We knowed the second day would beat the first.

Jim knowed hit too. Poor Jim, he didn't sleep that night—he

never seed the man upon the horse that night, he jest sat there, a-grippin' his knees and starin', and a-sayin': "Lord God, Lord God, when will hit ever end?"

Then mornin' came at last. This time we knowed jest where we was and what hit was we had to do. Our line was fixed by that time. Bragg knowed at last where Rosey had his line, and Rosey knowed where we was. So we waited there, both sides, till mornin' came. Hit was a foggy mornin' with mist upon the ground. Around ten o'clock when the mist began to rise, we got the order and we went chargin' through the wood again.

We knowed the fight was goin' to be upon the right—upon our right, that is—on Rosey's left. And we knowed that Thomas was in charge of Rosey's left. And we all knowed that hit was easier to crack a flint rock with your teeth than to make old Thomas budge. But we went after him, and I tell you what, that was a fight! The first day's fight had been like playin' marbles when compared to this.

We hit old Thomas on his left at half-past ten, and Breckenridge came sweepin' round and turned old Thomas's flank and came in at his back, and then we had hit hot and heavy. Old Thomas whupped his men around like he would crack a rawhide whup and drove Breckenridge back around the flank again, but we was back on top of him before you knowed the first attack was over.

The fight went ragin' down the flank, down to the center of Old Rosey's army and back and forth across the left, and all up and down old Thomas's line. We'd hit him right and left and in the middle, and he'd come back at us and throw us back again. And we went ragin' back and forth thar like two bloody lions with that cedar thicket so tore up, so bloody and so thick with dead by that time, that hit looked as if all hell had broken loose in thar.

Rosey kept a-whuppin' men around off of his right, to help old Thomas on the left to stave us off. And then we'd hit old

Thomas left of center and we'd bang him in the middle and
we'd hit him on his left again, and he'd whup those Yankees
back and forth off of the right into his flanks and middle as
we went fer him, until we run those Yankees ragged. We had
them gallopin' back and forth like kangaroos, and in the end
that was the thing that cooked their goose.

The worst fightin' had been on the left, on Thomas's line,
but to hold us thar they'd thinned their right out and had failed
to close in on the center of their line. And at two o'clock that
afternoon when Longstreet seed the gap in Wood's position on
the right, he took five brigades of us and poured us through.
That whupped them. That broke their line and smashed their
whole right all to smithereens. We went after them like a
pack of ragin' devils. We killed 'em and we took 'em by the
thousands, and those we didn't kill and take right thar went
streamin' back across the Ridge as if all hell was at their heels.

That was a rout if ever I heared tell of one! They went
streamin' back across the Ridge—hit was each man fer himself
and the devil take the hindmost. They caught Rosey comin'
up—he rode into them, he tried to check 'em, face 'em round,
and get 'em to come on again—hit was like tryin' to swim the
Mississippi upstream on a boneyard mule! They swept him
back with them as if he'd been a wooden chip. They went
streamin' into Rossville like the rag-tag of creation—the worst
whupped army that you ever seed, and Old Rosey was along
with all the rest!

He knowed hit was all up with him, or thought he knowed
hit, for everybody told him the Army of the Cumberland had
been blowed to smithereens and that hit was a general rout.
And Old Rosey turned and rode to Chattanooga, and he was
a beaten man. I've heared tell that when he rode up to his
headquarters thar in Chattanooga they had to help him from
his horse, and that he walked into the house all dazed and

fuddled-like, like he never knowed what had happened to him—and that he jest sat thar struck dumb and never spoke.

This was at four o'clock of that same afternoon. And then the news was brought to him that Thomas was still thar upon the field and wouldn't budge. Old Thomas stayed thar like a rock. We'd smashed the right, we'd sent it flyin' back across the Ridge, the whole Yankee right was broken into bits and streamin' back to Rossville for dear life. Then we bent old Thomas back upon his left. We thought we had him, he'd have to leave the field or else surrender. But old Thomas turned and fell back along the Ridge and put his back against the wall thar, and he wouldn't budge.

Longstreet pulled us back at three o'clock when we had broken up the right and sent them streamin' back across the Ridge. We thought that hit was over then. We moved back stumblin' like men walkin' in a dream. And I turned to Jim—I put my arm around him, and I said: "Jim, what did I say? I knowed hit, we've licked 'em and this is the end!" I never even knowed if he heard me. He went stumblin' on beside me with his face as white as paper and his lips black with the powder of the cartridge-bite, mumblin' and mutterin' to himself like someone talkin' in a dream. And we fell back to position, and they told us all to rest. And we leaned thar on our rifles like men who hardly knowed if they had come out of that hell alive or dead.

"Oh Jim, we've got 'em and this is the end!" I said.

He leaned thar swayin' on his rifle, starin' through the wood. He jest leaned and swayed thar, and he never said a word, and those great eyes of his a-burnin' through the wood.

"Jim, don't you hear me?"—and I shook him by the arm. "Hit's over, man! We've licked 'em and the fight is over!—Can't you understand?"

And then I heared them shoutin' on the right, the word

came down the line again and Jim—poor Jim!—he raised his head and listened, and "Oh God!" he said, "we've got to go again!"

Well, hit was true. The word had come that Thomas had lined up upon the Ridge, and we had to go fer him again. After that I never exactly knowed what happened. Hit was like fightin' in a bloody dream—like doin' somethin' in a nightmare—only the nightmare was like death and hell. Longstreet threw us up that hill five times, I think, before darkness came. We'd charge up to the very muzzles of their guns, and they'd mow us down like grass, and we'd come stumblin' back—or what was left of us—and form again at the foot of the hill, and then come on again. We'd charge right up the Ridge and drive 'em through the gap and fight 'em with cold steel, and they'd come back again and we'd brain each other with the butt end of our guns. Then they'd throw us back and we'd re-form and come on after 'em again.

The last charge happened jest at dark. We came along and stripped the ammunition off the dead—we took hit from the wounded—we had nothin' left ourselves. Then we hit the first line—and we drove them back. We hit the second and swept over them. We were goin' up to take the third and last—they waited till they saw the color of our eyes before they let us have hit. Hit was like a river of red-hot lead had poured down on us: the line melted thar like snow. Jim stumbled and spun round as if somethin' had whupped him like a top. He fell right toward me, with his eyes wide open and the blood a-pourin' from his mouth. I took one look at him and then stepped over him like he was a log. Thar was no more to see or think of now—no more to reach—except that line. We reached hit and they let us have hit, and we stumbled back.

And yet we knowed that we had won a victory. That's what they told us later—and we knowed hit must be so because when daybreak came next mornin' the Yankees was all gone.

They had all retreated into town, and we was left there by the Creek at Chickamauga, in possession of the field.

I don't know how many men got killed. I don't know which side lost the most. I only know you could have walked across the dead men without settin' foot upon the ground. I only know that cedar thicket which had been so dense and thick two days before you could've drove a knife into hit and hit would of stuck, had been so shot to pieces that you could've looked in thar on Monday mornin' with your naked eye and seed a black snake run a hundred yards away.

I don't know how many men we lost or how many of the Yankees we may have killed. The Generals on both sides can figger all that out to suit themselves. But I know that when that fight was over you could have looked in thar and wondered how a hummin' bird could've flown through that cedar thicket and come out alive. And yet that happened, yes, and something more than hummin' bird—fer men came out, alive.

And on that Monday mornin', when I went back up the Ridge to where Jim lay, thar just beside him on a little torn piece of bough, I heard a redbird sing. I turned Jim over and got his watch, his pocket-knife, and what few papers and belongin's that he had, and some letters that he'd had from Martha Patton. And I put them in my pocket.

And then I got up and looked around. It all seemed funny after hit had happened, like something that had happened in a dream. Fer Jim had wanted so desperate hard to live, and hit had never mattered half so much to me, and now I was a-standin' thar with Jim's watch and Martha Patton's letters in my pocket and a-listenin' to that little redbird sing.

And I would go all through the war and go back home and marry Martha later on, and fellers like poor Jim was layin' thar at Chickamauga Creek.

Hit's all so strange now when you think of hit. Hit all turned out so different from the way we thought. And that was long ago, and I'll be ninety-five years old if I am livin' on the seventh day of August, of this present year. Now that's goin' back a long ways, hain't hit? And yet hit all comes back to me as clear as if hit happened yesterday. And then hit all will go away and be as strange as if hit happened in a dream.

But I have been in some big battles I can tell you. I've seen strange things and been in bloody fights. But the biggest fight that I was ever in—the bloodiest battle anyone has ever fought—was at Chickamauga in that cedar thicket—at Chickamauga Creek in that great war.

9

The Plumed Knight

THEODORE JOYNER WAS old Bear's youngest son by his first marriage. As so often happens with the younger children of a self-made man, he got more education than the others. "And," said Zachariah whenever the fact was mentioned, "just *look* at him!" For, mingled with the Joyner reverence for learning, there was an equally hearty contempt among them for those who could not use it for some practical end.

Like his two more able brothers, Theodore had been destined for the law. He followed them to Pine Rock College and had his year of legal training. Then he "took the bar," and failed ingloriously; tried and failed again; and—

"Hell!" old Bear said disgustedly, "hit looked like he want fit fer nothin' else, so I jest sent him back to school!"

The result was that Theodore returned to Pine Rock for three years more, and finally succeeded in taking his diploma and bachelor's degree. Hence his eventual reputation as the scholar of the family.

Schoolmastering was the trade he turned to now, and, Libya Hill having grown and there being some demand for higher learning, he set up for a "Professor." He "scratched about" among the people he knew—which was everyone, of course— and got twenty or thirty pupils at the start. The tuition was fifteen dollars for the term, which was five months; and he taught them in a frame church.

After a while "'Fessor Joyner's School," as it was called, grew to such enlargement that Theodore had to move to bigger quarters. His father let him have the hill he owned across the river two miles west of town, and here Theodore built a frame house to live in and another wooden building to serve as a dormitory and classroom. The eminence on which the new school stood had always been known as Hogwart Heights. Theodore did not like the inelegant sound of that, so he re-christened it Joyner Heights, and the school, as befitted its new grandeur, was now named "The Joyner Heights Academy." The people in the town, however, just went on calling the hill Hogwart as they had always done, and to Theodore's intense chagrin they even dubbed the academy Hogwart, too.

In spite of this handicap the school prospered in its modest way. It was by no means a flourishing institution, but as people said, it was a good thing for Theodore. He could not have earned his living at anything else, and the school at least gave him a livelihood. The years passed uneventfully, and Theodore seemed settled forever in the comfortable little groove he had worn for himself.

Then, three years before the outbreak of the Civil War, a startling change occurred. By that time the fever of the approaching conflict was already sweeping through the South, and that fact gave Theodore his great opportunity. He seized it eagerly, and overnight transformed his school into "The Joyner Heights *Military* Academy." By this simple expedient he jumped his enrollment from sixty boys to eighty, and— more important—transmogrified himself from a rustic pedagogue into a military man.

So much is true, so cannot be denied—although Zachariah, in his ribald way, was forever belittling Theodore and his accomplishments. On Zachariah's side it must be admitted that

Theodore loved a uniform a good deal better than he wore one; and that he, as Master, with the help of the single instructor who completed the school's faculty, undertook the work of military training, drill, and discipline with an easy confidence which, if not sublime, was rather staggering. But Zachariah *was* unjust.

"I have heard," Zachariah would say in later years, warming up to his subject and assuming the ponderously solemn air that always filled his circle of cronies with delighted anticipation of what was to come—"I have heard that fools rush in where angels fear to tread, but in the case of my brother Theodore, it would be more accurate to say that he *leaps* in where God Almighty crawls! . . . I have seen a good many remarkable examples of military chaos," he continued, "particularly at the outset of the war, when they were trying to teach farm hands and mountain boys the rudiments of the soldier's art in two weeks' time. But I have never seen anything so remarkable as the spectacle of Theodore, assisted by a knock-kneed fellow with the itch, tripping over his sword and falling on his belly every time he tried to instruct twenty-seven pimply boys in the intricacies of squads right."

That was unfair. Not *all*, assuredly, were pimply, and there were more than twenty-seven.

"Theodore," Zack went on with the extravagance that characterized these lapses into humorous loquacity—"Theodore was so short that every time he—he blew dust in his eyes; and the knock-kneed fellow with the itch was so tall that he had to lay down on his belly to let the moon go by. And somehow they had got their uniforms mixed up, so that Theodore had the one that was meant for the knock-kneed tall fellow, and the knock-kneed tall fellow had on Theodore's. The trousers Theodore was wearing were so baggy at the knees they looked as if a nest of kangaroos had spent the last six months in them, and the knock-kneed fellow's pants were stretched so tight that he looked like a couple of long sausages. In addition to all this, Theodore had a head shaped like a balloon—and about the size of one. The knock-kneed fellow had a peanut for a head. And whoever had mixed up their uniforms had also got their hats exchanged. So every time Theodore reared back and bawled out a command, that small hat he was wearing would pop right off his head into the air, as if it had been shot out of a gun. And when the knock-kneed fellow would repeat the order, the big hat he had on would fall down over his ears and eyes as if someone had thrown a bushel basket over his head, and he would come clawing his way out of it with a bewildered expression on his face, as if to say, 'Where, the hell am I, anyway?' . . . They had a devil of a time getting those twenty-seven pimply boys straightened up as straight as they could get, which is to say, about as straight as a row of crooked radishes. Then, when they were all lined up at attention, ready to go, the knock-kneed fellow would be taken with the itch. He'd shudder up and down, and all over, as if someone had dropped a cold worm down his back; he'd twitch and wiggle, and suddenly he'd begin to scratch himself in the behind."

These flights on Zachariah's part were famous. Once launched, his inventive power was enormous. Every fresh extravagance would suggest half a dozen new ones. He was not cruel, but his treatment of his brother bordered on brutality.

The truth of the matter is that the "pimply boys" drilled so hard and earnestly that the grass was beaten bare on the peaceful summit of Hogwart Heights. Uniforms and muskets of a haphazard sort had been provided for them, and all that could be accomplished by a pious reading of the drill manual and a dry history of Napoleonic strategy was done for them by Theodore and his knock-kneed brother in arms. And when war was declared, in April 1861, the entire enrollment of the academy marched away to battle with Theodore at their head.

The trouble between Zachariah and Theodore afterwards

was that the war proved to be the great event in Theodore's life, and he never got over it. His existence had been empty and pointless enough before the war, and afterwards, knowing there was nothing left to live for that could possibly match the glories he had seen, he developed rather quickly into the professional warrior, the garrulous hero forever talking of past exploits. This is what annoyed Zachariah more and more as time went on, and he never let a chance go by to puncture Theodore's illusions of grandeur and to take him down a peg or two.

Separate volumes could be written about each member of this remarkable family. A noble biography for Robert, done with a Plutarchian pen—that is what he deserves. A lusty, gusty Rabelaisian chronicle to do justice to the virtues of old Miss Hattie. A stern portrait of Rufus in the Balzac manner. For Zachariah, his own salty memoirs would be the best thing, if he had only thought to write them, for he saw through everybody, himself included; and if he could have been assured that not a word would leak out till his death, so that no political harm could come of it, he would have shamed the devil and told the naked and uproarious truth. As for Theodore—well, we'll try to do our best in the pages of this book, but we know full well beforehand that it won't be good enough for Theodore. No book, no single pen, could ever do for Theodore what should be done for him.

Theodore should have had a group photograph taken of himself. He should have been blocked out by Rubens, painted in his elemental colors by fourteen of Rubens's young men, had his whiskers done by Van Dyke, his light and shade by Rembrandt, his uniform by Velasquez; then if the whole thing might have been gone over by Daumier, and touched up here and there with the satiric pencil of George Belcher, perhaps in the end you might have got a portrait that would reveal, in the colors of life itself, the august personage of Colonel Theodore Joyner, C.S.A.

Theodore rapidly became almost the stock type of the "Southern Colonel-plumed knight" kind of man. By 1870, he had developed a complete vocabulary and mythology of the war—"The Battle of the Clouds," Zachariah termed it. Nothing could be called by its right name. Theodore would never dream of using a plain or common word if he could find a fancy one. The Southern side of the war was always spoken of in a solemn whisper, mixed of phlegm, and reverent hoarseness, as "Our Cause." The Confederate flag became "Our Holy Oriflamme—dyed in the royal purple of the heroes' blood." To listen to Theodore tell about the war, one would have thought it had been conducted by several hundred thousand knighted Galahads upon one side, engaged in a struggle to the death against several hundred million villainous and black-hearted rascals, the purpose of said war being the protection "of all that we hold most sacred—the purity of Southern womanhood."

The more completely Theodore emerged as the romantic embodiment of Southern Colonelcy, the more he also came to look the part. He had the great mane of warrior hair, getting grayer and more distinguished-looking as the years went by; he had the bushy eyebrows, the grizzled mustache, and all the rest of it. In speech and tone and manner he was leonine. He moved his head exactly like an old lion, and growled like one, whenever he uttered such proud sentiments as these:

"Little did I dream, sir," he would begin—"little did I *dream,* when I marched out at the head of the Joyner Military Academy—of which the entire enrollment, sir—the *entire* enrollment, had volunteered to a man—all boys in years, yet each breast beating with a hero's heart—one hundred and thirty-seven fine young men, sir—the flower of the South— all under nineteen years of age—think of it, sir!" he growled impressively—"one hundred and thirty-seven under nineteen!—"

"Now wait a minute, Theodore," Zachariah would interpose with a deceptive mildness. "I'm not questioning your veracity, but if my memory is not playing tricks, your facts and figures are a little off."

"What do you mean, sir?" growled Theodore, and peered at him suspiciously. "In what way?"

"Well," said Zachariah calmly, "I don't remember that the enrollment of the academy had risen to any such substantial proportions as you mention by the time the war broke out. One hundred and thirty-seven under nineteen?" he repeated. "Wouldn't you come closer to the truth if you said there were nineteen under one hundred and thirty-seven?"

"Sir—Sir—" said Theodore, breathing heavily and leaning forward in his chair. "Why you—Sir!" he spluttered, and then glared fiercely at his brother and could say no more.

Is it any wonder that fraternal relations between Zack and Theodore were sometimes strained?

To the credit of Theodore's lads, and to the honor of the times and Colonel Joyner's own veracity, let it be admitted here and now that whether there were nineteen or fifty or a hundred and thirty-seven of them, they did march out "to a man," and many of them did not return. For four years and more the grass grew thick and deep on Hogwart Heights: the school was closed, the doors were barred, the windows shuttered.

When the war was over and Theodore came home again, the hill, with its little cluster of buildings, was a desolate sight. The place just hung there stogged in weeds. A few stray cows jangled their melancholy bells and wrenched the coarse, cool grass beneath the oak trees, before the bolted doors. And so the old place stood and stayed for three years more, settling a little deeper into the forgetfulness of dilapidation.

The South was stunned and prostrate now, and Theodore himself was more stunned and prostrate than most of the men who came back from the war. The one bit of purpose he had found in life was swallowed up in the great defeat, and he had no other that could take its place. He did not know what to do with himself. Half-heartedly, he "took the bar" again, and for the third time failed. Then, in 1869, he pulled himself together, and, using money that his brothers loaned him, he repaired the school and opened it anew.

It was a gesture of futility, really—and a symptom of something that was happening all over the South in that bleak decade of poverty and reconstruction. The South lacked money for all the vital things, yet somehow, like other war-struck and war-ravaged communities before it, the South found funds to lay out in tin-soldierism. Pigmy West Points sprang up everywhere, with their attendant claptrap of "Send us the boy, and we'll return you the man." It was a pitiable spectacle to see a great region and a valiant people bedaubing itself with such gimcrack frills and tin-horn fopperies after it had been exhausted and laid waste by the very demon it was making obeisance to. It was as if a group of exhausted farmers with blackened faces, singed whiskers, and lackluster eyes had come staggering back from some tremendous conflagration that had burned their homes and barns and crops right to the ground, and then had bedecked themselves in outlandish garments and started banging on the village gong and crying out: "At last, brothers, we're all members of the fire department!"

Theodore took a new lease on life with the reopening of The Joyner Military Academy. When he first decided to restore the place he thought he could resume his career at the point where the war had broken in upon it, and things would go on as though the war had never been. Then, as his plans took shape and he got more and more into the spirit of the enterprise, his attitude and feelings underwent a subtle change. As the great day for the reopening approached, he knew that it would not be just a resuming of his interrupted career. It would be much better than that. For the war was a heroic fact that could not be denied, and it now seemed to Theodore that in some strange and transcendental way the South had been gloriously triumphant even in defeat, and that he himself had played a decisive part in bringing about this transcendental victory.

Theodore was no more consciously aware of the psychic processes by which he had arrived at this conclusion than were thousands of others all over the South who, at this same time, were coming to the same conclusion themselves. But once the attitude had crystallized and become accepted, it became the point of departure for a whole new rationale of life. Out of it grew a vast mythology of the war—a mythology so universally believed that to doubt its truth was worse than treason. In a curious way, the war became no longer a thing finished and done with, a thing to be put aside and forgotten as belonging to the buried past, but a dead fact recharged with new vitality, and one to be cherished more dearly than life itself. The mythology which this gave rise to acquired in time the force of an almost supernatural sanction. It became a kind of folk-religion. And under its soothing, otherworldly spell, the South began to turn its face away from the hard and ugly realities of daily living that confronted it on every hand, and escaped into the soft dream of vanished glories—imagined glories—glories that had never been.

The first concrete manifestation of all this in Theodore was an inspiration that came to him as he lay in bed the night before the great day when the Joyner Military Academy was to reopen its doors. As he lay there, neither quite awake nor yet asleep, letting his mind shuttle back and forth between remembered exploits on the field of battle and the exciting event scheduled for the morrow, the two objects of his interest became fused: he felt that they were really one, and he saw the military school as belonging to the war, a part of it, a continuation and extension of it into the present, and on down through the long, dim vista of the future. Out of this there flowed instantly into his consciousness a sequence of ringing phrases that brought him as wide awake as the clanging of a bell, and he saw at once that he had invented a perfect slogan for his school. The next day he announced it at the formal convocation.

It is true that Theodore's slogan occasioned a good deal of mirth at his expense when it was repeated all over town with Zachariah's running commentary upon it. The father of a student at the school was one of Zack's most intimate friends; this man had attended the convocation, and he told Zack all about it afterwards.

"Theodore," this friend reported, "gave the boys a rousing new motto to live up to—earned, he said, by their predecessors on the glorious field of battle. Theodore made such a moving speech about it that he had all the mothers in tears. You never heard such a blubbering in your life. The chorus of snifflings and chokings and blowing of noses almost drowned Theodore out. It was most impressive."

"I don't doubt it," said Zack. "Theodore always did have an impressive manner. If he only had the gray matter that ought to go with it, he'd be a wonder. But what did he say? What was the motto?"

"*First at Manassas*—"

"First to eat, he means!" said Zachariah.

"—*fightingest at Antietam Creek*—"

"Yes, fightingest to see who could get back first across the creek!"

"—*and by far the farthest in the Wilderness.*"

"By God, he's right!" shouted Zachariah. "Too far, in fact, to be of any use to anyone! They thrashed around all night long, bawling like a herd of cattle and taking pot-shots at one another in the belief that they had come upon a company of Grant's infantry. They had to be gathered together and withdrawn from the line in order to prevent their total self-destruction. My brother Theodore," Zachariah went on with obvious relish, "is the only officer of my acquaintance who performed the remarkable feat of getting completely lost in an open field, and ordering an attack upon his own position. . . . His wounds, of course, are honorable, as he himself will tell you on the slightest provocation, but he was shot in the behind. So far as I know, he is the only officer in the history of the Confederacy who possesses the distinction of having been shot in the seat of the pants by one of his own sharpshooters, while stealthily and craftily reconnoitering his own breastworks in search of any enemy who was at that time nine miles away and marching in the opposite direction!'"

From this time on, the best description of Theodore is to say that he "grew" with his academy. The institution thrived in the nostalgic atmosphere that had made its resurrection possible in the first place, and Theodore himself became the personal embodiment of the post-war tradition, a kind of romantic vindication of rebellion, a whole regiment of plumed knights in his own person. And there can be no doubt whatever that he grew to believe it all himself.

According to contemporary accounts, he had been anything but a prepossessing figure when he went off to war, and, if any part of Zachariah's extravagant stories can be believed, anything but a master strategist of arms on the actual field of battle. But with the passage of the years he grew into his role, until at last, in his old age, he looked a perfect specimen of the grizzled warrior.

Long before that, people had stopped laughing at him. No one but Zachariah now cared to question publicly any of Theodore's pronouncements, and Zachariah's irreverence was tolerated only because he was considered to be a privileged person, above the common *mores*. Theodore was now held in universal respect. Thus the youngest of "the Joyner boys"—the one from whom least had been expected—finally came into his own as a kind of sacred symbol.

In Libya Hill during those later years it was to be a familiar spectacle every Monday—the day when the "cadets" enjoyed their holiday in town—to see old Colonel Joyner being conveyed through the streets in an old victoria, driven by an aged Negro in white gloves and a silk hat. The Colonel was always dressed in his old uniform of Confederate gray; he wore his battered old Confederate service hat, and, winter or summer, he was never seen without an old gray cape about his shoulders. He did not loll back among the faded leather cushions of the victoria: he sat bolt upright—and when he got too old to sit bolt upright under his own power, he used a cane to help him.

He would ride through the streets, always sitting soldierly erect, gripping the head of his supporting cane with palsied hands, brown with the blotches of old age, and glowering out to left and right beneath bushy eyebrows of coarse white with kindling glances of his fierce old eyes, at the same time clinching his jaw grimly and working sternly at his lips beneath his close-cropped grizzled mustache. This may have been just the effect of his false teeth, but it suggested to awed little boys that he was muttering warlike epithets. That is what every inch of him seemed to imply, but actually he was only growling out such commands as "Go on, you scoundrel! Go on!" to his aged charioteer, or muttering with fierce scorn as he saw the slovenly postures of his own cadets lounging in drugstore doors:

"Not a whole man among 'em! Look at 'em now! A race of weaklings, hollow-chested and hump-backed—not made of the same stuff their fathers were—not like the crowd we were the day we all marched out to a man—the bravest of the brave, the flower of our youth and our young manhood! One hundred and thirty-seven under nineteen!—Hrumph! Hrumph!—Get along, you scoundrel! Get along!"

The Works of Thomas Wolfe
Included in This Collection

O Lost. Columbia: The University of South Carolina Press, 2000. 5–24.

"The Web of Earth." *From Death to Morning.* New York: Charles Scribner's Sons, 1935. 216–19.

Mannerhouse: Prologue and Act 4. Baton Rouge, Louisiana: Louisiana State University, 1985. 29–39, 137–47.

Of Time and the River. New York: Charles Scribner's Sons, 1935. 76–83.

"The Four Lost Men." *The Complete Short Stories of Thomas Wolfe.* New York: Charles Scribner's Sons, 1987. 106–19.

The Good Child's River. Chapel Hill and London: University of North Carolina Press, 1991. 118–31.

"His Father's Earth." *The Complete Short Stories of Thomas Wolfe.* New York: Charles Scribner's Sons, 1987. 206–13.

"Chickamauga." *The Hills Beyond.* New York: Harper and Brothers, 1941. 77–107.

"The Plumed Knight." *The Hills Beyond.* New York: Harper and Brothers, 1941. 264–76.

OTHER MAJOR WORKS

The Web and the Rock. New York: Harper and Brothers, 1939.

You Can't Go Home, Again. New York: Harper and Brothers, 1940.